PRAISE FOR *SPARE AND FOUND PARTS*

"A piece of mechanical poetry, an intricate machine with
a fierce and fearless heartbeat." **V. E. Schwab**, author of the
Darker Shade of Magic series.

"A truly original creation: part magical realism, part steampunk,
it's a coming-of-age allegory that examines technological progress
and an individual's place in a stratified society." *Guardian*

"A unique feminist coming-of-age novel… Clever, beautifully
written and compelling. I loved it." **Marian Keyes**, author
of *The Break*

"A sweet and darkly hopeful tale of what it takes to build love."
Kiran Millwood Hargrave, author of *The Girl of Ink & Stars*

"The big dystopian talking point of 2018—the way The Power
was for 2017." *The Pool*

"This is a writer of such natural vivacity and spark, such eloquence
and invention." **Kevin Barry**, author of *City of Bohane*

"A dark and fierce thing, but one that also has much to say abo[ut]
hope and human ingenuity." **Joseph Fink**, co-author of
Welcome to Night Vale

OTHER WORDS FOR SMOKE

SARAH MARIA GRIFFIN

TITAN BOOKS

Other Words for Smoke
Print edition ISBN: 9781789090086
E-book edition ISBN: 9781789090093

Published by Titan Books
A division of Titan Publishing Group Ltd
144 Southwark Street, London SE1 0UP
www.titanbooks.com

First Titan edition: April 2019
10 9 8 7 6 5 4 3 2

A CIP catalogue record for this title is available from the British Library.

Printed and bound by CPI Group (UK) Ltd, Croydon CR0 4YY.

Reader, here are two things.

This is a book that took me 3 years to write. It is about fear and love but mostly it is about a haunted house. I learned from Stephen King that a haunt is a place animals go to feed. A hungry owl was the first image in this story to show up — and that owl is the heart of the story, still.

This is also a book about women & Ireland. If a whole country could be a haunted house, I can think of no more accurate site than this. The witches & women of this nation in many ways fuelled the story that lies ahead. I am indebted to them.

Thank you for reading,

Griff

For Helena

"Concentrate, and ask again"

THE MAGIC 8 BALL

Prologue

NOBODY knew what made the three of them from Iona Crescent up and walk out of the world. The rumors were different, depending on who you spoke to. Accident, attack—nobody could say for sure, except for Mae Frost and her brother, Rossa. They were there when it all happened, but they were sworn to silence in the way so many survivors of horror are: their tongues held by something beyond their control. Mae wasn't sure she'd ever be able to say any of it out loud, even if she was asked. That second summer, away up in the hinterlands where the suburbs kissed the mountains, had stolen the words from her. The language that matched her confession was lost.

Afterwards, when dear old Rita Frost and her ward, Bevan Mulholland, were gone, the national media descended on the twins. Microphones and cameras desperate to harvest their sorrow and turn it into headline ink. *Lucky* was what those headlines had called Mae and Rossa. Lucky, like spotting a bright penny on a pavement, lucky like two

1

magpies seen together for joy. Lucky, like the twins' escape had happened by chance.

Not a trace of Bevan or Rita was found. The twins were discovered by police and the fire brigade, sitting on the roadside at the end of Iona Crescent, holding each other. Streaked with soot, hands bloodied, but otherwise unharmed. Seventeen, the pair of them, wide-eyed and gaunt for months. They'd never be the same again, said the papers. It was a miracle, whispered the neighbors. Those lucky, *lucky* kids.

All they told the journalists was that they ran for their lives. They would cast each other looks, Rossa and Mae, as they said just about nothing at all under rapid-fire questioning. Shock was the disguise they wore, and it protected them from having to say much at all.

The only detail real Mae ever gave to the tall, coal-suited reporters as they grilled her was that she hoped Bobby the cat had managed to make it out into the mountains. They always liked that bit. Their eyes would come over sad; they would say she was so brave.

The neighbors on Iona had been far more forthcoming. Devastated, all: Rita Frost was such a sweet old lady. And young Bevan, tabloids were splashed with photographs of her, school headshots, the occasional clumsy selfie. A gorgeous, bright girl struck down before her life had really begun. Her former boyfriend, Gus, gave an impassioned missive to the national broadsheet about the strength of her character, her beauty. There never would be anyone quite like Bevan Mulholland again, he'd said.

Mae had agreed with him, when she'd read it. There wouldn't be anyone like her again.

While the papers flooded with tributes, it seemed to Mae that nobody remembered that Bevan and Rita had kept themselves to themselves. That Bevan had few friends, if any—that she was a quiet girl with something hard in her eyes. That Rita had been little short of shunned by the parish for operating as a psychic medium from her living room.

No use in remembering the harder things, the stranger things. Rita was kind and Bevan was beautiful, and Audrey—well, what would anybody at all really know about Audrey? Audrey had been gone for years.

Rita was kind. Bevan was beautiful—this is what remained. This, and the smell. They talked about it for years, told stories of how the sky above Dorasbeg had looked tornado-gray; a disaster in the air. Great billows of it carried on the wind down over the village and the motorway: smoke, sweet and dark.

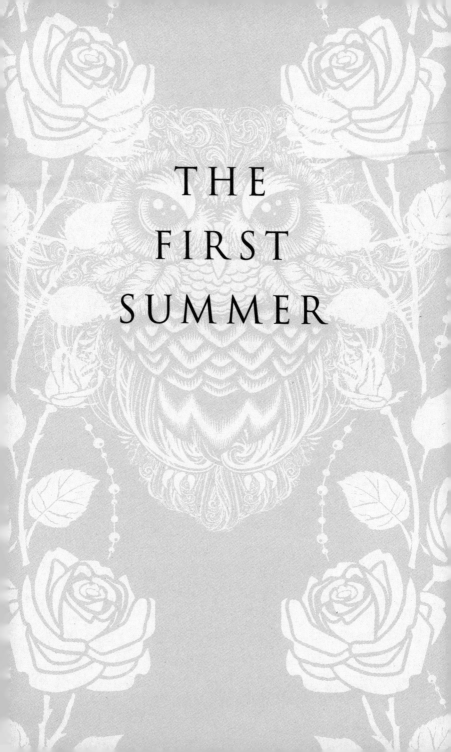

THE
FIRST
SUMMER

ONE

THE floor is tiles and sawdust, like dry, flaked snow. You shuffle your feet and make little heaps of the fine wood shavings, here and there. Your fruit gum tastes like nothing. You're last in the line. When the gray-faced old man and the woman with the pram are gone, it'll be just you and the butcher's son, Gus.

You haven't looked at him just yet; instead you inspect each cut of meat behind the glass counter. That's what you must look like on the inside, you think, running your gaze over the crimson flanks, the pastel translucency of breasts, the redness of mince.

Gray old man leaves, paper bag under his arm. The bell on the door rings as he opens it, closes it. For a moment, the cool of the shop is disturbed by the hot summer air outside. The woman with the pram moves forward, leans over the counter, goes, "Will you do us up a chicken with stuffing and a spice rub? Cheers, now, Gus."

Boring. You drag your fingertips over the glass, tap your

nails against it. You blow a small bubble with your gum, it snaps. An impatient sound. Gus looks over at you, takes you in. "I'll be with you in a moment, Bevan."

You hum back to him. "Whatever."

He tuts like he's exasperated, but you know he likes you. That's funny.

Gus snows the pimpled chicken skin with salt, pepper, something red from a canister. Stuffs it with bread crumbs and sage and onion and butter. Puts it in a little tin dish, wraps it in cling. Keeps flinging you looks while he works. The woman with the pram passes a fiver over the counter. His latex gloves are still covered in the rawness of the bird as he takes the green note. You lean back against the arc of the counter, the skin on your legs sticking to the glass. Chilly.

"What'll it be, Bev?"

Gus's voice is flat, like he's not interested in helping you— rather, like he's playing at not being interested in helping you.

"Bones again, if you have them."

You slide your eyes up him, his bloodied apron, his denim shirt. This is his da's shop. He's still in school, only working for the summer. He's got a pair of cheekbones you could sharpen a knife off. Starving green eyes. Cornfield-fair beard and woolen hat over tufts of straw hair. Safety hazard, that. His ma told Rita that he's got notions of moving to London after school, getting out of the family trade, starting over. Wants to do tattoos for a living. You can see a couple of inky surprises peeking from under his cuffs.

"More bones?" He is incredulous. "Using them to pick your teeth?"

"Soup." You flip out your phone, thumbing open the lock screen, posing indifference. "For Rita."

"Give it over. You're smudging the counter," he snaps, hands on his hips.

"Make me," you reply, popping another small bubble.

"What kind of bones?"

"Whatever you've got." You don't take your eyes off your digital feed, but you aren't reading it, not really. He loves it, your indifference getting right under his skin.

He hisses and disappears behind thick plastic curtains to get you what you're looking for. Good boy.

You start to sing along with the radio while he's in there, loud enough given there's nobody else around. It feels like the stations have only been playing four songs this summer, all of them bangers. You sway side to side along with the chorus, raise your arms above your head, kick the sawdust. Beat's easy, words dark. *Pay me what you owe me*—you sort of lose yourself in it, synth overtaking your limbs a little. It's cold in here to keep the meat fresh. The hairs on your arms rise.

Gus comes back, holding a blue plastic bag weighed down with bones. They'll be wrapped in cling, then yesterday's paper. You smile at him, still dancing. "Take a break? This is *such* a tune. . . ."

He shakes his head. "Christ, Bevan. Give it up, would you. Stop yourself."

You lean over the counter and he passes you the blue bag. It rustles. "Never. Dance with me?"

You don't really mean it or even want him to—you

know he won't—but hot red discomfort climbs his face. He sets his teeth, exhales through his nose. "Are you trying to be funny?"

You're not trying. You're hilarious.

"Suit yourself." You shrug, kicking up the sawdust at your heels like glitter as you leave the shop. The bell rings as the door opens and closes on the summer tune and the flustered boy, lit up like a Christmas tree in June. You did that.

On the walk home you try as best you can to hold on to the rush you got from his eyes on you. You stick in your headphones, scuttle through the village quick as you can. The village is what your ma and Rita call it. But Dorasbeg isn't much more than an intersection of a few busy roads. There's a looming church, three chippers, a school, two pubs, a string of shops, a Supervalu, a butcher, and a barber. A credit union, a pharmacy, a newsagent. All clustered together like a clutch of old ladies at the hem of the looming Dublin Mountains. It's nice here, sort of. Pleasant, but for the disquieting presence of the old Magdalene laundry* by the river. You'd always thought that was an uncomfortable thing, for people to live in the shadow of such a sad place.

This one in particular put your village on the map. The workhouse for unmarried mothers was closed down after a scandal was leaked about a pregnant teenage girl who died after escaping it, decades ago. Now it just stands there, leering history.

---

* A Magdalene Laundry is not a building. It is a threat.

But your ma always reminds you how fortunate you are to live in a place like Dorasbeg. You suppose you should believe her.

You power down past the river that runs under the church and take a sharp left into your housing estate. Rows and rows of semidetached houses, white with red roofs. Big ones, porches extended, tasteful gardens. Glamorous, or at least trying to be. Upper middle class and labyrinthine. You lope a few turns, then head down to the end of the last cul-de-sac, where your house sits. Well, Rita's house. You just live in some of the rooms of the behemoth. Your ma used to, too.

Behind the house is the long garden. Behind the garden is a wall. Behind the wall is the forest, then the mountains begin to climb.

You let yourself in, same as always. It doesn't feel that different now that ma is gone: for a moment you forget that her coat won't hang on the banister again; instead it is somewhere far away. It has only been a few months. You check for postcards—none, just a couple of pizza menus.

The house is pristine, like in a catalogue—this side of the building so different from Rita's. Your ma tried so hard to make it her own. You would have too, if you were her, but maybe not as cold as this, as orderly. Nobody really lives on this side, and it shows. Imelda kept nothing.

She was young, still. You're her only souvenir. The daughter with the face of a musician who let her into his dressing room after a show, then up and left. Your ma had always said you were like him, but then she up and left too, so maybe the pair of them were alike and you were something else.

You've thought a lot about leaving. But not leaving the way she did. Not slipping away full of apologies and promises that the time would come when you could join her. Not the tears-in-an-airport kind of leaving. Something better than that. Less cowardly.

Away up the stairs and into your room. Your soft bed, the big window. Pastels. The leaning mirror. The wardrobe. The room is nearly empty, one whole wall of the room totally featureless—no furniture, no interference. Barely a sign of who you are anywhere—this could be a hotel. A space that any person or any thing just passes through. The wallpaper is white roses and tawny vines and leaves, a textured and endless pattern.

You sit on the rug, your butcher-shop bounty in your lap, legs crossed. You look up at the wall, pop your headphones out, slide your phone across the floor and away. You swallow your gum. At last you scoot nearer, so your knees graze the sideboard. You pull the plastic open, then the newsprint, then the cling. The bones are a nest, pink and raw and slivered white. They smell metallic.

You pluck out a slender wand of bone and twirl it between your fingers, then place it against the wall like a painter with a brush full of crimson. You press, and the surface gives way like wet sand. It eats the bone and his voice says, **more.***You take another and push it in among

---

* It is happening again.

12

the pale roses, the delicate vines. They tremble. They begin to rearrange. **good.**

The paper garden begins to shift. A third bone. **yes,** he says.

"Yes?" you say.

And the owl arrives.

You are so glad to see him.

TWO

ROSSA was carsick. His mam was driving, the radio murmuring news. His dad had his eyes closed, just listening, leaning against the window, and the heat was stifling, making his nausea roll, his palms sweaty. Mae was glued to her Nintendo, silent and hunched forward, headphones in her ears. Rossa found himself a little shamefully glad that she was being quiet for a moment. He wasn't sure when he had started being grateful for his sister's occasional silence, treasuring the moments when she wasn't effusively gushing about something or other. It was recent. Their twinship, too, had become strange rather than comforting—the secret language between them had loosened at the seams. He blamed it on fourteen. He really wasn't into being fourteen.

It didn't help that Mae had half a foot in height on him, like she just woke up one day with her limbs mysteriously elongated without sending his a message to pick up the pace. The pair of them were made of the same stuff; surely that meant his bones owed him an explanation. He was three and a half minutes older, too, which had always felt like a winning argument before, but now was just another check on an ever increasing list of embarrassments about his body.

The car swung around a corner, his mother blindly pressing buttons on the ancient cassette player. Rossa jolted in his seat; Mae nearly dropped her game.

"Paul, put our Philo on there, I can't see if the tape's in and I don't want to drive us into a tree!"

Dad tutted, as though Mam's request was a burden. He shuffled through the glove compartment, tapes long older than the twins clacking, before stuffing the favorite into the mouth of the player. It took off midsong, and the rawness of Phil Lynott's voice filled the car. Rossa's nausea subsided a moment as a fanfare of trumpets cleared the tension. Mae didn't react, thumbs twitching against the d-pad of her small console.

"Love this," Mam half said and half sang. Her voice was metallic, pantomiming something she wasn't feeling at all. Even Rossa could tell that.

Dad said nothing, returning to his window.

There was a reason they were being shipped off to their great-aunt Rita's for the summer, though Rossa didn't know what it was. He was pretty sure that Mae knew, but he didn't want to ask her. Rossa looked out the window at the scrolling, dull landscape. Gray and moss green. Why Rita? She was practically a stranger. They'd only met her at their holy communion and confirmation, maybe one Christmas. Why this summer?

"Almost there now, babs!" Mam chirped, taking a sharp

left into the affluent, cloistered housing estate where his great-aunt lived. The houses here were far, far bigger than the poky little terrace that they lived in. There were hardly any people around, Rossa noticed, just stately houses and manicured lawns. He closed his eyes for the next few turns, a lurching roller coaster, trying to focus on what the still air and steady ground would feel like when they got out. An hour of his mother's driving—or more specifically, his mother in a terrible mood and unable to focus on her driving—and it was nothing short of a miracle that he hadn't thrown up in his lap.

To Rossa's sweeping relief, the car slowed. Mam parked at the end of a cul-de-sac. Rossa undid his belt and leapt out of the car with such speed it surprised even him. Mae exclaimed, "Jesus, Rossa, wait for me," unpopping her headphones, emerging from her digital adventure. Her brother didn't answer, just flopped down onto the path a moment, heaving great undignified gulps of air. The relief of it.

His mother and sister began unloading a summer's worth of meticulously packed cases. Dad did not help, rather let himself out of his door and strode up to the house. He was pissed off at Mam and wasn't even trying to hide it. Rossa couldn't help but stare at him, marching ahead like the rest of them weren't there.

Before Dad was halfway up the path, the hall door opened and Great-Aunt Rita stood there in the frame. She opened her arms wide at the door, a gray shawl draped over them, and her neat white hair in a knot at the crown of her

17

head. Glasses circular, earrings pearl, long fingers stacked with rings. And an alarmingly large black-and-white cat at her feet. Dad picked up the pace, waved clumsily to her—a boy again in her long shadow.

"Paul, the state of you," she laughed, embracing him. Rossa's father buried his face a moment in his aunt's shoulder.

Mae and Mam trekked towards the house.

"Rossa, you lazy bollix, get up and help us with the bags!"

"Don't call your brother a bollix, Mae."

"But he is one!"

"I know he is, but you're not to be swearing!"

When Mam and Mae weren't arguing, they were play-arguing. It was nice to see, but it gave Rossa an ugly pang of jealousy. Mae found it so easy to slip into a friendship with their mother when things were good. He begrudgingly pulled himself up off the pavement and went to heft his case from the back of the car. It was heavy, jammed with T-shirts and jeans and markers and paper and books.

"Rita has plenty of books!" Mam had scolded as he stacked his case.

"But she won't have *my* books," Rossa had grumbled in reply: his crisp, neat sketchbooks, his charity-shop salvaged old anthologies of nature magazines, his favorite issues of *National Geographic*—he never got bored of them. He wasn't about to adjust his taste along with his whole dislocated summer: at least he'd have portals to the places he wanted to go with him. His little paper hideaways.

By the time he'd hauled himself up the driveway, his

dad had detached himself from Rita, but she still clasped his hands in hers. Mae was making smooching noises at the cat, who had his eyes closed and was nuzzling into her hand.

Now that he was up close, Rossa could see that the cat was absolutely the size of a dog. It was unsettling—little fangs poking from the corner of its maw making it look more beast than pet. Rossa would not be getting as cozy with him as Mae was anytime soon.

"It's good to see you again, Evelyn," Rita was saying to Mam. "You look great."

"Working on it, Rita. And you've barely aged a dot."

They kissed each other on both cheeks, effortlessly sophisticated. Both acting. It was more than a little uncomfortable until Rita turned to Rossa and his sister. "Mae and Rossa, you're only giants!" Her gaze was warm on the pair of them. "You pair and me and Bobby here will have a nice relaxing time while your folks are—"

"Off gallivanting!" Mam cut her off. "Absolutely dancing it around the south of France!"

Rossa despised the strange urgency on the edge of her tone: something was wrong. Why didn't they just tell him? He was fourteen, not stupid.

And Bobby was a stupid, stupid name for a cat.*

Rita nodded enthusiastically, covering for herself. "Both of you be gone now. I've Bevan Mulholland from the other side of the house coming in to put the dinner on."

---

* Bobby was not his name. That was the name Rita and Audrey decided on for him. Bobby Dear, the cat that came in the window. Neither girl knew what he was called before.

"Little Bevan?" Mam cooed. "I haven't seen her in years. I'd say she's gone real tall!"

Rita smiled. "Lion of a girl. She's mostly with me, now. Now away with ye, off to the sunshine. Make sure to drink lots of water and use factor fifty on your skin. I don't want a pair of lobsters showing up here on my doorstep! Send us heaps of postcards!"

Mae sprang up and squeezed Mam. "I love you, I love you!" Then she ricocheted to Dad. "I love you, I love you!"

Rossa rolled his eyes. He hugged his mother, then his father—but for a moment longer. Dad's eyes were wet, his mouth heavy in what was undeniably sorrow. His big hands rested briefly on Rossa's back, and then he was gone.

The green car revved with a familiar clunk, and their parents were away. The twins and their great-aunt waved at the door; then Rita ushered them and their cases inside.

Something was cooking on the stove in the kitchen, and Rossa could smell it from the doorway. He was, quite suddenly, starving. His stomach had flipped nausea for hunger in that way a belly does when it realizes the world isn't moving too fast for it anymore.

Rita's hallway was familiar in the strange patchy way that so many of Rossa's relatives' homes were. He'd been here before, once, twice—but he'd never noticed the statues. All of them were the Virgin Mary: her blue robe, her white face, her lips too red. A cluster of them stood on the hallway table, a tall one by the stairs. All in a little line, sisters in blue on a shelf above the radiator next to a bowl of potpourri and a cone of incense spiraling dense tendrils of gray. Rossa's house didn't smell like this.

The carpet, sun-bleached maroon scattered with gold, was soft under his sneakers. The pattern looked like it had once been flowers, now abstract from age. There was a shabby grandeur about the house: a small glass chandelier presided over the hallway, reflecting scattered prisms here and there. Rossa was unsure he would ever be able to be comfortable in a place like this. Even though it was quiet and still, the place felt busy, somehow. Like there was no room for him.

Bags abandoned in the hall, the twins were ushered into the kitchen. It was a long, bright room, cupboards painted eggshell blue, renovated so the ceiling was almost all glass, facing up at a sky barely dappled with summer clouds. Two huge double doors were flung wide onto a patio facing the manicured back lawn, a green stretch.

"It's more of a sunroom lately, isn't it, Bev?"

The tall blond girl stirring a pot on the huge wrought-iron stove nodded. "I like it better this way. It was too dark before you had the roof put in."

Rossa blinked at her. How were teenage girls so tall?

"Bevan lives in the other side of the house—ye've met before, though you were probably too young to remember. She helps me with odds and ends of the business. Her ma, Imelda, moved away, so we keep each other company, don't we?"

Rita didn't explain what "the business" was, or where Imelda went, or why. She pulled a spindly chair out at the table. The table felt almost too big for the room, a little too tall for the seats and wearing an oilcloth covering, patterned with prints of lavender and oranges. Rossa wasn't sure how anyone could eat off something so ugly but supposed he'd better get used to it. He wanted to go home. He wanted to run out of the house and chase after the car and go to France with his parents and make them tell him what was wrong, why Dad was so heavy in the face, why his eyes were so red.

Rita produced a slim white cigarette case from under her shawl. She lit up and drew heavily, a satisfied breath.

Mae was on the floor, the immense purring cat in her arms. She stared up at her great-aunt a second. She blinked, then couldn't contain herself.

"Are you sure you should be smoking, Rita?"

Rossa glared down at her—she could be so blunt. And she looked silly, still holding the cat. It was almost like the cat was holding her, the proportions all wrong.

Thankfully, their great-aunt did not seem to take the remark seriously, and laughed through a silver plume. "Let me have this, child. I've no vices left at all."*

Mae shrugged. "Dad's back on them again."

Rita raised her penciled eyebrows and tapped some dead gray into a crystal ashtray, silent a moment. "They're an impractical and dangerous cure for stress, but we take the small things while we can still get them."

"You won't let me have one," quipped Bevan, her back still to the room, grinding black pepper into the huge,

---

* Besides. It reminded Rita of Audrey. With every single lit cigarette, Rita thought of her. That made it at least ten times a day.

bubbling pot. "I'm stressed sometimes, I'd like to be cured."
The kitchen at home was all stainless steel and practicality.
Bevan's pot was burned orange and ceramic; it looked
ancient. Rossa wondered if it was clean. It sat on top of a
massive black stove: he'd never seen anything like it in real
life, only in illustrations in books. In the core of the beast,
a fire burned bright behind thick scorched glass. Was that
safe? He shifted in his seat.

"Sure what have you to be stressed over? You're not
made for this poison." Rita exhaled a cloud and Bevan
gave a dismissive "Yeah, yeah . . ."

Rossa thumbed the sleeve of his hoodie. The two girls
and old woman were at such automatic ease with each
other. He thought about asking to be excused, or where
the bathroom was, or could he go and unpack. He thought
about texting his parents, promising that if they came back
and took him along, they'd never even notice he was there.

But he didn't. Instead he opted for politeness. It was rude
just to leave so quickly after arriving. His opportunity would
come along, he'd just have to wait. He let a numb swathe of
boredom wash over him as his sister, aunt, and new neighbor,
or housemate, or whatever Bevan was, chatted away to each
other. This feeling of being slightly outside of things was
what the summer was going to be. It filled him with a
gentle sort of dread, and when the soup—bright squash and
thyme—was placed in front of him with fat wedges of soda
bread, he couldn't even manage a single bite.

THREE

Wʜᴇɴ you finally get away from the visiting children, you call upon him again and he comes quickly, almost without ceremony.

Ah, doesn't your skin feel so much better for his presence, your bare legs folded on the floor, your hands resting on your knees, symmetrical? You didn't even have to give him a feed tonight, just called his name soft, and out he came, coaxed easy from the paper.

Something like delight uncoils in your chest as he arranges himself amongst the fawn roses of the wallpaper. His beak, so white and sharp, seems more smiling today— if bone could smile. His feathers twitch and shift and he opens his eyes. They are huge, buttercup yellow with slit pupils like pure obsidian. Near your feet, at the sideboard, his marble claws protrude: they are teeth without a mouth. The air hums a little like sickness, a little like sex—but mostly like magic.* He is a parliament of one.

---

* Magic is such a big word. Almost as big as "love." Almost as big as "afraid."

25

You are scared.

He knows.

Your scalp feels tight, your eyelids too, and silently your corkscrews of mad yellow hair grow, become thicker. You laugh as the spirals twist low below your elbows—an inconvenient waterfall, a rush of curl.

"Stop!" You are playful, and he laughs, and the air is charged electric from the sound of him. A current runs through you, your fingertips thrum, and your nails grow an inch, sharpening before your eyes. You have never seen anything alive change so quickly before: this body doesn't feel like your own. His laughter is a night animal and a man and a storm. Yours becomes distorted in the air.

"I'll have to cut them, James," you whisper, watching your fingertips extend, talonlike, curved.

what if you couldn't cut them, he rumbles, and there's pressure then, crushing heat, like trapping your hands in the steel door of an oven—heavier than that, even, trapping them under a brick, a whole building, a mountain. Your scream is caught in your throat as you stare. Your flesh glistens away into something else. Your nails are diamond, your fingers are diamond, long shining rocks—sharp and glinting and impossible and full of fractals, casting tiny prisms as the summer day pours iced-tea light into your room.

"Thank you!" you gasp.

again, he says.

"Thank you!"

good, he says, and you are relieved. You wish he would speak more, his voice so enormous, so great.

You sit there in the quiet for a while, watching the movement of his feathers and bones, glowing with your new gifts. He'll turn your fingers back to normal soon, won't he? Of course he will. You'll have to cut your hair and burn it so no one notices it's happened, but for now, you are magnificent and strong, a baby monster at his feet, growing from his power, the fear ebbing and flowing in you like a cosmic sea.

He pulses in the paper, blinks long and slow.

bevan, there are children in the house.

"Yes," you reply. "Two."

are they of the crone's blood?

The crone. A terrible name for Rita. Rita loves you, doesn't she? You love her too—or you think you do. But Sweet James can call her whatever he wishes. Rita who's minded you since you can remember, who let you stay when your ma walked away. Rita, your other mother. Rita who teaches you how to read cards and how to listen to the strange static channel in your head that hears car accidents in the city an hour before they happen. But Sweet James, you are sure, is the one who gave you the coordinates to that frequency in the first place. Before he was huge, when he was just a strange rustling of leaves and petals on your wall. When you were a child, before he truly showed himself to you—he taught you how to listen. Rita just about raised you, but Sweet James made you whole. You owe him so much: this gorgeous nausea, this vertigo between fear and joy.

"They're her great-niece and great-nephew. Twins," you say.

your closeness to her does not please me.[*]

"But . . . but I live here. It's her house. . . ." Your gut drops. You knew he didn't like Rita, but hearing him say it is rotten fruit, is foaming mold.

it is my house. you know this, and yet you still tend the fire, and the fire keeps me from her.

You do. You stoked it minutes before you came up to your room. You raked over the flames, fed it turf and kindling, watched it swell and purr and crackle. You feel that pressure again in your hands and you look down— your nail beds still shine, but they are blackening. They sear and sing with pain and bright heat.

there are children in the house and i am hungry.

"I can get you all the bones you like. Gus—Gus likes me!"

i do not want bones. i want pieces of the children.

"I can't do that!" Your hands, your arms, the ends of your hair, your eyelashes are in flames.

fire is a terrible thing, isn't it?

You can't speak.

this is how the fire in the crone's kitchen makes me feel. i am so hungry, bevan. the fuller i am, the stronger you will become. the things i will show you . . . make me stronger. bring me pieces of the children.

The heat cools. Your arms and hands restore as if nothing ever happened and all those sensations had just been a

---

[*] Sweet James had never really liked Rita. There had been someone else he'd preferred.

28

too-tangible hallucination. Then the owl does something you have never seen before. You've seen him almost every single day since you were a little girl, and you thought you understood all the ways that he could scare you, bargain with you. But before your eyes, he shifts himself into a door. The physics of your bedroom defies itself, makes space for something new, and your eyes struggle with it for a second, like your optic nerves can't translate what is happening before you. He is an owl no longer then, and a volt of fear runs through you as the wooden rectangular door unlocks itself and swings open wide, revealing a room that cannot be there.

You are shaking.

You step forward.

FOUR

NEON. That's all you can take in at first, the ugly electric hum of something too gaudy for the indoors, too big. A fairground. A billboard off the motorway. You rub your eyes, knuckle white disturbances against your eyelids, and then look around, hard.

The room is empty and long. Twenty feet ahead of you there is a wall, and in the center of that wall there is another door. It is closed, though you can see it has a handle. The walls are pulsing with veins of that neon light, a galactic juxtaposition of star bright against void dark. The floor is glass, and just beneath, black water rushes below you. The air smells of it too, the water. Not salty or fresh, like being by the ocean. More like rain, like wet earth, though there's not a trace of earth in sight. Maybe, you think, this room isn't even attached to the planet. You'd played in caves by the sea once or twice as a child, waves rolling slow at your feet as you'd scoured rock pools for small, sharp animals to collect as souvenirs.

This feels like that—like a mouth to someplace else.

You look over your shoulder, and the summer light of your bedroom, cream and clean and ordinary, is just a few steps behind you, framed in Sweet James's door of paper and bone and owl and wrong. You take a few steps forward, your bare feet padding against the glass floor, which is uncannily warm. How is it so warm? Not warm like the sun, or like a fire. Warm like a body.

"Sweet James, is there anything . . . does anyone live in here?" you call, your voice strangely dull, as though the room is eating the sound of you.

there are things you will find out for yourself. His rich and terrible call comes down on you from everywhere: as though you are inside him.

You exhale, trying not to protest his unhelpfulness. You're lucky he's given you this much, this taste. You walk about, cautious at first. But the place is so empty. You look up: a ceiling—or rather, no ceiling—stretches out above you, blacker than black, abysslike.

Perhaps the strangest thing about the room is how indistinct it is. There aren't any chairs, or tables. There aren't any shelves by the walls, just all that sick neon tubing. No signs of life. Nothing to do but roll in the uncanny of it.

You pace back and forth. Without meaning to, what must be quiet feelings of disappointment leave your body in a deep sigh.

you are ungrateful, he snarls, before the thought even crosses your mind.

"I'm, I'm not, I just—"

i show you the first link in the chain of the other world, and you are bored by it?*

"I'm not!" Your voice is getting louder than you can control. "I swear!"

you are lying, and i can tell. you can hide nothing from me.

With that, a sucking gust pulls you from your feet and you are launched with roaring velocity back into your bedroom, your shins almost burning as you skid along the carpet. You are whiplashed from the force, winded. Sweet James erases the doorway in the wall like a mistake drawn on a piece of paper. You cry out, "Please no!" and he says, **ungrateful**, and you are weeping, pleading with him to let you back in. It was too quick. It's not fair.

Your bedroom is too bright now. Too ordinary. The reek of those god-awful air fresheners your mother used to hide about the place is almost scorching in your nostrils, the longing for that water smell rises in you like something terrible. You just wanted a little longer to look around—what if something *was* hiding in there? What if you missed something, the most important thing—what if you missed the whole point? You didn't even get to touch the next door.

"It's not *fair!*" you wail, pounding your fists on the carpet, the ordinary carpet. The carpet of your bedroom, of your world—while another one lies there, just beyond the

---

* Audrey had never seen neon like this. Audrey had never felt like this. So frightened, but so elated. Sweet James had found that very pleasing.

wall. What if you never get to see it again? Your stomach rolls and you feel your face crumple—how could this be it? What if that was all you'd ever get and you barely had a second, barely a moment, to touch it?

The great owl reassembles himself, unbending from door shape and back into himself, and as he does so, he chuckles, low, like the clicking of joints.

"Why did you kick me out? I wasn't done!" Your hot tears are unstoppable.

you were not ready, bevan. you will be, soon. maybe things will be a little fairer when you give me what i want. when you show me you are strong.

"I am, I am strong!"

Your voice cracks. You hate this. Worse, you hate that you have seen it now—that he could keep this wonder from you.

bring me a piece of one of the children, and i will let you in again.

You stay on the floor awhile, the longing for neon and water racking your body. You have to get back there. By the time your tears stop and you stand again, the sun has come up. You will take something from the twins. Something *real* good. Better still, you will make sure that neither of them notices a thing.

FIVE

THE next day, in the long sprawl of the twins' first full afternoon in the house on the crescent, Mae tucked herself out of sight. She didn't want Rita to know she was getting bored already, restless without her usual routine. So she snuck away to the bathroom to spend a little time applying thick purple mascara to her eyelashes. Rita had given it to her—a considerate small gift, and Mae had thrown her arms around her bony great-aunt, so touched was she by the gesture. Rita had given Rossa some toiletries as well, like a kind of welcome package, a small box of "make yourself at home" or "just in case you forgot anything."

However, Rossa, typically, had been cagey about the small shaving kit and shower gels. It was relatively obvious to Mae that her brother was nowhere near capable of growing a beard and thus had no use for shaving utensils, and had no idea whether to thank his aunt or take moderate offense so he just grunted a thanks and shuffled away. Mae would have loved to tease him about it, but it wasn't worth the risk of him getting in a huff. Lately he'd been all scowl and silence—there was no point even trying. Fourteen had eaten all the buzz out of him.

Mae reckoned she could get at least twenty minutes out of figuring out how to paint the fine, mousy strands surrounding her eyes with the weird, spiky brush in the tube. Then she'd cozy up someplace and play her Nintendo. A good plan for the day.

So she wedged herself between the large, marble bathroom sink and the thick windowsill, moving some hand creams and seashells out of her way. She dragged the brush along her eyelashes slowly: it felt invasive and heavy on her eyes. She could see the tint of it out of her peripheral, an amethyst frame on the world as she looked out the window. The view of the forest and the mountains was like something from the screen of one of her consoles, a reeling world full of promise and adventure.

Mae imagined herself, sword and shield on her back, healing potions hung about her belt, scaling the heights into the unknown of whatever lay beyond the peaks.* She would befriend mystic hermits, courageously banish troublesome creatures.

Maybe she'd ask Rossa to go out on a ramble with her tomorrow—but he might say no. He'd become so serious: this fresh new fourteen had been a rupture in them. God, what would fifteen do?

---

* Wicklow lay beyond the peaks. That was all. The unknown was nearer by than that.

She missed him. His quiet was so opposite of how he'd been before, and the quieter he got the louder she felt herself becoming against him, desperate to pull something, anything, out of him. Even if it was a tantrum, even if it was a mean name. Even if he stormed away from her, at least she'd have caused some effect. At least he'd have seen her. She'd hoped that since they were away from their friends for the summer, somehow they'd come closer together. But this last twenty-four hours hadn't spelled good weather for them—he'd rolled his eyes at her *twice* over breakfast. She'd only been talking about how they never have marmalade at home and how it felt like it came from another time, an antique food that real people surely didn't eat anymore, except in books. Rita was interested and all. She'd only been making conversation like a normal person, but he had prickled and almost recoiled at the sound of her voice. Like he was becoming allergic to her from overexposure.

A real sadness came over her then—no use thinking like that. The pair of them were made of the very same stuff; a split in the fabric of reality made them both possible. Her mam had said that the stars had aligned and she doubled her luck. The stars hadn't felt very aligned at all for Mae lately. It felt like she and her brother were from different planets. Maybe even different dimensions.

Mae looked away from the lofty mountains and over the dense forest and into the green quiet of Rita's back garden. It was a good garden, far more colorful than the little patch of concrete they had back in town. All they had in their yard was a washing line. Rita's garden had plants Mae had never seen before—even from up here she could tell it was a botanic paradise, something out of nature documentary. She ran her eyes over all the greens, the freckled daisies on the lawn, the clusters of fire that might be nasturtiums. Roses, she could see them. A troupe of sunflowers, standing tall and there—there suddenly like a jewel on the lawn, Bevan sprawled out under the sun on a tartan blanket, her flat stomach to the sky. Her legs a hundred miles of tan.

Oh *no*.

The dull unpleasantness of Mae's worry about Rossa transformed just then. A tightness in her chest, an awareness in her fingertips.

Had Bevan looked that way in the kitchen yesterday? Over the boiling pot, sitting at the rickety table, just an ashtray and a saltshaker away?

It wasn't as if Mae hadn't known about girls before this moment. She'd known, always, this fact about herself: girls were it. The sky was blue, the grass was green, girls were the thing. She'd just never felt it so starkly, with such accuracy. As she stared out the window at Bevan, something flooded her, heady and obvious.

The crush of it. Surely, that is exactly where the sensation got its name. *Crush*.

Out of nowhere, Mae was drunk on some new cocktail of anxiety and wanting. A little bit shaken, in fact. How come she hadn't noticed Bevan's hair yesterday, melted gold in the summer light? How could a body even look that way? Would her own body ever look that way?

The door creaked open, and the pyramid ears and yellow

eyes of Bobby the house cat poked into the room, whiskers and fluff, purring low. Mae blushed, gathering herself. She liked the cat. They weren't allowed to have pets at home, not even goldfish. Or houseplants, for that matter. Bobby was bigger and softer than any cat she'd ever seen. Gentle, too, and friendly, starkly opposite to the way that cats were usually aloof and a little destructive. She'd watched videos of cats on the internet and occasionally displayed them to her mother as a sort of petition, a series of failed hints. But none of the cats had looked like Bobby. None had eyes so big and intelligent, none had paws so big.

"You lonesome?" she asked absently.

"Are you?" replied the cat.

In the garden, you look up at the bedroom window when you hear Mae's scream. You tut under your breath and put in your headphones. Must mean the cat had started talking to her. It was bound to happen at some point or another.

"Stupid kids," you sigh to yourself, rolling onto your belly and unhooking your bikini top, building towards an even, perfect tan. You daydream of dancing in neon rooms. You wonder how it is, exactly, you will get back there again—what the next door will feel like under your palm.

When Mae had finished vomiting into the toilet and leaned, sweaty and chalky skinned against the tiles, Bobby curled up at her feet. The once-gorgeous mascara was now two symmetrical purple streaks down her tawny freckled face. The pock and dapple of them stood out stronger against her blanched skin.

"I didn't mean to frighten you," Bobby purred, apologetic. His voice was somewhere between the air in the room and feeling like it was inside Mae's head. A deep voice. Too deep. She didn't say anything, gagging again—*what is happening did I poison myself is the mascara seeping through my eyelids and making me hallucinate*—

"I can go and get Rita for you, if you need her." Bobby looked up at her, those eyes too human. More than human.

Mae choked out, "I'm—I'm fine. . . . Who, or—sorry, what *are* you?"

Bobby stood up, stretching, his fur liquid for a moment. The light in the bathroom went strange and gorgeous—a flash diamond, a blink iridescent. Mae's jaw hung open.

"I suppose I'm a cat. I've been a cat for quite some time. I think it's best if I don't elaborate for you, just yet."

"Where are you from?" the girl managed, bravely extending a hand to stroke his fur. If she just breathed a little, got steady and treated him as normal, she could make this normal.

He narrowed his eyes in that pleased way that cats do, leaning in to her touch.

"Up in the woods on the side of the mountain."*

Mae laughed a little, an awkward nervous habit, a small burst of noise that she couldn't stop coming out every time

---

* This is not, exactly, a lie. It is what he told Rita at first, too.

she couldn't think of something to say.

"I'm the only one of me, in case you think there's a colony of talking cats living over the garden wall."

Mae nodded, and Bobby climbed into her lap. A new, soft light seemed to be glowing off him and refracted onto her shirt, her jeans. He emanated a rumbling purr, the frequency of it almost normalizing the fact that Mae was having a conversation with a domestic animal. Something in her chimed then, a beautiful shock—magic was real. Here it was, curled up on her, in the body of a sweet, purring animal.

"Do you feel less sick now?"

"Yes. Yes . . . look, can I, can I tell my brother about you?"

"I'll show him who I am in time. Rita wanted me to come and get you. Something is about to begin for you."

Though she didn't like the idea of keeping this all to herself, Mae agreed. She whispered, "All right, just let me wipe my face first." Her knees like jelly, she picked herself up. The girl and the cat made their way down to the quiet living room, past a statue of the Virgin Mary that was so tall it was almost to Mae's hip. Had it always been there?

Mae realized then that she had no idea where her brother was. If he was in the house, why hadn't he come to her? Had he not heard her scream?

The kitchen was too hot, the fire roaring as though it wasn't two in the afternoon in July. It was a December stove fire, too big for this day. The smell of it was more Christmas than summer holidays. Mae was knocked a little by it as she entered the room, spun even further out than she already was.

Rita was poised at the head of the kitchen table, shuffling long, slim cards in her hands, her eyes half closed. On the radio, an afternoon DJ answered calls from listeners, their back and forth unintelligible, a thrum. Mae pulled up a stool and Bobby hopped into her lap as Bevan waltzed through the double doors, pulling a hoodie over her head, a flash of flesh concealed quick. She closed the doors behind her and planted herself across from Mae, not looking at her. A small woven basket was in the center of the table, lined with a paper towel, where a cluster of custard creams nested. The ashtray was like a fallen city of slate and sandy cigarette butts. A heap of crystals lay on the table, too—some rounded out, like berries, others raw and spiked. A golden spoon with a long handle lay amongst them.

"Light the incense from the stove for me there, would you, Bev?" Rita asked quietly, not taking her focus off the cards. Bevan rose immediately and began plucking a bouquet of incense sticks, one by one, from tall mason jars by the pantry. Fuchsia, mustard, aquamarine.

Mae could hardly sit still. She was so fevered, so claustrophobic in this heat, so thrilled to have been invited into this quiet domestic coven. Witches! she thought to herself. They're witches! Could she be a witch, too? She tried to keep solemn, keep a broad smile from pushing its way onto her face. Maybe it was Christmas in July, after all.

Bevan pulled open the heavy iron door of the stove, the belly of it dazzling flame and fat bars of embers. A bellow of heat pumped through the room as Bevan tipped the crowns of each wand in to light them, then blew the bright flames out so the tiny ember could release dense, precious smoke. The stove sounded like the heavy breathing of a very old, very large animal.

Mae was sweating. Bevan closed the stove door with a clunk of the handle, but the room was still so close, almost stormy. Mae was too nervous to ask to open the garden doors again. Maybe this was how magic got made, she figured, make the house a storm.

"Do you know what these are?" Rita met Mae's eyes. Mae shook her head. Her great-aunt flickered a smile. "That's all right, sweet pea. This is a tarot deck. Seventy-two cards that together, and individually, tell the story of life. They're a language. A tool. They're my business, and since you're here with me for the summer, they should be yours too. I'm sure you'd rather this than aimless field trips to the zoo and museums, wouldn't you?"

Mae nodded.

"Good. These'll get you listening closer to your environment. Looking harder at your surroundings. Isn't that right, Bevan?"

"Yeah. They're like . . . cyphers." The tall girl had placed the tricolor of incense into holes in the back of a small brass hedgehog, and she sat it on the table by the crystal heap. She then broke a custard cream in two and absently licked the cream from the center. Mae shifted. "Do you know what a cipher is?" Bevan asked.

Mae felt uncomfortable and stupid at once. She lifted

Bobby off her lap and onto the table. He wasn't going to give her any clues.

"No."

"They're a kind of . . . a cheat sheet for the story of the world. Once you start looking for signs and symbols, you won't be able to, like, *un*see them." Bevan threw the clean rectangles of biscuit into her mouth, chewing inelegantly.

"Is that how magic works?" whispered Mae, regretting it immediately as Bevan snorted, "Magic! Ha!"

Bobby swatted her with his paw. "Don't be rude."

"Be kind, Bevan," Rita said. "No, Mae, this isn't about magic. This is about intention, and perception: seeing and feeling the secrets of the world. Opening yourself up to it. Now. Pick a card."

Rita fanned out the deck in front of Mae.

"Don't think. Just listen. See which one calls you."

With trembling fingers Mae reached out, the gaze of the witches and the cat on her, the heat in the kitchen clinging to her skin. She selected a card from the left side of the spread, a little out of sight. It wasn't exactly singing her name or anything, she just wanted this tense, judgmental moment to pass. The card came away from the deck like a petal departing a daisy, Mae thought. She loves me, she loves me not. . . .

"Turn it over," Rita instructed, folding the cards back into a deck.

Mae flipped the card and placed it on the table. Drawn in delicate black ink, a gray cygnet swam on a lake of fine black lines. At the bottom of the card, "Page of Cups" was printed in austere lettering.

"Cups, sure I told you so!" Bevan laughed.

Rita was smiling. "You did. Get up and put the kettle on, would you?"

The tall girl rose, cackling to herself. "That's hilarious!"

Mae was baffled, staring down at the little picture of the baby bird.

"Is that supposed to be me?" she ventured.

Rita nodded. "Somewhat. The tarot is partially broken into four houses, like a regular deck of cards, but instead of clubs, spades, diamonds, and hearts, the tarot has wands, swords, pentacles, and cups. Cups is the house of emotion, friendship, and love."

Mae wasn't sure that her temperature could rise any more than it already had. Her palms were sweating, her brow. She wasn't sure she liked the idea of a piece of paper opening up chats about her emotions—especially not with Bevan hovering by the kettle, so much hair, eyes too big for her face.

"Is that good?" Mae asked, scarlet.

Rita smiled and nodded. "Yes. It shows you have a way to go but are overflowing with potential and emotion."

"Well, she is like, twelve, Rita," Bevan remarked, over her shoulder. "Of course she's overflowing with emotion."

Mae almost gasped, she was that embarrassed, that quickly.

"I'm fourteen!" she squeaked.

Bevan rolled her eyes. "Twelve, fourteen, no difference."

Rita clicked her tongue and turned to Bevan. "What cards, remind me, did you draw most of when you were her age?"

Bevan turned, three empty mugs hanging from her fingers as the kettle began to scream.

"Pentacles," she replied. "What?"

"Pentacles and what, exactly. The cards don't know or care what age you are. They're indiscriminate," Rita continued. "Now stop being a brat, Bev, or Mae won't want to sit in with us."

Bobby made a noise and stretched out over the table, looking over at Mae. He winked at her. Mae didn't say anything, just looked back to the baby bird on the card. It was pretty. The cards couldn't all be that pretty, could they?

"Are there any bad cards?" she ventured.

Rita said, "No," and Bevan, pouring the scalding water into the mugs, said, "Yes."

Mae's stomach dropped.

The teenage witch and the crone stared at each other for a moment. Rita put the cards down.

"Don't lie to her, Rita," Bevan said. "There's a couple. There's definitely at least one."

Rita reached into her packet, took a cigarette from the slim white box, and lit up.

"No card is entirely bad. We can't exist under those terms. The Hanged Man, Death, the Eight of Swords, the Three of Swords, they—"

"The Tower?" Bevan interrupted.

"The Tower. They are all cards that denote difficulty or crisis or secrecy or change, betrayal perhaps—but these things are all part of life."

Bevan banged the mugs on the table. Rita smoked and

heaped sugar into her tea. Mae sweated and sweated. Bevan didn't sit back down; rather, she leaned against the counter, eyebrows raised.

"There's as many bad cards as bad things in life," Bevan said. "The Daughter of Cups can also signify naïveté. Immaturity. Inclination toward addiction. Dependence. I mean, you're a twin, so of course you're overly dependent. The Daughter of Cups makes promises she can't keep." Bevan listed these flaws out on her fingers, her eyes on Mae all judgment.

"That's enough, Bevan," Rita snapped.

Mae felt like a bowstring, too taut, about to break. There was a beat or two of awful silence as Rita took two long pulls off her cigarette. Ragged inhale, hiss exhale.

Bobby purred, nudging the biscuits toward Mae with his paw. "Bevan can be a little prickly. Teenager business. You've all that ahead of you."

"I . . . can . . . can we open the doors, please? It's very hot. I can't drink my tea—can I have something cold—please?" Mae's voice was shakier than she liked, but at least she'd managed to say something. She felt charmless now. Out of place.

Bevan swanned over and flung the veranda door wide, a swathe of air refreshing the room. "Let me ice that tea for you. You'll like it." She swooped up the cup from Mae and walked to the fridge, ignoring the hardness in Rita's face.

"Bevan sometimes can't quite look away from the negatives," Rita said. "You can focus in on the darkness too hard while you read the tarot. It's almost easy—like all shadows, they pull your vision."

Bevan set a tall, cold glass down in front of Mae, and Mae took a long drink. It wasn't sweet, but it was cold—and that was enough, for a few seconds.

"Have you been reading the cards for long?" she asked Rita.

Rita hissed a low sigh. "I came to the tarot after I lost someone I loved very much. I wasn't much older than Bevan. For a long time all I could read in the cards was tragedy. This house was a house of swords: I drew the Devil again and again."

She stubbed her cigarette into the ashtray and immediately lit another. Mae thought of Rita's age, her deep voice—Mae's eyes flickered to her rising and falling chest, imagining her lungs. How many cigarettes had she demolished at that pace? How much smoke was in her body?

"Where did you get the cards? Is there a shop for these kinds of things?" Mae asked.

"It's bad luck to buy your own cards," Bevan interjected. Rita let the statement hang.

"Superstitions will get you no place," murmured Bobby.

Rita held the middle distance in her gaze a second, then spoke again.

"These ones . . . dear Imelda, Bevan's mother, got for me when Bevan was just a child. They aren't my only deck, or my first. But they're my favorite. My—well, Audrey— my best friend gave my first deck to me many, many years ago, before she left Dorasbeg. I don't know where exactly they came from.* I've still never seen anything quite like them, they were full of strange figures in strange rooms. It was hard to find any light in them at all. They're long gone now, but each image is seared into me. Even in these cards I see those bodies, those rooms."

The ash grew long at the top of Rita's cigarette, climbing towards her fingers like rot. "Rita gave me a deck for my twelfth birthday and it's not even a little bit like either of those," Bevan remarked, diffusing the dark energy with her clipped, confident voice. Mae marveled at the control Bevan held over the space. Not necessarily over Rita, but over the mood in the room.

"What do yours look like?" Mae asked.

Bevan closed her eyes and sighed. "They're a traditional Toth deck. They're way weirder looking than these ones here. More psychedelic, or something. I'll graduate to a fresh deck at some point, but I kind of like these ones. They tell the story of life in a different way than Rita's cards. Besides, I'm not ready to read for anyone but myself yet, so they're kind of just for me."

"You are ready, you know," Rita corrected. "You just don't want to."

Bevan shrugged. "Well, that's more or less the same thing, isn't it?"

"Perhaps." Rita stubbed out her cigarette. "Look, Mae. We'll meet here in the afternoons, while you're staying with us. Most days I practice yoga on the lawn in the early

---

* She did know, but Rita knew a lot of things she didn't say.

morning. Then I visit clients or see them in the living room from around nine until midday. We can begin after that.

That was Rita's business. A medium, a mystic, and yes—yes, a witch. Mae let out a soft "Oh!"

"Before we finish up, will you perform a reading for me please, Bevan? Rossa can't possibly be out much longer, and I don't want him getting involved in all this just yet. He's quite a closed boy; we have to go gently. No use in disturbing him."

Mae almost snorted at the idea of Rossa being disturbed over anything. Though it didn't seem fair to her at all if Rita was just getting him out of the house so they could play with these cards without him seeing. Leaving him out felt bad to her, a rupture in something already weak. Why couldn't they involve him somehow?

Rita shook her head and began shuffling the cards again. "The little love offered to bring some parcels down to the post office, so I gave him a list of jobs to do for me in the village. He's a dear heart." Rita was smiling into the cards.

She drew one and held it facing her, the back to Bevan. Her expression was blank. The witches were locked at the eyes.

The tall girl crossed her arms and leaned back. Mae looked at her, then at Rita, then over at Bevan again.

"The Star. Inverted," Bevan said.

Rita set the card facedown on the table. She drew another. Bevan took more distance, moving across the kitchen, cocked her head to the side.

"The Page of Pentacles. Upright?" There was a query

in Bevan's tone, an inflection of uncertainty that surprised Mae. She sounded almost like a normal person.

Rita's face remained expressionless this time, as she put the card beside the last on the hideous tablecloth.

"One more," she said, drawing a final card.

The answer was instant this time.

"The Tower," hissed Bevan, almost as soon as Rita had the card upright. The brutality in Bevan's voice ran a jolt through Mae. Rita placed the card on the table and sighed deeply.

"Three for three," said her great-aunt, an air of resignation in her voice. "Though the Page of Pentacles was inverted, not upright."

Bevan thrummed her fingers on the table, impatient. "Can I please move up to six? I can do it. Just let me show you."

"Not yet. Last time we went to six you collapsed—your head missed the corner of the table by barely an inch."

"I want to know what happens after the Tower." Bevan's teeth were clenched. She wiped her brow. From the beads of sweat on her face, it was clearly physical work, all that reading. Mae was awestruck—she cast a glance to Bobby, who gave her a nod.

Rita shuffled the three plucked cards back into the deck. "You'll know in due time. Don't exhaust yourself. Look at you, ringing with the sweat already."

Bevan exhaled petulantly. Rita placed the cards back into a soft linen bag, bidding them goodbye with a kiss.

"Why don't you take a lie-down, Bev? That was a lot of hard work." An order framed as a suggestion.

"Sure," Bevan accepted. "Later, Mae. See ya, Bobby." For

a strange moment, she stood, towering over Mae, surveying the table one last time. An uncomfortable few seconds passed; then Bevan suddenly ruffled Mae's hair. Intense and invasive for a second, and then she turned on her heel and walked out of the kitchen. The door clicked shut behind her. She was gone.

"Bevan's clairvoyance comes easy to her, but pushing and asking her to see through surfaces exhausts her. In time, she'll get stronger."

Mae tilted her head to the side. "Can you do that, too? See things?"

"Your brother will ring the doorbell twice, in seven seconds."

Rita counted down with her fingers—seven, six, five, four, three, two, one. *Ding ding.*

Mae's skin nearly leapt off her body, but even so, she dismissed it as a silly fluke as she rose to answer the door. Rossa stood there on the steps, rain just beginning, a plastic bag in his hand.

"Howya."

"Howya," Mae replied as he stepped indoors. Was his voice different?

"What did you get up to today?" he asked, rustling his shopping bag at her. "Just missed the rain!" Bobby stalked down the corridor and nuzzled Mae's calves.

"Nothing much. Just listened to some music. Played cards."

"Sounds dull," Rossa said.

Mae shrugged. Bobby looked up at her, eyes like butter.

SIX

Yᴏᴜ kneel on the carpet, like praying. Isn't this prayer? A slim strand of the girl's hair is woven between your long fingers, almost cat's cradle. Your breathing is still uneven from the reading. You should sleep, but you cannot wait to call him with this—this small stolen thing, this piece of the child. This must be something like what he wants. It might have been safer to wait until after dark, when the house was sleeping—but you couldn't hold on for him much longer. Nobody has ever caught you. Why would they catch you today? You can't imagine someone just walking in on you, Christ.*

"Sweet James . . . ," you whisper, placing your left hand on the wall, the hair woven across your fingers, your palm an altar.

---

* When Audrey cut off all her hair, her mother began to get suspicious. The nuns in their gray habits came to visit her house some mornings. Audrey should have taken that as a warning. Getting caught doesn't always look like confrontation. Getting caught can be a gradual snare: all the doors closing until the room is a prison.

The air around you distorts electric, delicious. You pull your hand away and look up at him as he comes together in the paper, the clicking and crumbling and pulling sounds of it waking your whole body up. You wipe wet salt from your forehead.

He arrives fully, his toxic eyes on you, his pupils god-awful triangles. Today he catches the light, like more mirror than bone. As you let him fill your vision, you could almost swear you see his reflection in the scaffolding of him—an infinity that goes on and on. His laugh is deep and long, double bass and bad. Your skin prickles with delight.

what have you brought me?

He sounds different: amused. Strangely human.

"A piece of the girl twin," you say, holding up the hair, and he laughs again. But this is not good laughter, this is scorn. Heat gathers in your cheeks.

a lock of a child's hair. how archaic. do you think you live in a fairy tale, bevan? do you think i can feed on stray strands of a child? this waste?

Hellish, rolling laughter. Mockery. You are so stupid. You've never displeased him like this before. You are panicking. "I'm sorry, I'm sorry," you splutter, fat tears escaping your eyes.

eat the hair, he commands, and you do, brittle choking string in your mouth. It pulls at your throat, but you'd do anything to please him. You gag and try to swallow, you retch but force it down. You murmur sickened apologies while he laughs.

next time bring me something more, something

harder to steal. work harder for me. i give you so much.

He's right. He does. He chose you, he comes only to you. You have to be better for him. You have to give him more. You nod, his eyes pulling you apart at the seams.

"I can't bring them up here yet. Rita will be suspicious," you nervously admit.

What you don't say is that you don't want to share him, and you don't want to hurt them: you're not sure which impulse is stronger, but combined it is a blaring *no*.

He takes a moment to respond, his breath low and thrumming. He is considering the risk of Rita. You wish you knew more about their relationship. What happened before is still only hushed hints, some eternal rivalry percolating over that fire in the kitchen, burning away in the stove.

fair, he concedes. **bring me something better, something more of theirs next time. steal me something hidden.**

"Will you let me into the rooms again if I do?" you ask, longing swelling up inside you for that faraway air, that break in reality, the smell of running water, the neon— your hand on the doorknob, the shock of whatever comes next. Sweet James chuckles as you sweat there.

you can have one more room now for being such a good girl. you will work hard to come back, won't you?

You will. As he speaks, threat and order, he unfolds into the door. You are on your feet before you even know it, propelled by curiosity, by rapture. The only thing you

55

notice about the neon and water room is the smell, because you are bolting to the next door, your greedy fingers on the knob. It turns and opens and you step beyond, the glory of new light on your body. God, it is different here—this is what you craved.

The room is chalky white and long, ceilings arched, a fat tunnel. All over the walls bloom graying flowers, and you draw breath as they twitch, as their slate petals blink—they are moths, resting in clusters. Beyond the breathing flutter of their movement, you think you hear a bird singing somewhere. But you can't see any birds. Just moths. The air smells tropical, floral. Sweet James rumbles a soft laugh, and you are pleased.

"Yes!" you gasp. You are delighted. "Can I touch them?"

take one, he offers, **in exchange for your little present. be quick.**

You step forward and face the wall. Their soft bodies are the length of a thumb, marked in white and black—almost like dotted eyes and sharp teeth, almost smiling. Their wings open, a greeting. You extend a finger, an invitation. One little fool steps cautiously onto your skin, a thrill.

Each second that passes rings heavy in your veins, hurry hurry please don't let this end before I have you. The owl laughs again. Your finger is a gangplank the moth tiptoes up, boarding the trembling ship of your body. You have it. It is yours.

The air begins to pull around you, and you know it is over. You pray the gust of expulsion doesn't dislodge your tiny prisoner, your papery treasure.

You run, alight, your velocity disturbing the remaining holy creatures, their wings opening all at once in a quiet thunder but too quick you're back into the glowing first room and the new door slams behind you. The strange wind picks up further as you sprint, landing back in your room on your knees, carried by Sweet James's force. You look over your shoulder as the door begins to fold away.

You get up, skipping, elated, to your bedside table, an empty plastic water bottle, pink, waiting for use. An old gift from your ma. "Stay hydrated!" and all that half-arsed advice. You unscrew the fat lid with your free hand, awkward. The moth folds its wings, obedient now in your world. You lead him down this new corridor, this plastic trap, and promise you'll make him a new, better home tonight, after you rest. Moss, you think, maybe. A few little pebbles.

"In you go," you murmur, "in you go." He tumbles into the pink, and before he can spread his wings, you have the lid on. He flutters, rose colored and helpless in this prison. You leave the top a little unscrewed, for air. Does it need air? Was the air in that room the same as out here? You place your captive down on your locker and flop onto the bed, face into the blanket.

Sweet James says, **you are happy.**

You reply, "Yes."

He tells you to say it again.

"Yes," you say. "Yes . . ."

Your eyes droop closed, and a deep nap takes you in the fading afternoon light. The moth in the bottle stops fluttering. He gives up.

SEVEN

THE week rolled on, lazy days identical in their hush. Rossa sat alone in the guest room, fat sketchpad in his lap, headphones in. Sometimes he had to check what day it was, so similar were they. He was bored, but cozy in that boredom. A magazine depicting a burning forest sprawled out in front of him. A rapidly cooling mug of milky sweet tea and a clutch of chocolate biscuits on a floral saucer sat beside him.

It was still bright out, even at nine o'clock, waiting on sunset. This must be what his mam meant when she'd sigh at their kitchen window in the dark, long winter nights.

"We won't be long waiting for the grand stretch now, just a few more months," she'd say. Like she was solar powered, she only got strong in the bright light.

He led the soft coal of his pencil this way and that, pulling something that resembled a stag out of the air. He liked drawing animals; they were gentler to look at than buildings or machines. They had faces. He wanted to tell Mae that he was homesick. He could have, maybe six months ago. But he had no idea how to talk to her anymore. He pushed the pencil harder. Why was she so different now? Something was going on with her and Rita. This week he'd caught them whispering in the kitchen two afternoons in a row. And both times, they paused upon his entry to the room, before a dramatic, too-loud change of subject. Mae had no subtlety. Why wasn't he being included? Did he do something wrong?

He scowled, splintering a pair of antlers on the page in dark lead. Was it because he was a lad?

He could really do with a few quiet rounds of Star Fox or Mario Kart with his dad right now. He couldn't remember the last time they'd done that together—or maybe they'd only done it once or twice, and he was stretching the memory out as far as it would hold. Rossa didn't even need to have chats with him. Just to be near his smell, fabric softener and Major Gold cigarettes. Rossa was mortified at himself, red cheeked and wet eyed with homesickness in an old lady's house, barely over a week into his stay.

Bowie's weird minor trills just made it worse, and he pulled his headphones out, resentful. The stag was just an outline. Wonky. Rossa struck him out then, a bolt of thick black, a strike of frustration. He got up to shake it off. Where was Mae now, anyway? She'd skirted off with that bloody cat and he hadn't seen her since. He'd go and find her and confess, straight out, that he was homesick. Anything not to face weeks and weeks of this strange silence, this not knowing, this being left out. Maybe if he nipped it in the bud, this could be an adventure summer for him. If he gave Mae a secret, one of his very own, maybe she'd tell him some in return.

He stepped out of the room into the hallway and there she was; had she grown another three inches? Her jeans were too short on her, her feet bare, mop of curls just like his but in an unwieldy scrunchie on the crown of her head. The cat, too large, was under her arm, her phone in her hand. The bright white of the messenger screen cast light up onto her face. A ring of short, slim Virgin Mary statues was right by her feet, as though they'd just sprung up there, like mushrooms. Had he just not noticed them before?

"I found a spot of coverage. Da says they're settled in the villa, it's gorgeous and sunny," she said, careless, not looking up. "I'm going to send him a selfie of me and Bobby."

Rossa flinched, pulled his phone out of his back pocket. No messages.

"He texted you? He didn't text me," he said, voice catching, cheeks on fire.

Mae shrugged, putting her phone away, adjusting her grip on Bobby so she was holding him like an enormous, unwieldy baby. His deep purring was audible across the hall, and it only incensed Rossa even further. He didn't say anything, the twins staring at each other there in the corridor.

"He probably just thought I'd tell you," Mae said, eyes flicking to her brother's reddening cheeks, his fists clenching and unclenching. "It's not a big deal."

"It wouldn't be a big deal if it was the only thing!" Rossa exploded. "Why is nobody including me!"

Mae didn't flinch, matched his volume. "Because you're pissy and moody and no fun! You don't include yourself! Why would anyone bother talking to you?"

"Because . . . because . . . ," Rossa stammered. "Because you and me are meant to be the same!"

"We *were* the same, Rossa, until you got all grumpy and weird. I'm still just myself, you're the one who sulks all day."

"I don't sulk!"

The cat watched the argument ricochet back and forth.

"What were you doing before I came up?" Mae asked, cocking her head to the side, accusatory.

"I was drawing and listening to music!"

"Sounds like sulking to me. You've been up here since after lunch."

"That's because, unlike you, I don't need to be in everyone else's faces all the time, sucking up to Rita, putting weird makeup on your eyes."

"Being nice and polite isn't the same as sucking up." Mae was starting to go red now herself. He'd hit a nerve. "And my mascara looks savage!"

"You're not going to impress them. They'll see through you eventually, it's plain as day that Bevan thinks you're a sap—"

"You shut your mouth!" Mae was scarlet then, quieter, eyes shining. Her grip around Bobby tightened.

"She's not going to be your friend. Mam and Dad and Rita can fawn over you all they want because you're a girl or whatever, but Bevan knows you're just a child."

Mae didn't say anything back this time, hot tears spilling

from her eyes. She lowered the cat softly onto the floor and turned away from her brother. She began to walk away, down the stairs. Rossa watched her go, steadying his breath. Bobby padded after her.

Only when Rossa heard the swing of the living room door did he let himself cry. Just for a moment, one ugly moment; then he wiped his tears away with the sleeves of his hoodie. He hadn't been fair. Mae got the worst of their parents. But she also got the best of them, and that made him angry, and he had to keep quiet about being angry all the time. From down the stairwell he could hear the rise of the weird easy listening oldies she was, he assumed, passive-aggressively blaring.

He didn't want to go back into his room; he needed air. The garden, he thought. He scurried quietly down the stairs and off through the kitchen. Rita sat, smoking, with a book, news rolling mutely on the little television, the sound of Mae's emotional orchestra bleeding into the room.

"Headed outside?" Rita remarked, not looking up.

"Yes, wanted to . . . catch the sunset. I'm—I'm coloring it." Rossa's voice caught as he turned the key in one of the glass doors. He left the kitchen, stepping out into the coral pink light.

The air was beginning to cool now, and it soothed him. He exhaled deeply and stepped down the patio onto the winding cobble path, past the small, empty chicken run, the lush waterfalls of wisteria flowing from the shed's roof. There, on the bench at the back wall, sat Bevan. Christ's sake, thought Rossa, here we go.

★

Christ, you think. Here we go.

She was reclining, legs stretched out, golden and muscular, drinking something from a pink water bottle. Does she ever just wear jeans, like a normal person? Rossa wondered. A glossy magazine was open in her lap, ignored, her phone angled toward her face. Rossa despised her, so proud and willowy, her easy demeanor a taunt.

"Want something to drink?" she offered, without so much as a hello. Rossa was sure this was the first sentence she'd ever said directly to him. He looked at the pink bottle again: it was full of a dark liquid.

"Is that . . . alcohol?" Alcohol. Nobody calls it alcohol. Nice, Rossa. Real smooth.

Bevan snorted. "No. As if I'd give booze to a child. It's actually something a little better." She took a long swig, resumed staring at her phone, as if Rossa wasn't there at all. Anger prickled through him. He was still upset over Mae, and this was the last thing he wanted or needed. He clenched his jaw. "What's in it, then?"

"Tea." Bevan didn't look at him this time. "But, like, magic tea."

Rossa scoffed at her. "It's not fair to take the piss out of me, Bevan."

"Don't say piss. You're only twelve. No cursing." Still no eye contact whatsoever. "Do you want the magic tea or not?"

64

"I'm fourteen."

"Whatever."

The boy hissed an exhale. "Tell me what's in it."

Bevan sighed dramatically. "Fiiiine. White tea leaves, dried rose petals, three jasmine pearls, elderflower cordial, a spoonful of brown sugar, and one gray moth." She drank deep from the bottle. "And a whole rake of gin. I lied. There's alcohol."

"A moth?"

"Yeah. I caught a moth a few days ago. Then I took a nap, and when I woke up it had gone to powder, so it was either snort it or drink it, and here we are."

"You are so weird." Rossa took a step back.

Bevan laughed. "Yeah. I suppose." She drank again and Rossa flinched, picturing skittering moths on a ceiling, their flaky wings.

"At least sit down. You're so awkward, you're worse than your sister."

Rossa flushed, wanting to stay standing just to spite her, but took the other end of the bench, almost autopilot, obedient despite himself. A few more disquieting silent beats passed. She took another swig.

"Fine. Give me a shot of it then," Rossa demanded, gruff.

Bevan handed the bottle to him, her wrist an indifferent hinge, barest sly smile on her face. Rossa unscrewed the top and without pause, took a long drink. Vile, sweet, strong liquid in his mouth—he forced a swallow—was that a rose petal caught in his throat? Or a piece of a wing? The weird spike of alcohol, he knew immediately. It was like something innate, though this was his first-ever taste. Maybe he was only imagining his head lighter, his limbs looser. Why was he grinning with his whole mouth, what was this laughter?

Bevan stood up, looming over him, her skin rippling iridescent. Like a fish, like a seashell, like terrible, like *oh no*.

"What . . . what was in this?" Rossa slurred, full of a rolling, strange joy—frightened, elated—and Bevan just laughed. She placed her long fingers in her own mouth but somehow Rossa felt them in his, something moving and deep and sore in the back of his jaw. A god-awful pulling, the metallic undeniability of blood on his tongue.

Mae had knocked out one of his teeth with a television remote when they were five and that same disgust rolled up now, the sureness of something leaving his body before it was ready. Bevan was doing this, taking this—she was pulling a dormant tooth from the back of his mouth.

His eyes were fixed open on her form, fingers in her mouth, glimmering all wrong in the sunset. He couldn't make a sound. He couldn't stop her.

She's a witch, he thought. She's a witch.

The tooth broke free then, a severing bolt of agony in his mouth. He gagged and burbled it out, spit bright blood into his palm and down his chin. He retched and Bevan thrust the bottle at him again.

"Finish it," she said, her voice deep and unholy, and Rossa obeyed her.

She plucked the tooth from his open hand and wrapped it in a square of kitchen towel—she was prepared, she had planned this—but the bottle was to his lips, that sweet sharp tea quelling the deep ache at the right side of his jaw, washing away the copper, flooding him with hazy good again.

Rossa drank deeper. The bottle emptied, a loss greater than any tooth, how he'd have loved just a few drops more. But Bevan took it from him and picked up her magazine from the bench. She thrust another slice of paper towel at him, patterned with strawberries and lemons and apples cut in half.

"Stay here for ten minutes. Clean your face, then throw this over the garden wall. You won't feel like anything is missing. Actually, you won't feel a thing. Not a single thing," Bevan instructed, turning on her heel to walk back into the house.

"Why? Why did you take my tooth?" Rossa managed, tongue heavy.

Bevan didn't turn around to answer, just said, "Stop asking questions. Do as you're told." Then she stepped into the kitchen, sliding the door closed behind her.

EIGHT

IN the afternoon, the day after the fight, Mae sprawled out on the living-room floor in a fat beam of sunlight. A bright record turned on the stereo, and Doris Day breathed sweetness through the air. Bobby lay beside her on his back, his belly to the ceiling, and Mae absently stroked the plain of his body. He purred happily.

She still felt a little strange talking aloud to him. A cat. She was always sure that eventually he'd just not talk back, that she would have been imagining it.

"When can I tell Rossa?"

She was still upset with him. Really upset. But maybe sharing something like this would bring them closer together—if Rossa was angry at her for having secrets, perhaps giving him one, like a gift, would mend things. He'd been cruel, but she could tell from his eyes that he was hurting her because he was hurt himself.

Bobby stretched. "I'm not stopping you from telling him. But we can get better work done if this is just you, me, Bevan, and Rita."

Mae furrowed her brow. "I'm not so sure. It's not really fair."

Bobby spoke through his purrs. "I am not sure he would be open to me."

He wasn't wrong. Mae didn't know much about her brother lately, and if he wasn't open to her, he wasn't going to be open to a talking domestic animal. He would have loved it last summer, back when they were still telling each other stories and having actual conversations instead of merely exchanging syllables. These days it felt like Rossa hated the sound of her. She could almost see his scorn.

She didn't say anything for a moment or two, listening to the sugary crescendo of Day's voice, something about secrets, something about love. She thought, despite herself, of Bevan then.

Maybe she should ask Bobby about Bevan. Get up the courage to say the girl's name aloud. Inquire. Gently. All right.

Couple of deep breaths. Then, "Is she nice? Bevan?"

Bobby chirruped, something like a laugh. "No, she's not, but that won't stop how you feel."

That stung. Not that he said it, but that it was true. Day changed key, and her voice swelled up. Mae's stomach lurched. It felt good and bad all at once.

The cat nuzzled his head into her side. "Love's a funny one. This is just your first go-round. You'll love again when it's over."

Love. The word was too big for the shape of the room, too big for the shape of her. But no sense in denying it. She knew it was love, like she knew colors and numbers. It was obvious. Fine, let love be what it was. Calling it other names doesn't change how it feels. Even when it feels shameful and kind of sad and worst of all, absolutely impossible.

"That doesn't sound very hopeful, does it?" whispered Mae.

"No." Bobby made eye contact with her, and she was alarmed by how human his gaze was, even though he wasn't at all human—or all cat.

She sighed and sat up, the record clicking and hissing to a halt. "I think I'm going to listen to that song again."

"You'll listen to it all summer, then every time you hear it again you'll think of her. Even when you grow up." Bobby rolled over and stretched out, flexing his fat paws.

"You're a cat. How do you know how I'll feel?" Mae buzzed over to the record player. They didn't have one of these in her house, a hefty machine from long ago. Using it had a certain ceremony to it, the flat black moons of vinyl like relics, full of mystery. She leaned her face low and checked to make sure she kept the track just right, lifted the needle, and placed it carefully. Hiss, then melody, gorgeous.

"I'm so old, and you're so young," Bobby replied, over the music. "I know lots of things, and one of those things is that love is love is love no matter what kind of soul you are or where you're from. I saw all of Rita's heartbreak. This won't be so different."

Hold on. Rita's heartbreak?

This was gossip. Mae *loved* gossip. Gossip is lessons learned through other people's mistakes. And if they were talking about Rita, they didn't have to talk about Mae herself anymore.

"Ohmygoodness." Mae leapt over to him and rubbed that endless snowy belly again. "Tell me the story."

Bobby shook his head, "No, no, no . . . not yet."

Mae could envision Rita and some handsome young man in the days gone by. He must have left and she must have stayed behind, how tragic! Maybe he left on a boat for America, or took the ferry to England for work. Maybe he promised her he'd return,* but never did. Maybe he promised he'd write letters, maybe he wrote her one or two but then forgot† all about her! Mae was wistful already.

"Please?" She scratched Bobby's chin, and he narrowed his eyes in that lovely cat way, that happy way.

"No way, girleen, it's not my story to tell you."

She flopped back down beside him and sighed. "It's not fair that you know my big secret but won't tell me any."

"I am a secret, isn't that enough?"

He didn't even look at her, but he said it with such certainty that Mae was stilled by it. She was in the presence of something cosmic, and yet trusting it was so easy. Liking Bobby was so easy, he drew all this sweetness out of Mae. He was right, though, wasn't he? He was the secret she got to keep. That was a fair deal, wasn't it?

"I suppose. I suppose it is."

Someone stopped in the living-room door and Mae froze, bolting upright.

---

* There was never a promise of return.
† There was never any forgetting.

Bevan leaned against the frame. Was her hair that long yesterday? There was so *much* of it. She took in the scene with big, icy eyes and removed a tube of lip gloss from her hoodie pocket. Pastel pink, like a doll. Her shorts were denim and Mae was absolutely not under any circumstances looking at her legs, the sheer length of them. Her heart was absolutely not beating in her chest, pounding heavy chords on the piano inside her. There was, in fact, no piano inside her. Her mouth was not dry. Her mouth was normal. Everything was normal. She was just hanging around on the floor waiting for the rain to stop. She was just talking to the cat. Bevan knew the cat could talk. In this house, talking to the cat was a perfectly ordinary activity. Nothing suspicious was happening here and yet, Mae felt like she'd been caught cutting into a birthday cake not meant for her.

"Mae. Bobby," Bevan said coolly, and Mae forgot how to breathe for a second. Then she forgot how to talk.

Then she remembered again, but a little too late. Awkwardness cloyed its way into the room.

"Hi, Bev—Bevan."

Stupid voice, Mae admonished herself as Doris Day's voice swelled again in the background. The blond girl raised her eyebrows. "Listening to some absolute bangers there, yeah?" She managed to speak in some strange cadence in between sarcasm and sincerity. Mae had no idea if she was taking the piss out of her or not. She flushed and her stomach flipped. How was she supposed to answer that? Why was everything about Bevan so impossible? She opted on the side of sarcasm, just in case.

"Yeah . . . yeah. Rita has lots of weird stuff around."

Bevan nodded, slowly applying thick and glittering gloss to her lips. Mae wondered if her own mouth would ever look like that.

"Rita's wicked cool," Bevan said. "And her music is deadly. Doris Day's gorgeous, like. Do you want anything down in the shop? I'm buzzing down to get some groceries, for dinner and all. You can come if you like, if you want a change of scenery."

The universe paused around Mae for a moment there on the carpet, and Bobby looked up at her, holding the stillness of time in his gaze. The pure thrill of this invitation was like nothing she'd ever felt. An invitation to step out with Bevan into the town, two girls on a mission. Walking through the suburbs under the mountains, side by side. But this watercolor impression of a romantic afternoon was splattered by an immediate bolt of insecurity: what if she said something stupid to Bevan during this walk? What if this was the instance during which Bevan decided Mae was annoying and unworthy of her company in the future?

Mae wasn't ready for a whole walk to the village with Bevan yet. She had to rehearse a little more. Get better at saying words out loud, for a start—maybe even practice a few cool things to say, a few interesting questions to ask. They had Doris Day in common, at least, and that would be a start. If she was going to spend time one-on-one with Bevan, it just couldn't be a mess. It needed to be perfect. And the way that Mae was feeling right now—terrified, just about breaking out in a cold sweat—this was not perfect.

Bobby yawned. "Well? Cat got your tongue?"

Mae stammered, made a couple of noises in attempt to say no, but even those two letters couldn't land together.

Bevan trilled a laugh. "Be sound, Bobby, give her a minute."

"No, no—I'd just—I'll stay here, thanks. I don't need anything in the village." Mae managed full words, somehow, a miracle. She didn't think it was too harsh a refusal. She might be slightly shy. Shy. Shy was likable, wasn't it?

The tall girl shrugged. "Cool. Suit yourself. See you at dinner." And just like that, Bevan was gone. Footsteps to the door, the latch opening, the hinge swinging.

Mae exhaled a deep breath when she was sure Bevan was gone and rolled over onto her stomach, covering her burning face with her sweaty hands.

Bobby made a sound, like a snicker meeting a purr. An almost snort. Mae guessed that this was as close to a laugh as you could get from a cat. The record had gone silent, and Mae let it hiss there. Bevan had asked her to go to the village. And she had said no. She had missed out on a gal adventure.

But she had played cool. Surely that had been the right choice. Mae groaned aloud. She didn't like any of this at all. Head wrecked. Fourteen, she decided, was actually terrible.

"Don't laugh at me, Bobby. That's not kind," Mae said into her hands.

Bobby made his way over and lay down by her side, his body seeming to take shape next to her like liquid, his purring a good low tone. "Unrequited love has to be at least a little funny sometimes."

"Don't say unrequited, that feels terrible." Bevan couldn't see Mae as a person. Like it or not, to Bevan, she was a child.

"Can't you just enjoy it?" Bobby asked. "It's a big first."

"No," Mae said. "No. It's not fun. It hurts. I want it to go away."

"It won't. It'll get huge, for a while. It'll walk around your veins and your stomach. You might even feel it in your rib cage, or your heart, like the songs say. But eventually it'll get smaller and smaller and will run out of steam, until it's a tiny thing that you barely remember. It'll get replaced by other loves."

"I wish you'd stop saying love."* Mae groaned again. He sounded like he knew what he was talking about, but that didn't make it any easier.

"Well, you're thinking it, aren't you?"

"Yes, but that doesn't mean I want to hear it out loud. Makes it more real."

"Love is the realest thing, Mae. The world around you will become realer the more you feel it. Doesn't music sound better already? Isn't there more meaning? There's a reason you had that song on loop. It's deepened."

"I suppose." Mae sighed. He was right. "I'm still not sure how a cat can be such an expert on, like, emotions, though."

Bobby nuzzled her. "Don't think too hard about it. I'm here to talk whenever you need me."

Mae stayed there for the rest of the afternoon, only

---

* Rita said this once, but not to Bobby.

periodically getting up to put the record on again. She talked to Bobby a little, but mostly listened to the swell of the music. How it exactly mirrored the new weird rush of color that Bevan had lit in her. How the chorus of voices behind Doris Day's mirrored the way her bones felt, bright and sad at once. How could songs written so long ago exactly match how she was feeling there on the living-room floor, far away from the world the music was written in?

When Bevan came back into the house, she didn't stop to say hello to Mae, just headed straight into the kitchen. Mae hoped she didn't notice that the same song was playing—but then again, what did it matter if she did? Hopeless. The whole thing. Hopeless.

NINE

WHILE the rest of the house slept, Rita sat by the
fireside, the glow of it crawling over her. Four a.m.,
wrapped in a shawl, whiskey in her right hand, her rings
clinking on the glass. A poker in her left, moving the small
hot coals in the furnace this way and that, stoking the heat.
Bobby in her lap, purring heavily, ambient with the fire
crackling. Both of them wide-awake, as they so often were
at this hour.

Bobby leapt soundlessly to the kitchen floor, the fire
casting his shadow long on the checkered tiles. There, in
the strange light, he stood up on his hind legs and grew.
A straight back, a shrinking tail, skin. A black suit folded
around him then, his eyes yellow and shocking in the
night. Rita felt tears on her cheek, and when she lifted
her hand to wipe them, her own skin felt smooth, her
crevices softening, becoming supple. Hair fell long and
straight around her face. She was seventeen, suddenly,
in the dark of the kitchen. The years came off her with

79

Bobby's power. All the stiffness in her bones lifted.

The cat, now a young man, pressed his lips to her forehead. "We are ancient, both of us. A marvel, that."

Rita said nothing. She had not seen Bobby like this in years. He'd stopped changing for her shortly after Audrey had gone. Since then, she'd always had to ask him to.

Bobby knelt by Rita and she ran her fingers, her rings loose, through his shiny hair.

"My dear friend," she whispered. "I've missed you like this."

The light flickered and Rita watched her hand glitch old and then young, something broken in the reality around them.

"I'd suggest we dance, but I think music would wake up the twins." Bobby chuckled, standing. "Skies above, it's good to be upright. I don't like being one of the smallest things in the room."

"Then why stay a cat? You don't have to." Rita laughed, knowing full well Bobby's preference for invisibility, for sleep, for sneaking. Her voice sounded off to her own ears, unroughened by smoke, juvenile—too pure.

"We have to stay as we are," he rallied back. "All the power goes to keeping him up there, and even that isn't working. This shift will knock it back, some. But we've to take our graces when we get them."

Rita shook her head. "Seventy-odd feels more right than seventeen—even if seventeen feels good."

Bobby shrugged, then pulled his arms straight above his head, cracking his shoulders, exhaling. All the blinds were closed in the kitchen, the truest dark; even the eagerness of summer dawn couldn't break through. Rita couldn't have looked for her reflection anyplace in the room, and she didn't need to. She was always seventeen: that long, bad year—the one that froze in time without hope of ever really moving on. The year that Sweet James caught Audrey for good, the year Rita's heart left her body with the girl who walked through walls. The year Rita refused to follow her, even when Audrey swore she'd never come back. She never had come back. But Rita knew she would see her again. Everything she'd done in this house was for that chance.

Rita's parents had died young; her brother had died too. She was the oldest Frost left alive. She'd had adventures outside of Dorasbeg, for a time. It hadn't been the organic loss of family that froze her, or the monastic centering of her life around this house, or the necessary ritual of keeping the fire burning. It was Audrey. And before Audrey, it was Deborah, but even Deborah's name wracked Rita with grief, let alone what befell her in the end. Rita was the sole survivor of the three. The only one who knew what had happened.

She drank from her glass. Her young mouth didn't like whiskey. She and Audrey would mix stolen white wine and lemonade back then. How thirsty for it she was, suddenly, the sugar stupor of her and Audrey O'Driscoll. All this was for her, for Audrey. All the strength she was harvesting, all this keeping monsters in her house.

Here Bobby was before her, all young and man and gorgeous, and yet the misery in her former body left Rita wrecked. She could barely stand to touch him. This body was still in love with the girl who left.

"So, what will we burn for Bevan? She is having a strange time of it lately. James has her almost truly thralled," Bobby asked, pulling up a chair of his own, pouring himself a teacup of whiskey from the crystalline decanter. He was handsome; the only feline thing left about him was the slope of his cheekbones. She'd open the curtains soon, Rita thought, let the daylight in; then he would disappear into the form she knew best, too-large housecat, a purring thing.

The witch rose and gathered the makings of a spell from her pantry. Four aromatic leaves from the basil plant on the windowsill. A slim wand of dried sage from a tall, dusty mason jar. A barrel of flaky sea salt, blue and domestic. Tiny shards of clear quartz.

Bobby, meanwhile, set about lighting tall, lean black candles all about the stove. The plastic lighter hissed and popped in the quiet as Rita stood over the table, marking each leaf of basil with the felt-tip pen she usually used for her grocery list. Tiny stars, connected by a ring—pentacles, Rita thought, Bevan and her pentacles. What an awful thing to be a psychic child. How large a power for a creature with no lived experience. Rita could never protect her, not truly. She sighed as she marked the soft leaves, precise. A folly, all this. There was something inevitable ahead. But she wove the leaves together, still oozing life, with a piece of twine and tied them tight to the wand of sage all the same.

From her pocket, Rita retrieved a black silken pouch, then placed the sage–basil moth inside. She doused the bag with salt and crushed the almost-candy shards of quartz between her firelit young fingers.

"It's made," she said over her shoulder to Bobby, tying the drawstring tight, trapping the protection spell as it began to flutter against the fabric.

Rita brought it to the hearth as Bobby lit a fat cone of frankincense, heady and rich. She sat amidst the arc of candles, humming to herself, pulling blessings forth for Bevan. Rita did not have a prayer, only a single plea. She whispered to the bag, "I need a little more time. Keep her close to him, but do not let him eat her. Keep the want-to-leave in her."

She placed the bag into the fire, and it flared, hungry for this new taste of magic. The bag burst and shone, the winged-moth spell dancing, fluttering above the flames. A tease, refusing to be fully eaten. Rita slammed the door of the furnace, a little too loudly for the quiet of the dawn. Bobby looked at her, sad eyes. She took his hand and he lifted hers to his soft, human mouth.

"This is all we can do," he said. "One last try."

"We should rest. I don't want to be too tired in front of the children."

Bobby sighed, leaning his head into his hands. "I'll see you this way again soon." He looked hopeful, somehow, in a way that broke Rita's heart a little.

"Of course you will." And he folded back into the big cat he usually was. Rita took him in her arms and left the kitchen, her familiar age washing over her as she drew away from the fireside, all the while thinking steady on loop, It is happening again. It is happening again.*

---

* It is happening again.

TEN

YOU roll the tooth between your finger and thumb. It feels too light to be what it is, too blunt. A piece of chalk. A penny sweet. You have been sleeping heavy and long these last few nights, unmoved by dreams. Maybe there was black water, but nothing more than that. You stand before Sweet James's wall, the piece of Rossa in your hand, but you can't feel a thing.

He's not coming.

You whisper into the paper roses. "Sweet James, I have something for you."

You are talking to yourself. The silence is long and embarrassing. You are immediately angry at him—what is the meaning of this? Has he found some other girl to—to . . . whatever the hell he's been doing with you? Is it Mae? Has he been talking to her? How dare he send you off on an assault mission and then ignore your return. Hot tendrils of hysteria rise in your gut, your breath accelerates, and you swear, dragging your nails against the wallpaper.

"Come on," you urge. "What do you want?"

You sink to the carpet and hold your face in your hands. He's never refused to show up like this. Not a trace of him in the air. Your head spirals questions: Did you do it wrong? Is it not enough? Do you need to go and get a piece of Mae before he responds again? Is this offering so unacceptable to him that he won't even deign to breach the atmosphere of the house for you? You don't remember when your room was last so void of his static presence.

He has to come back at some point, right? Right. Too much is at stake. Well, for you there is. Maybe not for him. You've always had this paranoia lurking on mute that he was merely entertaining himself with you—that the paper-glass-bone-mirror owl who took up so much room in you was a strand of something bigger, just toying with you. A tooth between the fingers of something so big and terrible that if you wondered too hard about him, your temples started to ache.

You haven't brought him any meat in a few days. You used to feed him every day. Maybe if you brought him some extra sustenance he'd come back? It feels feeble after all you've been through with him lately. This isn't like forgetting to feed a goldfish. He doesn't really need the bones, does he? Oh god, what if you've starved him out?

You pull yourself up off the floor and swiftly switch pajamas for shorts, your hoodie, your pink sneakers with the flames on the side. You turn away from the wall as you change, but glance over your shoulder. It's not like he hasn't seen you before, but you don't trust this absence. What should Sweet James care for your naked body anyway? It's not like he has the same gaze as a human. It's not like he's a man. He's a something else. A monster, you think. A monster, you are sure.

Your legs are rough and unshaven. You prefer them this way, the hair just a texture, barely visible though this year's tan. You grab your little coin purse, your phone, big pink sunglasses, and bound out of the room, a girl on a mission.

You knock through the hallway to see if Rita wants anything from the village, but her side of the house is eerily quiet. Rossa has been avoiding you since the weirdness of the other night. You smirk to yourself. That, now—that had been delicious. He was so afraid.

You throw your head around the door to the kitchen. Mae is sitting at the table, lost in a video game. Bobby is lying on his back in a beam of sunlight sliced diagonal across the table. You sigh.

"I'm going for a walk. I'm wasting the summer in these walls," you lie. Mae looks up at you with her big, perpetually distressed eyeballs.

"Can I give you a fiver for a chicken-fillet roll? I've been missing them. Back home I used to get one every couple of days as a treat." She's nervous. The sap.

"Chicken-fillet rolls make you fat." You deliver the statement flatly, more just to see her face than because it's true. Bobby snaps his eyes open and looks straight at you, furious.

"Oh." Mae's voice is all warbled. "Never mind."

Eyes back to the screen.

Bobby kneads the tablecloth, claws on the vinyl, staring you down hard. "Get a slice pan if you're in the village," he says. "The bread in the cupboard is gone all stale. Rita would appreciate it."

How is it that the wretched cat can just stay around, but Sweet James disappears? You stomp to the door, fumbling with keys and earbuds. Maybe someday Sweet James will be for you what Bobby is to Rita, a companion, a familiar. A friend.

That was, though, if he hadn't found some other house to corrupt by then. Some other wall to lurk in.* She should have moved more quickly. Shouldn't have held back from him, should have given him the tooth gift immediately.

Nothing feels right on the warm morning walk to the village. Everything is his absence. I'm a fool, I'm a fool, you think to yourself, your own anxiety blaring over any potential cheer your playlist may have had to offer. You can't feel the pavement under your runners. You can't feel the summer on your skin. You can only feel his refusal to come. The potential of never seeing the other world again. The future, in which you forget all of this. In which all of this is just "that one summer," the years ahead in which you become Susan, who cannot remember Narnia and doesn't even want to. Susan who was all right without it.

You pass the newsagents and the post office and the shut-down video shop, one of the pubs—the butcher shop is right there. One foot in front of the other. Get the bones.

---

* Audrey had once asked him if he had ever been in any other houses. He had laughed at her. Said, **what do you think?**

The butcher's son, Gus, is smoking outside, reclining against the window. How is his da not taking the head off him for smoking right there, right in front of the shop? You can smell the toxicity of the cigarette: different from the smoke Rita exhales. Lighter. You stand a little straighter as you approach him. Did you even check a mirror on the way out this morning? You are suddenly self-conscious. Well, you don't need Sweet James's energy following you everywhere to be impressive. It's not like you are possessed by him. You are always just you. Right?

Right. Gus looks you over. Eyes charting you. You can't read him. Your heart and gut are doing something you don't like.

"A'right then, Bevan. Here to torment me again?"

Was his voice always so deep?

You nod. "Just looking for bones. For Rita." You shrug then, rubbing your arm for comfort, aware that you look nervous. You can't stop thinking about your body, his eyes on it.

"Jesus, what's up with you?" Gus is genuinely puzzled. "Are you sick or something?"

You don't know what to say. People don't often ask you how you are. Maybe you are sick. You feel sick. What kind of person gets sick for monsters, sick with the pleasure of it?

"I . . ." You're stammering. "I didn't sleep so well last night."

"What, were you out tearing up the town till all hours or something? On the lash?"

You blink.

"I'm underage. I can't go into town."

You feel very small as he smirks.

"So am I," he replies. "Doesn't stop me."

If you'd had Sweet James's influence you'd have said, "I suppose you think you're rapid then, yeah?" But he is gone, gone gone, so you just say, "Cool."

"Did the high-and-mighty Bevan Mulholland just call *me* cool?" Gus exclaims in mock surprise. You giggle—a noise you barely recognize from your own throat. You're mortified. He stubs out his cigarette, victorious looking, takes his phone from the pocket of his starched white apron.

"What's your number, Bev?"

He's bold now that all the nerve's gone out of you. You say the line of digits. You're not even a little coy. You don't ask him for his number. His eyes are piercing. Very blue. You hadn't noticed before. You can't believe yourself.

"I'll bring you the bones, so."

He walks past you into the shop, the bell chiming. You wring your hands, awkward, unable to follow him in. If Sweet James had just shown up like he was supposed to, you wouldn't be feeling like this. You're not sure you can remember ever feeling this way before. You kick the wall of the butcher shop and fold your arms. Gus emerges, familiar plastic bag in his hand, weighted by bone and scraps of clinging flesh. You take it and thank him.

"I'll give you a text," he says, by way of goodbye.

You don't care if he does or doesn't, but you say "Cheers" anyway.

★

Back in your bedroom, Rossa's tooth in one hand, a fragile pink wishbone in the other, you spread out your arms and press your body against the owl's usual manifestation site.

"Come on," you whisper into the surface. "Please!"

It takes a few fearful, silent minutes before the wall warps a little, before the strange wind picks up and the air around you fills with that gorgeous, awful, familiar pull. He's come back for you! At last!

Fat hot tears bead down your cheeks as you feel the wall's consistency turn to quicksand, as Sweet James takes the wishbone. He sucks it in.

more, he says, though his face has not come through yet, though the light is doing wrong things where he is trying to arrive. You rip open the bone bag and push fistfuls of the red waste into the wall. Tiny sacrifices at this unformed altar. He murmurs and groans.

i cannot come to you, he says. **the crone has put a hex on the house, she has tried to slow me. it is working.**

Your blood stops moving through your body. "No!" you cry. "Don't leave me!"

The wall looks like a shattered television screen. Too much color and liquid, all disturbance.

i need more of the children bring me blood and i will show you how to put the fire out we have to put the fire out we have to put the fire out you have to

And just like that, the wall is a wall again. The air is ordinary, still, home. You are alone with a tooth in your fist and something terrible to do.

Your phone chimes in your back pocket. You ignore it.

ELEVEN

WITH a fat knife, Mae spread thick butter onto a slice of Madeira cake and watched Rita, alone in the middle of the back lawn. Rita stood lean and elegant, on one foot, like the blade of a sundial. Her thin shadow angled out past her yoga mat and onto the dense grass. Her eyes were closed, so Mae didn't feel bad staring. She'd been there, posed on one leg for as long as it had taken Mae to procure the cake from the cupboard, slice it, butter it, and take two bites. Mae was considering fishing out some lemon curd from the pantry, and Rita was still motionless.

Mae's legs hurt even looking at her.

Bobby was splayed out, seemingly more liquid than animal, near Rita's foot. Mae took her phone out of her pocket, adjusted the screen for the blinding summer light, and snapped a picture. She reckoned maybe Dad would like it. Like a postcard.

Mae typed, "auntie rita is more fit than me and rossa put together," with a little monkey laughing emoji at the end, attached the image, and hit send. Rita slowly lowered her leg and opened her eyes, as though returning from some other realm. She saw Mae in the window and waved, smiling a little sleepily. Mae opened the window, the thin gauze curtain pulling slightly, a little inhale of the summer breeze. Rita came and leaned on the windowsill, adjusting her hair.

"You were very still for a long time," Mae said. "Would you like some cake?"

Rita smiled. "I'll have a couple of saltines—above on the shelf, the blue box. And there's lemon curd in the refrigerator, down the back."

Mae blinked, a piece of sweet fluff crumbling from her slice and falling on the counter. She inhaled and exhaled, pretending she wasn't at all alarmed by Rita's knowing expression, or the possibility that her great-aunt was casually walking into the corridors of her thoughts. She put down her remaining hunk of cake to retrieve the crackers and curd.

"Of all the things this garden does, of all the surprises it's given me, a lemon tree just won't grow here. A long time ago, back when I lived in San Francisco, we had one in the yard." Rita produced a cigarette out of nowhere and lit it. "We used to make curd in the summer with the fruit, and gallons of lemonade. The place reeked of citrus, we were practically rotten with them."

"Is that where you learned to stand on one leg with your eyes closed for, like, six minutes at a time? San Francisco?" Mae asked, meaning, "Is that where you learned to read minds?"

"It is," Rita said, letting her reply hang in the air a beat. "But this house is where I perfected my practice. I only lived over there for a few years, until Mother* and Father† died, and I had to come home to take care of things. Your granddad, Brendan, had his own family to take care of. I'd always intended to go back, but—sure, look."

"I don't know why, but I can't imagine you anywhere but here, in this house." Mae clacked out a handful of saltines onto a saucer, trying to envision a young Rita somewhere in the pretty, hilly city she had only seen in a handful of movies. "Do you want anything on these?"

Rita shook her head. "This house is where I've always belonged."

How certain she seemed, Mae thought, wondering what it felt like to belong somewhere at all. Might she ever belong here, on Iona Crescent? Could this be her home? And her brother's—though she hadn't seen him all day. Hadn't seen that much of him since their fight. What was it about this house that felt like it was pulling them apart?

Days later, Mae held a well-worn 1970s copy of *Tarot for Beginners* above the peaks of bubbles in her bath. The pages were yellowed and thin already; a soak might be the last thing to happen to it. The tub in the master bathroom was enormous, claw-footed, and currently filled with so much

---

* Brid first, in the corridor. A heart attack. They found her beside a radiator upstairs.
† Jim, a week later. In the bath. A heart attack, too.

Epsom salt that Mae was having trouble staying anchored to the bottom. Rita had handed her an industrial-looking white bucket of the shimmering substance and suggested a long soak after four consecutive days of twice-daily yoga had made Mae stiff and achy. Two small, ornate Marys stood on the windowsill amid expensive-looking soaps and lotions. Mae had turned them to face away, out toward the mountains. It had taken her almost ten whole minutes to lower herself into the bath because her body was so done over by the yoga.

"How come doing this makes me feel like I've the body of an old lady and makes you feel less like you are an old lady?" Mae had protested, gingerly stretching her arms above her head, her muscles roaring back at her for even attempting it.

"That's because your limbs are just waking up. In time you'll feel strange if you go even a day without it."

Mae had made a face. She'd hurt all over, stiffness and pain in parts of her body she'd never even known were there before: her sides, the backs of her arms. But as she floated in the tub, it all began to soothe, the steam rising around her and making the book warp in the wet air. She'd intended to play her Nintendo, but the more she studied with Rita, the less she'd needed magical worlds on a screen. Her own world had become magical. Certainly, it *was* studying: iconography to memorize, lists of terms and definitions—it felt a little like school, but good school. Not boring, difficult school.

The bathroom door creaked a little, and Mae peeped

over the edge of the bath—Bobby had invited himself in.

"Jesus, Bobby!" she yelped. She was almost totally submerged and wrapped in foam, but it still felt invasive for a talking cat to be hanging around when she had no clothes on. "Would you learn to knock?"

"No," said Bobby. Mae scowled at him as he jumped into the empty sink, somehow filling it perfectly. His large white paws folded neatly on the lip, the pads black, like little beans.

"What suit are you on?" he asked, nodding at the book.

"Pentacles," said Mae. "Money and power and all that."

"Put down the book and I'll test you," he said.

"Bobby, I'm trying to relax here!"

"You were studying!"

"Studying isn't the same as being tested!"

"Don't splash me! Cats don't like that!"

Rossa was frozen in place down the landing from the bathroom, door slightly ajar, where his sister was having an argument with a grown man. An interloper. A stranger. A thief? A murderer? Yes. A murderer in the bathroom. His heart hammered against his chest. Mouth dry, ears pounding, he pushed against his terror to get his phone out of his pocket. He was going to be sensible. He wasn't going to intervene. He'd call the police. Or text his parents. His hands felt useless, but he got it—no coverage. Okay, he'd do something else—maybe he'd record what he was hearing, to have some proof at least. He thumbed around on the screen, finding his camera, pushing record, but the screen began to fuzz and glitch as he held it. Then the phone tumbled from his shaking hands to the carpet, each bounce down the corridor gracefully muffled.

Foot by foot, he managed to back himself against the wall, his sweating palms flat against the wallpaper. He realized his knees were giving out, but before he could convince his body to try to pull against the gravity of his terror, he was sliding to the floor. The daylight turned sinister, panels of bright drama in the corridor. All Rossa could think now was how to keep his lungs breathing, keep alive—if an intruder was present he'd have to pull his bootstraps up, the action-hero adrenaline would have to fountain suddenly through him. He blinked heavily, in slow time with his breath. The landing felt wrong. He couldn't make out what the man in the bathroom was saying to his sister. It sounded like questions. It sounded like an interrogation.

Across the carpet, on the wall facing Rossa's trembling body, a radiator sat, cold. Rossa counted the indentations in the white metal as he breathed himself back to sanity, each corrugated ridge his breath, an up and a down, a pattern—until it wasn't. Until the white metal became matte, like bone. Until each ridge was no longer even, but toothlike, all wrong, a white mouth of fangs in his vision. A sinister origami of white.

Rossa knew what it was like to be afraid. He'd known the dark crawl in his belly when his parents thundered in the kitchen, his fists balled into his duvet, his head under the covers, praying that his bedroom door wouldn't open to a furious parent in its frame. He'd known the paralysis that came over him sometimes when his father's explosive anger was directed down at him or Mae, how that turned his stomach to cement, stole his voice from his throat. Rossa had been afraid, all right. But this was different. Worse.

The radiator had formed into the lines of a face—but not a human. A beast, a dragon—no, an owl. The sharp sloping beak, the white metal becoming feather. It clicked and groaned and Rossa's body went numb, darkness flickering across his vision, like the glitching of his phone screen. Dark fractals of truth slammed into him—he'd never be able to help Mae, he'd always be too afraid, he was useless, weak, a coward. . . .

He didn't feel himself faint. Nobody ever does.

Rossa woke to the cold of a wet cloth on his face, Mae towering over him wrapped in a towel, reeking of sandalwood. Bobby's fat paws rested on his chest.

"He's awake," the cat said, voice deep and human, like a newscaster or a man on the radio: he was no intruder, he was the man talking to Mae in the bathroom. Not a man. A cat. Maybe not a cat, even. Something else.

Rossa turned his head, retched, retched a second time, and then the black curtains fell in his mind once more. He was out.

★

When he came to again, in his bed, Rita was lighting candles on the bedside locker. It took him a moment to find the question, the hundreds of questions folded into one that he wasn't even sure his aunt would answer.

"What is going on in this house?"

Rita smiled down at him, the white lighter in her hands, but there was something crooked in it, something he barely recognized, or maybe was just seeing for the first time.

"If your great-aunt is a witch, wouldn't you expect her to have a talking cat? Wouldn't you expect the house to be a little funny?"

Rossa didn't say anything, and his aunt lit a cigarette as he lay there. It seemed strange to have someone smoking in a bedroom—there was too much fabric around that could catch light if a hot ash dropped at the wrong second. The smoke was too dense, too heavy around him, and he didn't like it, but he couldn't find words. This was her house, after all; she could smoke wherever she wanted.

"I was very scared," he admitted to her, voice tiny, hoping beyond hope that she might stub out her smoke and hug him, stroke his hair, tell him she was sorry for not warning him about the talking cat and weird hallway. Tell me it's okay, he willed her. Tell me it's okay.

For a second it almost looked like she was about to laugh.

"Are you still scared?"

He was, but he said, "No."

She did laugh, then. Short, hard, and sharp enough that it hit Rossa between two of his ribs like a bad little knife.

"You'll get braver in time. In order to become brave, we

must feel all that fear has to offer, then rise above it. Do you think you can do that for me? Now. I've a cup of tea here for you, it'll make you feel much better."

And Rossa took a small copper cup from his aunt. It did not at all taste like the black tea they drank down in the kitchen, but it was warming his belly by the time that occurred to him. And then he was beginning to sleep again, his consciousness dropping calmly away from his eyes, like sinking back into warm, dark water. He was sure he could still smell the smoke, still hear the click of the door closing him in.

TWELVE

MAE was in the living room, missing Rita's hour of morning yoga in the soaking sunshine of the garden. Her great-aunt, brother, Bobby, and Bevan were out stretching and meditating, and she was spooning a paisley cushion on the floor. In the days since Rossa's faint, Rita had been trying to include him in things a little more, keeping a closer eye on him. Mae wasn't sitting out on purpose—she'd only had her period a handful of times before and it was still a fresh and alarming inconvenience to her: the pain still slightly mystifying. She hadn't learned to expect it, or feel comfortable at all while it was happening, despite Rita's dispensation of floral teas and strong effervescent painkillers.

To Rossa's credit, he hadn't ever been weird about it. He was weird about almost everything, but not about this, giving her a hug and a half apology that morning: "If I could swap it out for the awful stuff that happens to me, I would." That had made Mae laugh as she held her nose and downed the fizzing glass that Rita promised would take the edge off the dull ache in her abdomen. Mae didn't want any of the gross goings-on that her brother was dealing with to happen to her, or anything. The last thing she needed was more bodily mysteries to unveil themselves to her. This, she reckoned, she could just about handle. Yoga she most certainly could not handle, and she was kindly excused.

Rossa offered to sit out and keep her company, but Mae shooed him away. He was good at yoga, and it put him in a better mood. It suited him, and Rita was encouraging. Even Bobby was encouraging. Rossa liked being good at things, and when they weren't in school and he had nowhere to prove himself, it put him on edge. It was good, too, for him to spend a little time with Bobby, now that he was in on the secret, even if Mae felt a bit put out. But trying to bend and stretch and breathe seemed impossible right now, her body an inconvenient, sore knot.

All Mae wanted to do was lie there with her half ache and the strange glint the painkillers left on her mood, letting the music wash over her. Playing out scenarios in which Bevan would be her best friend . . . then, as their closeness deepened, her girlfriend. Then her wife. She envisioned them as old as Rita, two soft suburban witches.

A familiar, leggy shadow cast down over the floor. Of course this wasn't her great-aunt or her brother. Vanilla and shea butter against the incensed air of the house, of course it was her. Mae was getting used to the rhythms of the household, even though it had only been a couple of weeks.

She recognized how the atmosphere felt thicker whenever Bevan entered her orbit. She barely had to open her eyes.

"Mae, do you have your ears pierced?"

Mae's eyes shot open—Look at the ceiling, don't look at Bevan, you'll be useless. "No. Never thought about it."

"Really?"

Bevan crossed the carpet and sat with a thump right beside Mae. Mae had to look at her. She'd been so good at avoiding any time alone with her. So good at distracting herself. Until now.

Bevan's hair hung in dense blond bunches on either side of her head, her neck long, two gold hoops hanging from her earlobes. Heather-gray hoodie. Denim shorts. No shoes. Pink toenails. Eyes for a hundred years. Chewing gum. Unfair, impossible legs. She held a fizzing glass, not unlike the one Mae had drunk to ease her pain earlier. She sipped it as though it was a soda.

"Why aren't you out in the garden?" Mae asked, eyes still half closed. Bevan was too much too look at.

"Period. Too sore to stretch."

"I'm . . . me too." Mae still found the word "period" very adult, it still didn't fit in her mouth right—or her body. Awful. She buried her face in her cushion. She was scarlet for herself. This wasn't the chat she wanted to be having with Bevan. She didn't want to be near Bevan. Not at all.

Bevan gave a throaty laugh and slapped the floor. "That's so funny. You know girls sync up, right? You probably gave me mine early."

Mae had read about this in a pastel medical-looking

pamphlet somewhere, and was only marginally as horrified by the idea of "syncing up" back then as she was in this moment. She peeked out from the pillow.

Bevan knocked back the fizzing glass. "This, though. This really helps. Rita probably shouldn't be giving it to us, but it's better by miles than the pain. Can you believe we can bleed for days and stay alive? Women are, like, miraculous."

"I wish we didn't have to." Mae snorted into her cushion. She wished she could crawl into the soft quilt of it and disappear.

"Sorry, babe, this is our lot until we're like, almost Rita's age. Better get used to it. Twelve times a year, every year, more or less—unless you get pregnant." Bevan made a cheers gesture with the last dregs in her glass and drained it. Mae was uncomfortable, but reached for her cooling mug of tea and raised it in response, limp.

"Christ, you're miserable," remarked the older girl. "Don't sweat it. Upside is that your pain threshold goes through the roof while this is happening to you. Isn't that amazing?"

Mae took a sip from her tea. Her mouth was so dry and her ears were ringing. Bevan was very close to her. Her earrings glinted, so large you could put a hand through them, big brassy things at odds with the softness of her outfit.

"In fact," Bevan continued, "if you did want your ears pierced, I could just do it for you today, and you'd barely feel a thing. You're basically superhuman when you're on your period. It'd barely be a pinch."

Mae wished Bevan would stop saying "period." Actually, she wished Bevan would just go away and stop offering her things like conversation and piercings so she could just lie in the sun listening to music and imagining a different Bevan, a Bevan who belonged to her, a Bevan who didn't scare her. Mae didn't say anything at all, just sipped her tea.

"Do you want me to do it?" Bevan was extremely persistent. Gleeful at the idea, almost.

Mae wrinkled her nose. "I'm not sure."

"Of course you're sure. It'll be like a bonding experience. A rite of passage."

This flare of interest from Bevan was disconcerting, but the mention of bonding had Mae far more sold than she wanted to be. Mae felt something bad, something like foreboding, but she batted it away: pierced ears and heartache were what summer at fourteen were all about, surely. She'd seen it on TV shows, read it in books—she was doing what she was supposed to be doing.

"All right then. Sure." Mae nodded, trying to sound casual, hoping it worked—like no big deal, just spear a piece of my flesh with some metal and stick some jewelry in it, grand, it's cool.

Bevan grinned, enormous. Mae wasn't sure she'd ever seen her smile before, let alone like this.

"I knew you were up for mischief, Mae. You're going to look great. I'll even give you a pair of my earrings."

You're going to look great, you're going to look great, you're going to look great, you're going to look great, you're going to look great, you're going to look great, you're going to look great, you're going to look great—

The next thing Mae knew, she was sitting on the edge of

the tub in the bathroom upstairs and Bevan was assembling a sinister-looking set of tiny domestic items with which to perform the piercing. Mae blinked at her, the light in the bathroom whiter than the warm of the living room. Bevan's hair caught in the light, impossibly gold as she stood over the sink with a short glass of something that smelled terribly strong and clean—rubbing alcohol? Or just alcohol alcohol? Vodka? Mae didn't know, she'd no experience with either. In the bottom of the glass were two long safety pins, silver and open, the pointed tip dangerous even at this distance.

Bevan was beautiful and bold, but that did not qualify her to go around sticking holes in people's bodies. She was washing her hands with a bar of rose-smelling soap the shape of a seashell. An apple and a knife lay on the windowsill. Four round-edged cubes of ice melting in a glass. A cluster of cotton swabs. Had Bevan been preparing for this? How had she known Mae would say yes?

Of course Mae was going to say yes. Mae would do whatever Bevan told her, and it was exactly that obvious. Obvious enough for Bevan to turn the bathroom into a soapy operating theater in advance, all her tools laid out. An amateur, strangely enthusiastic surgeon.

"Right." Bevan rinsed her hands, steam flourishing from the piping water in the sink. "I'm going to ice your ears first. Then I'm going to take a slice of this apple and place it behind your earlobe, and very quickly stick this safety pin through your ear. Then I'm going to pull it out, and before you know it, you'll have one of these lovely shiny things in there. Last, we're going to put a load of this alcohol on a cotton swab and hold it there while I do the other one. Sound all right to you? Just, like, don't move. You won't feel a thing. You're going to look so cool." The tall girl sliced the blushing pink apple as she spoke.

You won't feel a thing, you're going to look so cool, you won't feel a thing, you're going to look so cool, you won't feel a thing, you're going to look so cool, you won't feel a thing, you're going to look—

The pain was white hot. It was absolutely not a pinch. Mae bit her lip and didn't scream, but her eyes swelled with tears and her breath hitched and she did everything she could not to pull away.

"You're doing so well. You're so brave!" Bevan moved to Mae's other side, ignoring the tears on Mae's face.

Mae didn't feel brave. But she'd do anything to make Bevan like her. Anything. Mae scrunched her eyes shut and didn't see the blood on the pale slice of apple as she took a heavy wet piece of cotton that stank of harsh, clean alcohol.

"Just hold this to your ear," Bevan continued. "The earring is gorgeous on you, the other side'll match in just a second."

The rubbing alcohol burned her right ear—a temporary distraction from push and burst and throbbing on the other side. Mae couldn't believe she was crying in front of Bevan, but Bevan was soothing her with praise. "Pain is beauty, petal."

The clumsy, bloody ceremony was quick and sore. Then Bevan wiped away Mae's tears, because Mae was holding cotton to both earlobes and couldn't do it herself. The two girls' faces were very close—one face made up, big-eyed, the other blotchy, profoundly fourteen. Two long slices of apple, stained with clouds of dark red, sat in the glass where the ice was. What were they even for? Mae had cold water from the shrinking ice all over her wrists and arms, all down the back of her shirt. She was a mess—sniffling, a little faint, just about keeping it together. This was stupid, this was so stupid.

"All right then, take away the cotton for a sec. Take a look at yourself."

Bevan produced a mirror with a long handle and flashed it at Mae.

Two silver studs with bright purple gems at their center sparkled in pink, sore earlobes. Mae was surprised. Her body was different now. She'd done this. It made her feel a little sick, but a little older. A little stronger. She gave her reflection a forced, watery grin.

"That's the spirit!" Bevan chuckled, turning the mirror on herself, fixing her hair, pouting at herself. "You're a new woman now."

Mae had no idea what that was supposed to mean, but was helplessly ready to sign up for becoming a new woman—especially if Bevan had anything to do with it. The taller girl gathered the glasses and leftover cotton.

"You go snooze that off. When you wake up you'll feel miles better."

And with that, Bevan was gone. The ceremony done, the ritual complete. Mae held her earlobes alone in the bathroom, unsure of what to do with herself. This didn't feel like the beginning of a friendship, but she'd take it over nothing. She was sore. She was elated. She was a new woman.

THIRTEEN

W HEN everyone is asleep, you light some candles, a cone of incense. The tooth and the apple slices lie on a tea tray from your ma's kitchenette. You don't need the tray, you know, but a little pomp and circumstance never felt wasted on Sweet James. The room is electric already. You can feel him on his way to you.

How did you get away with this? You tremble with delight as you kneel before the floral wall. He's going to be so proud of you. Rossa's tooth is white and small and strange, and the apple is now almost black, but holding enough stolen blood for it not to matter. You press your palms on the wall, whispering his name. You can feel something rolling under the surface, like an insect under skin. You can't stop smiling. Finally, he's back.

The noise of him is the crunch of broken glass underfoot and the howl of remorseless wind and how these things spell relief for you you'll never know, how something that sounds so bad can feel so good. The tooth and the apple slices rise from the tray to your eye level and the wall opens like pincers and eats them from your palm. The owl assembles himself before you and your hair lifts on your arms, your vest billows around you, the hoops of your earrings pull up instead of down, your hair moves as though under water. Light pours from Sweet James's eyes, gleaming beacons, and you bask there. It is better than any sun.

thank you, he says, and you could scream victory at him but you hold it, you hold the size of that thank you and let it feed you as you have fed him.

"You're welcome," you whisper.

the blood was enough. you brought me blood.

"It was easy," you say, your smile creeping wider.

you are getting stronger.

You nod, knowing this to be true.

i want you to go to the corridor after the third room. i want you to take water from there and bring it back here. i want you to take the water and pour it in the stove in rita's kitchen. can you do that for me, bevan?

"What will happen then?" you ask him.

you will be able to walk the paths of the other place for longer. you will be able to do whatever you please.

"Will you change into something new?" You can't believe you are asking him this, this stupid greedy question you've been saving for a time when you were especially in his favor. You are drunk on the relief of seeing him again, him speaking full sentences to you, him seeing you.

He laughs! He laughs deep and earthy and unearthly. **something new?**

You run your eyes up his paper and mirror and bone. "Would you ever turn into a man?"

His laughter is huge, then, and the energy in the room shifts again. The light around you warps—it glints and your knees lift off the ground. You are suspended. But you are not afraid. He's never been like this before and you laugh with him.

put out that fire, bevan, and i will love you as you need to be loved.

The four letters shoot like good, hot bullets through your body. You do scream, this time. Yes, you say, yes.

Sweet James lets you onto the floor again and unfolds the door, wide open.

you can take all night. nobody will know. you must come back with water. do not disappoint me.

You have no intention of doing anything like it. Your knees are wobbly and you can't quite stop the tremors of laughter coming from that good place behind your ribs. You grab an empty mug from your bedside locker and dash through the door.

It closes behind you.

At the other end of the house, Mae wakes, ears throbbing. She rolls over in the bed and thinks about the cottage she'll share with Bevan when they are grown up, the life they'll have together, her eyelids heavy, battling nausea, hoping against hope she doesn't bleed all over the sheets. Mae closes her eyes and imagines herself tall and thin, chest flat. Her hair short, wearing an artfully big shirt. Barefoot on the shore of the lake. Bevan at her side, a floral dress, a straw hat. They have a dog . . . the light is pink around them—then she's gone, asleep.

Across the hall, Rossa is awake with a thudding in the back of his mouth that he can't quite place. Bevan had done something to him in the garden. He's been awake with it for days and days. A heavy emptiness. He wants to go across the house, wake his sister and tell her that he thinks something happened, but he can't. What if the corridor went strange again? He wanted to tell his sister, but he knows how she looks at Bevan, he's not stupid. He doesn't want to cause any trouble. Rossa stays awake.

You hardly pause at the first room. Same watery stench, same strange neon. First door, swung open like any in your house. Through the gray-and-white corridor—through the papery moths. You pluck one like a berry with wings and put it in your mouth, swallow it like a treat. Sweet James says nothing, though you know he's watching.

You place your hand on the next door like something holy. And then you twist the knob and push and it gives, and the next room is all yours.

Twelve white baths stand in two straight lines of six, steam rising from four or five of them. Each tub stands on four little brass claws. White tiles, slick with condensation, make up the floor under your bare feet, the walls, the strangely low ceiling. The air is clean and bleached and different from the other rooms. Your heart beats like a drum. This room is your favorite, though you imagine every new one will feel like your favorite. Up beyond the rows of baths, there are new doors on the left side and the right side. Two doors. Two ways to go.

You can't touch either yet, you know, clasping your cup in both hands, but how you want to.

only bring cold water, he says, **do not scald yourself. you are useless to me without your hands.**

His voice sounds unusually quiet and far away. Not as immense as it does when you are in your own room. So one of these baths must be cold, you think, walking the aisle between them, casting your eyes over the surfaces of the still water in their bellies. You want to lie down in one, soak yourself, be heavy with the water from this strange place—but you'll have plenty of time for that, soon. You walk all the way to the end of the room. The last bath on the left-hand side is giving off no steam. You lean close to the clear water: yes, it's cold. It smells like fresh rain and something strange and you scoop a handful and drink. It's icy and you are refreshed and nourished—this is the bath, you think. This is the one, and you swoop your cup into it.

A door behind you opens and closes and you spin around to look. A girl.

A girl?

A girl is standing in the room with you. A pale girl with cropped black hair and a red mouth wearing a slim black suit and a bright white shirt, barefoot, holding a white towel. She screams. You scream. The noise of your fear bounces off the tiles, broadened by their surface, by the water—the way singing in the shower sounds, if the singing were fear, not music.

For a moment, you are both screaming. Neither of you moves until your breaths run out and it is silent for a heartbeat, and then you both scream again. Shrill and electric screams. You are terrified, she is terrified. You run out of air just as she does, but before you have a chance to think about how language even works, she barks, "Who are you?" and strides towards you.

You size her up a second—she's slight, shorter than you by far, you could take her if you needed. You clench your fist around the handle of the mug, synapses firing all fight and no chance of flight.

"I'm Bevan fucking Mulholland, who are you?" you roar.

She stops dead in her tracks.

"I'm Audrey O'Driscoll, and this is one of my rooms, so get out and go back to wherever the hell you came from!" Her voice pitches high and she squares right up to you, her chin pointy, her eyes steely blue, her teeth small and straight.

"These rooms don't belong to anyone, I'm here on an errand from Sweet James!" You shove her and the cold water from the mug splashes over both of you, shocking and freezing—she yelps and staggers. But immediately she pulls herself back up, her pupils contracting into dots, her mouth contorting.

"Sweet James?" she hisses. "Sweet James in the house at the end of the crescent? Rita Frost's place?"

You don't answer, you don't think you need to.

"That mug . . . that—let me see that!" She snatches it from you, too quick to stop, more water spilling on the tiles around you. You let her have it a moment. If she breaks it, you'll break something of hers. Your eyes flick to her wrist—a slim, soft target. She holds the mug up to her face. "This is from Rita's ma's kitchen. This is, this is . . ." and she sinks to the tiles.

She cradles the mug and begins to weep. You wish she'd stop. A fight would have been easier than this. Her cries bounce over the tiles, and the room of baths is now a chamber full of her unrestrained sorrow. You pick up her towel and hand it to her. She sniffles and takes it from you, wiping her eyes, heaving deep breaths. She looks up at you, bleary-eyed and pink nosed. "Are you her daughter?"

"Whose daughter?" you ask.

"Rita's. Rita Frost's." Her voice warbles. "Dark brown eyes. Freckles, left-handed. Rita Maeve Frost."

You shake your head. "No. I'm Imelda Mulholland's daughter. I live in Rita's house."

"Is she still there? God, how long has it been—is she ... she's alive, isn't she?"

You aren't sure what to tell her. Her name sounds familiar, sure, maybe Rita's mentioned her once or twice— but you're cautious. What is and isn't real back here? What if she's not a person, but a trap? You tread lightly. "Yes, she is. She took my ma in when she was pregnant, and we live with her and Bobby now. Well, I do. Ma's gone."

Audrey laughs against her tears. "Bobby! Bobby, our cat!"

"Yours? Like, the both of you?"

Your heart is thundering and your stomach is lurching and you sit on the tiles beside her because you're not sure your legs can take all this. She puts a bony hand on your knee—she's freezing cold.

"Yes, the both of us. She's my—my best friend. How is she? Did—did she get married?"

"No, Rita never married. But she's fine. Smokes too much, I guess, given her age, but otherwise fine. I cook for her and help her around the house—she, em . . . teaches me with cards, and how to see things. She's like my other mother." This admission sears you a second, given the nature of your quest into the wall—the betrayal of it.

Audrey's eyes are still sparkling wet. "She's still smoking, that's hilarious! God, you don't have any cigarettes, do you?"

You shake your head. "Sorry. She won't let me smoke."

Audrey sniffles, and smiles. "I gave her her first one, you know. I'm glad she's still reading the cards. She . . . she was supposed to come with me here, but she never did. Has she ever mentioned me to you?" There is too much hope in that question.

You pause a second. "I'm sorry, but no."

She closes her eyes and sighs softly. "I don't suppose she did. Safer that way. Always safer to say nothing."

You both sit there in the quiet for a while and you wonder where Sweet James's voice has gone. The room is stilled of his presence.

"Why are you here?" Audrey asks you then, quietly.

"Sweet James sent me to get water to put out the fire in Rita's stove. Said if I did he'd . . . well—let me come farther in here. Whenever I wanted," you whisper, shameful, your cheeks heating up.

"He'll never change." Audrey shakes her head. "He's a sly one. You know, once you're in here, far enough, he can't do anything. This place charges you up. Makes you strong and strange. He and I were friends once—if you could call whatever it was we were doing friendship. I hear echoes of him in some of the rooms, every so often. Old fool."

A bright green streak runs through you, sharp jealousy. You knew. You just *knew* there were other girls. The fondness in her tone enrages you and you swallow hard as she continues.

"He promised me the world in exchange for my time, pieces of my life, pieces of me and Rita. He knew all our secrets, and when he had his fill, in I came, and I never turned back. There's so much in here. It goes on for a hundred thousand miles. Time feels strange. I haven't talked to anyone in a little while: I don't bump into other travelers often. In fact, you're the first one I've met who knows his name."

"Other travelers?" you ask.

"Yes, heaps and heaps of them around. They've come in through different cuts in the world from all over— different places, different times and tragedies. Some turn sets of rooms into towns, settle down and build worlds that look just like the worlds they came from. That's not for me.

I left for a reason, and if Rita wasn't coming, I was going it by myself. I'm a lone wolf." She winks at you, her smile bright. Too bright.

She's got a vulpine quality to her, a mischief that you are at once attracted to and profoundly envious of. She makes you feel huge and at first that had been in your favor, but now her delicacy feels like a taunt. She's been as close to that great paper owl as you. He made you big and strong like a lion but must have made her small and sharp like a diamond. She's gotten what you want. You have a thousand questions, but they are dulled against the nausea of jealousy.

"You don't think Rita would . . . would come, do you?" A flash of desperation colors Audrey's question.

"She didn't come with you back then?"

Audrey sighed. "She nearly did. She would love this. She would love this, and we'd have a life here. But we argued and the door in the neon room closed and—that was that."

"What age were—are you?"

"I was—am—seventeen. My body isn't reacting the same way it would back there. Nothing is the same here. God, she'd love it. She'd love it." Audrey shook her head and wiped a few persistent tears from her face. "I don't mean to be crying. I haven't cried in forever. I just, I've been so far from her for so long. I wonder if she remembers me at all."

You sit silently for a bit, together. The mug is still in Audrey's hands, and you're reluctant to ask for it back, but you came here on a mission and it's the only cup you have. You're waiting for Sweet James's whisper to roll down on you at any time. You're waiting for that suck of gravity to pull you back through the door you came in, but there's nothing. None of his pull in the air.

"Why don't you come back with me?" you offer, despite yourself. "I'm sure Rita would be happy to see you."

Audrey flinches. "I can't go back there. There's no room for girls like me back home. I don't fit there."

"Girls like you?"

"Yeah. Like me." She thrusts the mug at you and stands up, all her vulnerability evaporated. "Go back to your mission. This won't be the last time we meet. Next time, bring me some cigarettes, won't you?"

She turns on her heel then and strides back to the door she came from, opens it, and steps through into the blackness. It slams shut behind her. Just like that. Alone again, an empty cup in your hand. You sit with it awhile before standing and going back to the cold tub, dunking the mug into the icy water, then leaving. Your head spins all the while.

Goodbye, room of baths. Goodbye, corridor of moths. Goodbye, neon water.

hello, bevan.

Hello, Sweet James.

FOURTEEN

THE man in the office looked up from his desk. A caged canary peeped, some pages rustled, and Audrey leant against the door, panting. The man regarded her breathlessness, the new sweat on her brow.

"Follow her," he said, and went back to his notes.

Audrey steadied herself, her palm damp on the handle of the door. After all this time, another girl who had come in through Sweet James. And it wasn't Rita. What was Rita doing? Letting some stranger have access to their owl, *her* owl—letting her all the way in here, not even having the nerve to come in herself? Was Rita still that spineless?

Long seconds passed, the canary chirping like a tiny feathered clock, and the man at the desk looked over his shoulder again.

"If you don't move now, you'll lose your chance."

His eyes scared her terribly, they were leaden with too much knowledge. He was never wrong. She gritted her teeth and nodded firmly, then ducked out of the office and back into the bathing chamber, her feet padding along the tiles quicker than her heartbeat.

Audrey O'Driscoll knew herself well: after the years she had spent alone, she seldom surprised herself anymore. Her perception, reactions, her courage—they had all been tested in the strange, endless landscapes she had sacrificed everything for. But, of all the things she had seen in these corridors, of all the forests and fields and cities and hotel rooms and caves and casinos, she had never felt like she did at the sight of the girl holding Rita's cup. That was new. It turned her pulse to voltage.

The moth corridor blustered around Audrey as she dashed. She had not gone this way in a very long time. She hissed at the papery little creeps to keep away, but they gathered, in front of the door to the neon room, blocking her way. They giggled in a choir, their thousands of together-voices replying, "What do you think you're doing back here?"

"None of your business!" Audrey barked, batting the handful that flitted around her away. "Let me through. Now."

The moths tittered again. "So be it. The yellow-haired girl was very pretty, wasn't she?" and they came apart, revealing the door ahead. She opened it and stepped into the neon wet room, the room that had woken up her hunger in the first place. God, the smell of it brought the hair on the back of her neck on end and the door on the next wall ahead rippled a tease. It hung open ever so slightly.

"I know you're in here, sweet thing." Audrey's voice

shook despite her attempt to keep it steady and confident. "Come talk to me. I'm lonesome."

The wall in front of her trembled again, but that deep and terrible voice she hadn't heard in so long did not answer her. She knew she should turn around and walk away, but something in her, something old and impulsive, drew her forward to the door she had not stepped through in years, so many that she wasn't sure she could count them. She placed a hand on the warm surface and pushed.

FIFTEEN

THE clock rolls four. The house is silent as you creep into the kitchen, alight and trembling, the mug of water clasped in your hands. The room is amber lit from the stove. The fire rumbles in that low growling way it always does, seeming louder in the night.

Your bare feet pad softly on the floor, chilly, each step a commitment to your cause, each footfall a departure from consequence. This will give you what you want. You kneel down in front of it, opening the door, the rush of heat on your face. You are transfixed a moment, the flames seeming so small in the night, untended since Rita went to bed. They always falter near morning, hungry for breakfast to grow big again, to enact whatever it was they did over the architecture of the house—whatever kept Sweet James from his fullest form. It would be his house soon.

You look into the flames for what kind of man he would be for you, try to imagine his body there in the red and gold. You try not to wonder about what Rita will

129

say when she comes down to wet, smoking ash. Or about the shudder that will take the house when all this strange protection falls. About how it will feel never to be able to take this back. The mug is still cold in your hand. What will it feel like when he gets loose of his confines? You are afraid, and thrilled. A wildness new.

You tip the mug of water from the other world into the fire,* and foul smoke rises and the fire hisses. There shouldn't have been enough water to extinguish it, but the elements are no longer just water and flame, cold and heat. They are opposites, older and stranger than both.

In the grate among the turf ash lies a bundle of cards, barely charred, but wet now. You consider reaching in for them, drawing one for your own. A flash of a tower rises and falls before your eyes like a bright, bad camera flash, and you turn from the ruin. Your knees click a little as you stand, and you feel your way in the dark toward the table. Rita's cigarettes sit there. You pluck one from the pack and put it to your lips, delicious celebration: that's what Rita gets for telling people what they can and can't do, what they can and can't have.

You flick the lighter, plastic and white in your trembling hand—you wish you weren't shaking, but you are—and the tiny dancing flame sparks up for a second, then dies. You try it again, a catch, a spark, a tiny fire that disappears before you can ignite your victory treat. Your skin goose pimples; a low roll of nausea follows, like dread. The air drops in

---

* Her pupils go from circle to slit to triangle to slit to circle again.

temperature again. On your bare limbs it almost stings.

The walls groan and a reek of something rotting creeps into the air. You feel sick but underneath the sick you feel huge, tilting, that tower behind your eyes becomes your body. Sweet James is free now, crawling from where the holy heat had kept him contained. It creaks low and deep, the walls, the pipes of the place unmistakably laughing. That bad nectar, you *love* it.

The house lurches and you fall to your knees, a bruising crack against the kitchen tiles, your knuckles stinging from impact on the floor as you clench Rita's smoking tools, unable to let them go. The whole world leans askew* and Sweet James laughs again and a laugh rises up out of you, too. The air from your mouth turns vapor, cloud in the air. The cold is biting, and good.

Bobby knew what was happening before he even opened his eyes, pupils pyramid now, furious. He was curled up, a ball of cat at Rita's feet. The slowness of her breath told him she was still asleep, but the cold would rouse her, if not the poison in the air. He leapt silently to the floor, wound across the heaps of books there, and nudged the door open with the tip of his nose. Out into the hallway, he stalked, noiseless, full of rage.

*

---

* This trouble did not go unnoticed elsewhere.

Rossa had sauntered to the bathroom to pee. He'd been wide-awake all night, held hostage by the sensation of having forgotten something important, his tongue chasing the weird hollow in the back of his gum. He was torn for at least half an hour between the soft warmth of his bed and the discomfort of needing desperately to relieve himself, and ultimately his body won out over the bed. He padded down the corridor past Rita's room, past Mae's room, past the door to the hot press—past another door. And another. The bathroom was along here someplace, surely? Across from that awful radiator he'd fainted beside. He hated walking around this house in the dark. He didn't trust it. Bleary-eyed from lying with his eyes half closed, he felt like the night and the house had teamed together and were playing tricks on him.

There, a radiator on one side of the hallway, a door on the other. He opened it up and no—that wasn't the bathroom at all. Another linen closet? How many did the old woman need? He took his phone out of his pajama pocket and shone a light into the nook and immediately wished he hadn't.

It was a narrow closet, but rather than neatly pressed stacks of linen and towels, each shelf was crowded with statues of young women shrouded in blue, eyes red, faces numbed by sorrow. Statues of the Virgin Mary huddled together, casting long shadows around their little kingdom as Rossa shone his digital light upon them, staring, staring until some will rose up in him and he slammed the closet closed and flung his back against it, as though his sapling strength might be able to hold these statues in. How had he never noticed that door before? Why were there so many statutes?

Maybe his eyes had been fooling him. The radiator wasn't at all facing this new, slim door. It was a little way up the hallway—and the bathroom door was open enough that Rossa could be sure of his destination. He scurried up and slammed the light switch outside the bathroom door. The light glared, an assault on his retinas, but a safe one at least. He locked the door behind him, unlocked it, then locked it again. Doubly sure. The blanch of the tiles felt clean and safe and familiar, though every time he blinked Rossa could still see the white outlines of the virgin figurines.

After relieving himself, Rossa washed his hands in the steep old square sink—but the warm water wouldn't run. Both taps gushed water so cold it stung his hands. The house was normally so tepid, almost clammy: Rossa did not like this. None of this. He'd get back to bed—make sure he didn't open the Mary closet again—and put his head under the covers where he would be safe and warm, where he could get his heart to stop pounding, his ears to stop ringing.

Or he would have, if the door hadn't suddenly stopped being a door and instead shifted darkly into something else. If the bathroom floor hadn't tilted slightly and the light hadn't bent so hard that oily shadows spilled from the sink, the toilet, the bath. Rossa for sure would have been back in bed in no time if he wasn't trapped not only by the house gone wrong, but by a paralysis that began to creep up his body like cold, wet tendrils, pinning him in place. All he could feel was the cold bleed of fear.

The tiles around Rossa shone too bright then. Bone and teeth and viscera, he could swear the walls around him had turned feathered—white and dappled tawny. Beyond the screech of tinnitus in his ears, he could have sworn he heard low, bad laughter just before his knees gave way. He crouched on the floor. He closed his eyes tightly and listened to the rumbling laughter and found something in himself, beyond the freeze of fear: if this thing was evil, then he was good, and he must be able to overcome it. He just had to find the courage—he knew it was in there somewhere, but he couldn't grasp it.

Laughter rose and rose as he crouched there, mocking, callous, terrible until it became words, the madness of a voice manifest from everywhere and nowhere at all.

what good is being good if you're a coward, rossa?

Mae, down the hallway, dreamed of moths and mouths and in her sleep tucked the duvet close around her against the cold.

You pull yourself up from the floor to the table against a new, icy wind. You can barely catch your breath, but you can feel his presence, and strength floods you despite the chill. You willed him to appear. You have never wanted anything so badly. A man who was once an owl, with a deep voice. A man who knows you.

But when the door swings open, it is not James that barrels through: it is Bobby, and you are furious. He is huge and loping, his energy bigger and less orderly, monochrome but for the mustard gold of his eyes. Very almost a lion, you think, for a second, before the creature snarls.

What do you think you are doing? His voice comes down on you from everywhere, like the room itself is furious at you—like you betrayed the whole house.

"He asked me to. He wanted to get out, he promised me—"

Of course he did! Of course he did. Show yourself, James. Show yourself!

The floor quakes and the walls warp psychedelic and wrong and the snuffed-out old stove, with all its pipes and the hob and the fatness of the chimney, begins to worm and shift in the way that you know all too well. Oh, James. His laughter bellows as black iron and glass and wire become beak and eye and feather, as his body becomes the kitchen wall, the kitchen ceiling. He is huge, his face a stove, his wings spanning to cradle you and the table and Bobby, too—until Bobby roars something cosmic and ferocious, leaving your ears ringing, and the owl shrinks back, ever so slightly. Two titans and you are just a child caught between them, out of your depth. You have made a terrible, terrible mistake.

SIXTEEN

THERE was a stark little silhouette in the kitchen doorway.

"Sweet James and Bobby Dear, what do you think you're doing to this child?"

Three pairs of eyes, all pupils triangular, flung toward Audrey O'Driscoll as her voice rose. She dug her fingernails into the palms of her hands. She was as strong, at least, as the bird and the cat now, she reminded herself, though here in this kitchen she felt no more than a teenage girl with one dead best friend and another . . . well—best friend who didn't love her enough to run away with her.

She felt human for the first time in decades. It was awful.

Sweet James chuckled low and smug, and turned his furnace face to her, the house shuddering with his movement. **i left the door cracked open, i knew you'd come.** Audrey rolled her eyes. "Oh, I suppose you're not in the slightest surprised to see me, are you?"

there are no surprises, said James the furnace.

I was wondering when you'd come back, said Bobby the lion.

Audrey walked into the kitchen, full of new machines and old tiles. Rita's parents were long gone from here, she could feel it, sense from Sweet James that he had had something to do with it. And worse, in the deepest fibers of her, somewhere under her bones, she missed him and was glad to see him. He'd saved her. He'd given her a whole world.

"What do you think you're doing here?" Bevan said, her voice sudden and panicked and young. Audrey, James, and Bobby may have been living in a world without surprise, but Bevan most certainly was not.

Audrey looked at Bevan, the deep influence of the cat and owl all over her, and she was struck by the familiarity of it. A girl handing it all over to the beasts. Maybe she wanted freedom, too, or maybe something else, something bigger. She was a house for the monsters, herself. Audrey's heart broke a little, and she extended a hand to Bevan. There could be hope for her, yet. She had a whole life ahead of her beyond this.

"James, if I offer you something, will you leave the girl alone?"

Bevan made a spoiled, angry sound. "Who are you to him anyway? This is mine, all of this, not yours!"

Audrey sighed deeply. She let Bevan's protest die in silence, let the indignation of it turn childish in the quiet. How she remembered that feeling. How badly she wanted to possess the thing that possessed her. That hum under her bones rang again, that owl-shaped gap in the fibers of her. He already knew what she was going to say, he was already laughing.

surely you have nothing to give me now that you have gone out and beyond, he said, knowing full well that she did, the same offerings she had made him time and time again all those years ago.

"You leave this one alone, stop what you're doing to her, and anybody else who comes through this house—and I will visit you once a week and give you exactly what you need. She's weak, James. She hasn't seen what I've seen. She won't last like this. And . . . there are others in this house too—they deserve a chance at a life without whatever it is you do. I'm past it, but I can still feed you."

Bevan made a noise of protest, but she was ignored.

And aren't you going to try to stop me, Audrey? Bobby asked, swishing his tail, a sneer curling his maw.

"I don't care what you do," Audrey said to him, not faking her bravado now. "Rita can have you. You deserve each other."

The owl and the cat laughed the low roll of those who had known Audrey for too long.

you will make a far better feed than anyone else in this house. even with such a long time passed, it is all so fresh in you. i feel fuller already.

"Then come back with me, James. I will come to the neon room on Sunday mornings and I will tell you five things and they will satisfy you more than the small tragedies of this house. Seal up the door behind you. Do not darken the world of this little one, or the children upstairs, again."

"He's not yours to take," said Bevan, brandishing the empty cup.

"Well, he certainly isn't yours," replied Audrey, turning around and heading back into the hallway. She knew this was torture for the girl. That this taking away of her poison and power was a looting of the highest order, but better a stickup than a grave robbery. It wasn't too late for Bevan. She could let Sweet James go and move on with her life in this world. Audrey loved her corridors, but she wouldn't wish a departure like hers on anyone else. She never knew how long they searched for her; she never would.

Up the stairs Audrey strode, away from the kitchen in the eldritch freeze of the house. Sweet James followed her, a great wrong lump in the ceiling, in the walls. A parasite under the skin of the house, up along the landing that felt too long, like there were too many doors, too many identical radiators punctuating the sprawl. Too many little tables where clusters of tiny Virgin Marys stood, and Audrey could barely look at them because she knew well why they were there, what Rita was trying to call with their presence. They had not spoken in decades and decades, but that woman in the blue cloak was one of their coven, too. As she walked, Bevan was roaring drama and calamity after her, following her like this wasn't an inevitability, like there was anything she could do or say that would change a damn thing. Poor girl didn't realize that it wasn't all about her. She would, in time.

At one bedroom door stood a gawky, skinny little teenage girl. Audrey met her eyes in a flash; the girl's mouth hung open in terror. At the bathroom door, on his hands and knees, a boy who looked just like the girl. Were these Rita's children? There was Frost in them, but they weren't quite like her enough. Where was Rita, was she hiding? Here Audrey was, leading a procession of fear out of her house, having stepped back in, having done something she swore she would never do, and Rita didn't even have the decency to sense her presence, wouldn't even come out and greet her—until, doorway after doorway in the freezing rumble of the hallway, there she was. Old, thin, gray—but undeniably her. Audrey stopped a moment, as did the swelling paper rot in motion that was Sweet James as he followed her.

Audrey looked in Rita's eyes, and Rita looked back and they were silent. Audrey opened her mouth to say something, but Rita caught her first.

"You didn't give me enough time." Her voice was ragged from adulthood and smokes, but under it was the cold bright spring that Audrey recognized, the freshness of Rita that she once wanted to drown in. Funny how you can come face-to-face with a conversation you've needed to have for your entire life and not be able to find language for it, how all of the imagined arguments you have with the ghosts that broke your heart fall to silence. So she didn't reply. She just turned her head and walked on, the great rumble of the owl following her, Bobby and Bevan far behind—the house warping in response to their parade.

The room she had come in through, Rita's old bedroom, stood before her. Sweet James rumbled into the room and

Audrey said, "You'll seal up this place, now. Not just the door to the neon gate, this whole room. Hide it away. Make it wall. You won't need it: you will be strong and fat from my pain."

promises are for humans, said Sweet James.

"I'm not sure I am one anymore," Audrey replied, and he laughed, because he knew it was true.

The corridor slowly flattened back to itself. Bevan and Bobby—still the size of a lion—reached the spot where the door to Bevan's bedroom should have been: but it was gone, wallpapered up. Bevan placed her hands on the wall and jerked away with a yelp—her palms were seared a bright and terrible red, glowing with a hot poison. It hurt deep like a burn, but the ache of it traveled up her wrists and arms and shoulders and down right into her chest. They almost illuminated the corridor a second with their heat, like something had been transferred into Bevan's hands. The house had taken her room and she could not even touch where it once was.

Audrey had taken Sweet James. Bevan's nerves flashed a merciless electricity, her hands roared with pain, he was gone, he was really gone. He had offered her access to the universe and she had done everything he said and now he was gone. She had betrayed Rita, harmed the twins—she had talked to him in worship and prayer. He had made her powerful, clairvoyant, removed her need for anyone else in her life—he had given her so much. She opened and closed her fists, her mouth hanging open. Her whole life had been in that room and just like that, it was no more. The house was freezing and it was July. Her heart was not a heart but a cannon firing rage and sickness through her body.

Before she knew it, Rita and the twins were standing around her. Bobby began to shrink, and the world began to drain of that huge, wild energy and her hands dulled red to pink to almost opalescent scarred white.

Rita's voice was clipped and careful, void of the soft majesty she usually sang into the world. Bevan knew she was calculating something. A truly unmagical spell, to protect the twins. A lie.

"Mae, Rossa—it is no secret this house is strange. The world here is weakened by old tragedy, and things come and go through that weakness. Things like what you just saw. You will not see the likes of that girl or that beast again, and perhaps neither will I."

Bevan thumbed the bottom of her shirt, looking at her fingernails, the floor, anywhere but the strange space in front of her where her room used to be. Her eyes looked too big for her head. Rita placed a hand on her shoulder, sympathetic for a second.

The twins exchanged intense glances with each other, the kind of looks that wanted to be a silent language, one they had long lost in their growing up.

"Bevan, we will need to get you some new clothes. I am sure there will be another bed for you, somewhere around here. This room is gone, now—and we will all be better for it."

There was a fragile silence in which the twins did not ask any questions, in which Bevan did not scream, though she looked very much like she needed to. They all just stood there.

"We should take breakfast," said Bobby then, a brittle olive branch of a suggestion. As the five walked back down the corridor, Rita produced a fat wand of sage from her dressing-gown pocket and lit it with a cigarette lighter. Thick, medicinal smoke billowed from it, and she held it aloft as she walked. A tiny cleansing over the corridors, the twins shoulder to shoulder, confused and scared, Bevan on a hard comedown, Bobby silent, and Rita mourning.

The kitchen looked as it had when they had all gone to bed that night. The stove was cold, but Rita promptly lit it again, as though nothing had happened. As though it were any old fire, not a sacred flame, not a wasted protective source. The twins sat down side by side, silent and shook—and Bevan noticed that they were holding hands under the table.

There were pancakes, talk radio, and eventually, conversation—though none of it about the girl in the black-and-white suit or the sickening beast that had followed her through the hallway. The only questions were the ones thrumming through every vein in Bevan's body, the desperation of "What am I going to do, what am I going to do?"

VIGNETTES
FROM
OTHER
SUMMERS

Question:

What is a summer?

Answer:

A summer is not as simple as a band of good weather when school is closed and the days are longer. It can reach all the way to October, or be as shining and tiny as a midday to three o'clock stretch. When we talk about summer, we are not talking about time. A summer is a bright wound that splits the year open like a hinge and leaves you exposed for who you really are, in the heat and pause and stretch of it. A summer is an agreement whereby something happens between people, between us. Something changes, something comes alive, only to die by winter. You will know it when it comes, you will be sure of it when it is gone.

Mae, One Summer Later

MAE had no idea what it was that came over her and gave her the courage to lean into Orla and kiss her for the first time. It could have been the fact that they were sitting by the ocean and the whisper rush and salty air was enough to make just about anyone a little braver, a little more elemental. It could have been that they were seven hours away from home, cloistered away with two hundred other strangers speaking the Irish language day in, day out: so even the act of sitting on a wall by the sea speaking English felt like a conspiracy. Especially because it was ten p.m. On a Friday. While everyone else was at the disco. And Mae hadn't even told her brother where she was going.

So call it oceanside bravery, being somewhere nobody else knew they were: whatever it was, it was the most gorgeous first kiss Mae could have asked for. Jackpot. Both girls laughed, and kissed again, cold fingers locked together. It felt to Mae as though the waves were roaring in celebration of them. How lucky this particular skirt of water was to be spectator to their romance. How lucky the girls.

Orla, early in the morning, waking Mae up and dragging her out of bed before breakfast. Orla, trying to cartwheel on dewy grass and slipping and falling, raising sleeping birds from trees with her laughter before the rest of the world had woken up. Orla, who let Mae out of herself little by little, who grabbed her wrist and dragged her to the discos in the parish hall and the film screenings in the old handball court because she had a song she wanted Mae to hear, a movie she wanted Mae to see, because she wanted to talk to Mae. She wanted to be with Mae. And Mae wanted to be with her, her heart a live creature in her body every time Orla's hand grabbed hers. This was the opposite of the sickness Bevan had filled her with. This was fun. This was what love was supposed to be, and Mae knew it the second it rose under her rib cage. Unmistakable, love.

Just once, after her evening shower, when the crush had gotten too big for her to contain, Mae caved. She sat on the bathroom mat wrapped in a bright yellow towel, her hair in sopping ringlets over her forehead, and drew herself a three-card spread.

The card on the left would represent her, the card on the right would represent Orla, and the card in the center would determine whether or not she should actually kiss her that night, or at all, or ever. Risk severing the hilarious kinship she'd been lucky enough to find. She'd take the cards as the signifier; she had nothing else to go on. She had no idea if Orla liked girls. She was far too shy to ask. They didn't talk about that kind of stuff: they were too busy laughing to ever be serious. Mae didn't want to be serious. She just wanted to kiss Orla. She would like to continue everything she was doing with Orla and also kissing. That wasn't a lot to ask.

She pleaded with the cards. Let this work out. Her damp hands turned them over one by one.

The Chariot.

The Ace of Cups.

The Wheel of Fortune.

Mae shrieked a little to herself, clasping her hands over her mouth. Chariot for courage, that was her. Ace of Cups for abundance of emotion, between them. The Wheel of Fortune was by the very nature of the thing, a wild card: Orla all over.

One of the other students hammered at the door to get her to hurry up, and she hurriedly shuffled the three cards away, hid the deck in her toiletries bag, and made her way back to the dorm, light on her feet, a chariot in her chest. Mae would take her chances.

That chariot, maybe, was what pulled Mae's body closer to Orla there on the wall. Maybe it wasn't the ocean or the sneaking away or the nighttime. Maybe it was a golden chariot of bravery, a destined thing. Mae would take it, either way.

For a year after that night, she barely thought about Bevan at all. It was only when Mae knew things with Orla were over, when love was a promise she could no longer keep—when the absence of love was as stark as the first rush—did she hear the footfall of the older girl in the background of her dreams.

Forty-Something Summers Previously

A UDREY, Deborah, and Rita lay on their backs in the glade up in the woods near Rita's house—not quite a meadow, but a place wide open, empty of trees. The one with the grotto in it. The Virgin Mary was the fourth of them, though none of them really believed in God or Jesus Christ—though they would only tell each other this. It wasn't a proper—or even particularly safe—thing to be rolling your eyes during the constant, droning hourly prayers at school.

But it was summer now, and the trifecta could talk at will about whatever they wanted. Not that the girls came out to the glade to be blasphemous or anything of the sort; they had a kind of love for the Mary. They were, of course, being educated at a convent, the classrooms of which were pocked with almost identical blue-robed girl figures with sad faces—sometimes one up above the blackboard at the front, and one above the clock at the back. With four mournful eyes on a classroom of gray-smocked teenagers,

Mary seemed omniscient. So even weeks after school broke up, here in the thick of July, the three girls went over Rita's parents' garden wall and down to the woods to see her. This Mary was wilder. Unconfined by the convent walls, out of the long shadow of the laundry, this Mary's cloak was bluer, lips redder. She was one of them, had been accepted into their coven despite her chastity.

Whenever the three gathered out in the woods to talk, Rita always felt like they were daring Mary to listen. To report them back to God for being bad, awful girls who wore black nail varnish and lipstick. Rebellious, occasional thieves who listened to punk rock. Very un-Catholic. By the small-town standards of Dorasbeg, downright dangerous. That kind of behavior was fine for the crows down in the city, but up here in the hills the air should be purer and the girls better behaved. Surely nothing they did could be that bad.

This was the precise thought Rita was having when Deborah told them that her period had stopped. Not just stopped recently, stopped four months ago. Stopped. Rita's head spun. The Mary would hear Deborah's soft posh-end-of-the-village voice and then would somehow tell the Mary in the church, who would tell the Mary in the convent, and then her gray army of hard-faced sisters would come and scoop up Deborah and put her away. Probably Audrey, too. Probably even Rita herself.

The girls lay there in the bad quiet that fell: something had been breathed into the air that had changed their whole reality. Worse, when Audrey said, "We have to tell someone," it was as though the clearing split open beneath them.

None of them moved. Three girls breathing in the glade, quiet until finally Deborah said, "I don't want to. Unless it's someone who can, you know . . . fix it."

Audrey sat bolt upright, glaring down at Deborah on her back. "Fix it? Who the hell do we know who can fix it? You need a doctor, Deb."

Rita looked over at Deborah. How had she been stowing away a little creature in there, how had she held her silence? Who was the man? But there was no time to ask these questions, the burden shared suddenly became something else, something worse than burden: danger. Audrey stood up, ferocious.

"We'll get it sorted," she spat. "We can't do this on our own."

And before Deborah could talk her down, Audrey was gone, back out of the forest, downhill, toward the houses. Her panic was a loaded gun. Deb's eyes flashed with terror. Rita took her hand. Both of them knew everything was about to change.

Rossa, Two Summers Later

ROSSA was sitting on Sam Batra's couch, eating a heaped bowl of jasmine rice with a spoon. The rest of the Batras were out at some family affair, and the boys were left to fend for themselves. They were waiting on pizza, but Rossa was famished, so he went through their fridge for what could be eaten and not particularly missed.

"Does your family not feed you?" asked Sam, landing down next to him and handing him a cold, cheap beer (acquired via Sam's older sister, Diya, in return for two neatly rolled joints), "You could eat for your country."

Rossa shook his head and swallowed the rice. "I'm sure they would if I stuck around there long enough for them to try." On this particular Friday night, Rossa had not been home in four days.

He had sent sparse text updates to Mae, who was becoming increasingly pissed off at him. He'd taken one call from his father, ignored six from his mother. He'd stayed with his pal Jordan for two nights and was crashing with Sam for two. He'd go home in the morning, he promised himself. Just steel the nerves first. The upside of being gone a long time was, well, being gone a long time. The downside was that when he got home, the fallout was worse. And now Mae was annoyed at him too. He tried not to think about what it might be like for her in the house without him, though she'd been hanging around with that girl from the Gaeltacht a lot since last year. Maybe she'd found somewhere safe to go, too.

He'd felt bad for not taking her more places with him, but he reckoned it was easier to crash at people's houses if he was just one, not two. Mae was strong. She could fend for herself, more or less. She'd have to, he thought, scooping the last grains from the bowl. Seemed when he was trying to protect her it only made his parents worse. Angrier. Less in control. If there was only one of them there, she might get off easier.

The boys cracked open the cans and switched on Netflix, waiting for the pizza and then a small cohort of mates to come over with more cans, louder conversation. The screen glowed in the dark of the living room.

"Look, Rossa," said Sam, sparking a joint. "My mam says you can stay for as long as you need if things are shit at home. Just wanted to let you know."

Rossa let silence fall between them, suddenly not hungry, the beer more sour in his throat. His heart thudded. The only thing worse than having to deal with his parents' fights was the creeping realization that he couldn't keep it totally secret. Cracks would open up. People would know. Their school was small. Maybe his couch surfing was giving him away. His exit route too obvious. He found a last thread of dignity, somewhere in his person, and pulled it taut. "Ah no, man, it's grand, thanks for offering, though. I'll head back over there tomorrow."

Sam did look at him for a second then, and Rossa saw genuine pity flash across his wide brown eyes.

"Whatever you say, man."

And he handed Rossa the joint, a tiny red light in the dark.

Forty-Something Summers Previously

THE stone eyes of the Mary couldn't see the warp and twist of the air in the glade. It happened in the middle of the afternoon, in the sun drench of the early summertime, long after the worst had happened. Just at the beginning of the continuing lives of those who had lost their friend. The most powerful tragedy is the first time one is forgotten, even for a minute.

There was a weak point: the kind of injury upon reality that unearned pain and unspeakable punishment had left on this mountainside. The world split, a hairline crack in reality that shone like iridescence and madness.

The two of them slid out, like tears or drops of blood or spirits—or monsters—or calamities. They were starved, and this place was a fertile plain of agony and ecstasy. There

161

was so much grief around this mountainside. They would follow it to its source.

One came in the body of a cat. The other in the body of an owl.

Behind them, a cut in the world. An entryway. An exit.

Forty-Something Summers Previously /
A Number of Hours Later

A SLOWNESS had taken Rita when the sisters had come for Deb, not long after she had confessed her pregnancy that day in the glade. Not long after Audrey had asked her mother for help. And after Deborah was found in December, Rita's limbs had felt like they weighed more than a human's should, her tongue lifeless in her mouth. Audrey had cut off all her night-black locks of hair, some act of shame, some apology that would never be heard.

And yet here, nine months later, on the cusp of August, the two girls were hand in hand in Rita's bedroom, expressing something in themselves to the lilting, thin tunes on the record player. It wasn't the first time their bodies had known to go to each other for comfort, but this was the first time they had danced. It didn't come naturally to either, but they had risen off the floor where they had been lying, hushed as usual, and come together to the rhythm.

The weight came out of Rita's arms, and she closed her eyes. She wondered: would she spend the rest of her life listening this hard to the grief in her body, trying to find a way to make her flesh her own again? Would she ever forget the headlines, some nameless girl dead in childbirth beneath the statue of the Virgin Mary? Hearing radio presenters discuss how exactly this nameless girl, Girl X, they called her, got out of the laundry, instead of why she was put in there in the first place. Like a criminal. She was nameless, X, there at the end of the alphabet. Would Rita ever stop wondering if it was she herself who was the criminal? Or Audrey, for speaking? All these terrible queries ran through her as she moved with Audrey, but something, as always, in the soft electricity of the other girl's touch almost, almost alleviated the pain of them. At least they had each other. At least they had this.

When the tap came to the window, Rita recoiled and Audrey strode forward, flinging up the blind to look into the night, challenging whoever had the nerve to disturb their tiny moment of reprieve.

Upon discovering the bright yellow eyes of a cat on the windowsill, and the even yellower eyes of the owl, she cast a look over her shoulder at Rita and opened the glass pane. She took the owl in her hands as though it was a tame thing, let the cat pad in after. The two creatures tentatively explored the room, sniffing the air, investigating, staring at the girls with their pupils too clever and all wrong.

Audrey said how sweet the little bird was, hopping around the blankets on the bed, arranging himself. How he looked like a James. A Sweet James. The cat had knocked his head off Rita's shins, rolled a deep and happy purr to her, and she said that he was a little dear. Bobby, she said. Bobby Dear.

you'll have to keep us now that you've given us names, said the owl.

We're terribly hungry, you see, said the cat.

Rossa and Mae, Three Summers Later

"ROSSA, I am going to sit on my hands until this conversation is over because I cannot believe what you're telling me and I might throw something. You are going to get me in so much trouble."

Rossa stood over Mae as she sat on the floor of her room in the spindly little townhouse they were raised in. Their home. Down below, their parents were arguing again: only for once, Rossa knew exactly what they were arguing over. He had made a comment. A stupid comment. One stupid comment about Mae that had flipped an ordinary evening into one of *those* evenings. Well, it was one of those evenings for him. For Mae it was even worse.

"I didn't think it was a big deal? I thought they knew. I mean, it's kind of obvious—" This was the cowardly way. Minimize it, make it smaller, that way her anger couldn't get too big. Trick her into thinking it's not a big deal, or at least try.

"What the fuck is that supposed to mean?"

"Well, you know. You cut off all your hair? You don't like, wear a lot of makeup or anything. You and Orla were together all the time . . ."

"Sorry, Rossa, but I literally cannot believe that we were born in the same year let alone came from the same fucking cells. That is so ignorant."

"Well, I thought they knew, all right?" Hands in his pockets. He knew he was wrong. He knew they didn't know, and he told them anyway. Mae had been so moody since she and Orla broke up, and he just wanted to find a way to talk to Dad about it. That meant telling him, and Rossa'd reckoned if he just mentioned it, like no fuss, it wouldn't be a problem. He didn't see the issue with Mae liking girls. But Dad had summoned their mother and accused her of knowing already.

She hadn't.

The information dropped like a bomb. Mae had come into the house for dinner after what Rossa had assumed was a long, morose walk and had been confronted by both of their parents, arms folded.

"It was very dishonest of you to have kept your relationship secret from us."

"If this is some kind of rebellion, you need to get over it and get over yourself."

"If we'd have known you were this way, we would never have let you spend all that time with that girl."

Mae hadn't even responded. Just walked up the stairs and shut the door of her room. Rossa had let himself in and now wished he hadn't.

"You knew full well that I hadn't told them yet. I was going to tell them eventually. Just not now, when things are so—"

Down below them, something crashed, their mother's voice roared something unintelligible. If this house was the kind of house that could shudder, it would have.

"I just didn't think it was a big deal. . . ."

"It doesn't matter if it's a big deal or not. It's not a big deal to you, or to our mates. But no matter what size it is, it's my deal. It's up to me to tell people."

"But—"

"But nothing, Rossa. This wasn't yours."

"But—"

"Nope. Get the fuck out of my room. Don't talk to me."

Rossa didn't even try to bring her around. He shrugged his shoulders and left in silence. Down the stairs in twos, coat snatched off the hook, pockets checked for keys— and he was out. Didn't stop to check in on the parents. Just left them to it. Mae'd have it worked out with them in an hour or two.

He turned the redbrick corners of the tiny housing estate they lived in, a left, a left, and a right, until he made his way up toward the small sloped park that marked the beginning of the concrete labyrinth. None of the lads were around, odd. It was sunset and the tide was up on the river, he'd sit and have a look at the swans. One of the lads would come by with a football at some point, maybe a few cans. A distraction.

Rossa kept walking, hands balled in his pockets as he

walked, didn't look at the birds again, just tongued the hollow in his toothline, thought about sending Mae a text apologizing, guilt at his back like a chill wind in the balmy August air. He felt like all the old ladies knew he'd just done something unfair and unkind to his sister. Like over their teacups and fans they whispered, "Some people just don't know how to keep their mouths shut," "I'd be snapping if I was her," "Sure it'd be a wonder if she ever forgives him." He couldn't take this one back, so was there any point in trying?

Up the concrete steps, down the center of the green and to the walkway by the river, he leant then over the high wall erected to stop the basin of the estate getting flooded by heavy winter rains. Today it was fat and full, a silver-pink dragon of a river that led right down to the Liffey. Swans flecked the surface, mute and vicious and gorgeous. More violent birds, Rossa thought to himself. Don't go near them, they'll break your arm, his ma had always warned. Maybe she wasn't just talking about the swans, maybe that childhood advice was about gorgeous things that only want to break you in half. The hollow where his tooth had been panged again.

He thought about how easy it was simply to exit the house. To disappear into the world. How nobody tried to stop him going, even though he was sure his parents saw him get his coat. He took comfort in that, there by the skinny urban river as the bad day bruised to night. Things might go wrong, but he could always walk away. He could always just leave.

Bevan, Three Summers Later

"WHAT did you just call me?" she whispered, low, hot tears prickling in the corner of her eyes, her fingernails digging into her palms.

"Crazy," Gus sneered. "No wonder you have no friends. Making up stupid stories. Do you think that makes you more interesting? An owl in the wall. Christ."

Crazy, a bullet.

Five Things Audrey Tells Sweet James,
Every Sunday For Three Years,
Until One Day He Does Not Show Up

I am afraid *she has forgotten me*
I am afraid *I will never forget her*
I am afraid *if they find me they will put me away*
I am afraid *I will never love again*
I am afraid, I am afraid, I am afraid

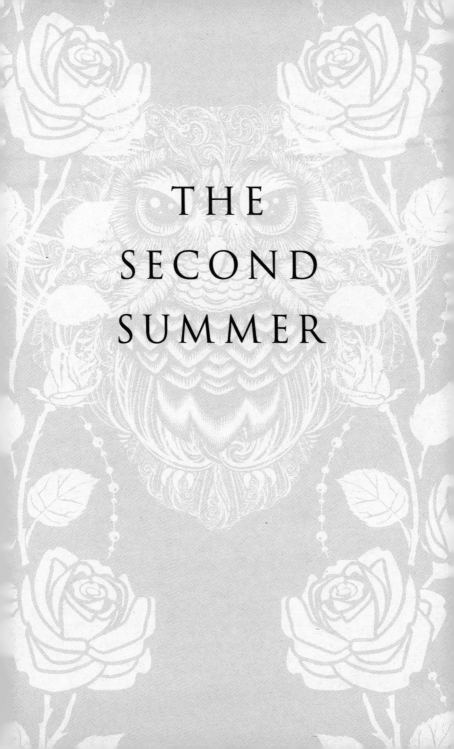

THE
SECOND
SUMMER

ONE

THE year the twins turned seventeen gave way to a vicious, roaring family collapse. Mae started to find gray hairs springing from her temples like tiny shining weeds. One in her eyebrow, one in her armpit, too. She'd taken to plucking them with tweezers. As the car approached Iona Crescent for the first time in three summers, the tweezers were nestled in the front pocket of her backpack with some pens, a lipstick, her little Nintendo, just in case. She laid her head against the window of the car door as her mother silently sped her and Rossa through the leafy suburbs.

The twins had only been informed three days before that they would be spending the rest of the summer with Rita, in order to stay clear of proceedings. The disassembly of their family home was proving traumatic for everyone concerned. Rita's impartial cool had offered their father great solace—he told them she'd keep an eye over them while he and their mother worked the last things out.

Neither twin said anything of missing teeth or broken hearts or talking cats or radiators that went all strange when you looked at them for too long. They were glad to be out of home. They'd take the wrongness of Iona Crescent over the escalating anxiety building in their little terrace house. How strange was this mutual, silent agreement that maybe something was badly wrong in Rita's house, that they'd seen something awful there that they couldn't quite name, but somehow they felt more able to manage that wrong than their parents.

Mae and her pompadour of curls, her tiny nose stud and skinny jeans, was three years from the gawky adventurer she'd been last time she was down this end of the world. Beside her, Rossa wore corduroys and a long, narrow cardigan—his own curls wound into a neat bun at the back of his head. Mae had shown him how to make sure it looked effortlessly hip.

"I'm not having some scruffy hippie for a brother. At least try to make it look cool, would you?"

"The beard balances it out," he'd replied gruffly.

His patchy attempt at growing facial hair was mostly ginger, a profound mismatch to the mousy dishwater brown of his mop, but he was dedicated to his cause.

The car was quiet and moving too fast. No radio. Mae knew not to ask to put it on. Mam would take off her head for even suggesting it. There'd been an argument: Dad had wanted to see Rita and their mam hadn't wanted to share the car with him, so Dad had stormed off to the pub at midday and their mother had stood blankly in the kitchen, car keys on the floor, for half an hour while the twins sat on the stairwell, like children, silent, shoulder to shoulder.

Without fanfare or comment, they turned through Dorasbeg village. Three years and it was just the same, cradled by mountains, in the shadow of a gray stone church. Mae reached her hand across the back seat for Rossa as their mother took a sharp turn away from the Crazy Prices and down into Iona, rattling toward the crescent. Her brother's hand eventually met hers and squeezed, silent recognition.

The woman driving the car was so far from what Mae thought she knew of her mother that sometimes Mae felt scared. Not least when Mam was behind the wheel. The breakup had made Mam brittle: touch her at the wrong second and she could cut you right open. Long gone was the buoyant optimist, the lady with all the answers who couldn't ever seem to stop singing. Gone, and the woman in her place was razor fury, who couldn't wait to see the back of them. Mae wondered if that loving woman had only shown up a time or two, in her memory. That the singing may have only been once or twice, the optimism an illusion disguising the knife drawer.

The car screeched to a halt outside Rita's house. Rossa jolted forward, his seat belt pulled taut. He clenched Mae's hand a little too hard; her knuckles cracked. They locked eyes, both pairs watery blue, identical, both feeling the very same thing in that quiet second. They were older now, though they didn't always feel old. But they were grown enough surely to handle whatever dark, rotten thing remained in Rita's house—if any of it remained at all. This moment of eye contact said more about what had happened in the house than either of them had said aloud in years.

They'd nearly talked about it that morning, when they'd been packing, listening to the screaming match on the ground floor of the house. Mae knew Rossa wanted to talk about it. She could sense it. The questions in her throat were in his, too.

Out of the car and into the still suburban air. Rita at the doorway. Two suitcases, two backpacks, left on the footpath. A perfunctory, brief hug each from the ghost of their mother. She didn't linger. When Mae let her go, she nearly burst into tears. It was less of a hug than a handshake.

"Be good," Mam said to them both. "No drama."

She paused a second. "I'll see you in three weeks. Well, either me or your dad will see you in three weeks—once we, well . . . once we know." She was less talking to either of the twins than she was to herself. She waved up at Rita, formal, almost a salute, one hand on the car door. She looked at her children again and said, "Be good," once more, and then got back into the car and pulled away. Just like that.

Rossa turned to Mae. "Well, things can't get any worse from here, can they?"

Mae inhaled deeply. "Here's hoping."

They pulled their cases over the pavement and up Rita's driveway. Their great-aunt stood there in the porch door, arms outstretched, Bobby by her side.

"I barely know ye," she laughed.

Mae and Rossa embraced her at once. Now this, this was a hug. She smelled like sage and stove. After a moment,

Mae felt a nudge at her ankles. Buttercup eyes looked up at her as she descended to her knees and kissed Bobby's small pink nose.

"You lonesome?" she asked.

"Never for a moment," he whispered in reply. Above them, Rita fussed over Rossa's hair and he let her. The twins were comforted by the unbridled warmth there on the doorstep. Maybe they would be safe this summer.

The house was the same as it had been, mock-holy ephemera that at first glance felt tacky, but held more power than that. On closer inspection, the small painted Holy Virgins wept tears of blood. Had they always done that?

Mae scooped up Bobby in her arms, his purring a balm—until she was in the hallway and heard movement in the kitchen. She knew exactly who it was, no doubt preparing soup. Lighting incense. Boiling the kettle. She'd recognize that footfall anywhere: a deer in a forest looking up at the sound of a wolf stalking a mile away. Mae put her nose in the scruff of Bobby's neck, her stomach a pit. The relief was nice while it lasted. But she kicked off her pumps and walked the long corridor towards the scent of herbs and garlic. Toward the barely audible choreography danced out in that kitchen day after day by Bevan Mulholland.

Rossa, somehow able to tell, leant over her shoulder and whispered, "She's only a lanky bitch anyway, Mae." And he meant it kindly, but Mae nearly turned on him. She drew a sharp breath and didn't reply. Rita led them into the kitchen.

The patio doors were flung wide, the kitchen saturated

with summertime, and there, at the stove, she stood, blond curls in bunches, too tall, legs tan and thick, a wooden spoon in one hand and a teacup in the other. Glasses she hadn't worn the first summer, thick, framed in tortoiseshell, perched on her nose. Still the center of any room. Still making Mae's whole stupid heart beat like a drum.

Bevan spun from the pot, a toothy smile across her impossible face. "Mae and Rossa! Would you look. You two are so tall now! C'mere, sit down—I'd say you're starving!"

The thudding of Mae's pulse dulled. Rita had reported that Bevan had "gotten over herself," but this almost manic brightness was a little too much. It felt false.

Mae looked to Rossa to exchange a silent *whaaat?* look, but he was already helping the titanic girl gather soup bowls from the shelves, setting the table, suddenly quick and helpful, chirping small talk while Mae stood there, stock-still.

Bobby leant into her and said soft, in her ear, "It's all over, Mae. Bevan's unwound herself. She's nothing to be afraid of anymore."

Mae stroked him and nodded, but her eyes were on Rossa, whose eyes were on Bevan. She wasn't afraid. She was kind of angry. The cat rumbled.

"I've missed you, old man," Mae said to him, by way of distraction.

The four humans sat around the table, and Bobby padded over to lie in the shaft of light by the wide garden door. Bevan chatted brightly to Rossa and Rita: she'd decided to give up college, it wasn't her style; besides, who would look after Rita? She wasn't going to leave her here on her own. She was booked out the gills with readings and someone had to do the organizing, a little accounting, didn't they? Bevan saw no point in being holed up down the country at some university when she had all manner of studies to undertake up here anyway. Rita bantered back with her, Rossa laughing along, charmed.

Mae blinked and absently dipped crumbling soda bread into red soup, the iced tea untouched by her side, dripping condensation. She felt like she was watching the whole scene unfold from the ceiling. Bevan talked so much now. Where was the scowling maelstrom Mae had fallen in love with? Had she made it all up? There was so much about that first summer that Mae could have made up, but if the talking cat was real—

"Are . . . are those tattoos on your hands? Do you mind me asking?" Rossa's question snapped Mae back to the table.

Bevan raised her hands up to her eyes and there, on her palms, were two bright blue markings. Eyes in themselves, in inked dots and swirls over her lifeline, her love line— patterns obscuring the organic puzzle of her hands. She closed her fingers over her palm and opened them—a blink. "They are!"

Rossa laughed, Bevan laughed. Mae stared.

"My ex-boyfriend did them for me. Rita hates them, don't you, Rita?" Another comic hand-blink or two.

Rita rolled her eyes, Rossa chuckled.

Mae didn't know what shocked her more, the tattoos,

the phrase "ex-boyfriend," or the *laughter*. In Mae's memory Bevan was largely a scornful giant, and here she was, giggling. Mae's appetite evaporated, and she dropped her soda bread into the bright soup, surrendering.

"I just don't know why you have to mark yourself like that," Rita tutted.

Bevan kept her eye-hands up. "She hasn't even seen the other one yet!" Bevan said, and theatrically winked one hand, dipping her head and elbow for effect.

"Did they hurt?" Rossa asked. His eyes had almost left his skull, and Mae was half tempted to lean over and click his jaw closed for him.

"Not really," Bevan replied, taking her hands down and presenting them to Rossa for examination. "I burned my hands years ago. I reckon since then my body doesn't really, like, compute pain. Actually, you were here that summer, do you remember that?"

Mae was uneasy with this. She remembered one bad night, one weird breakfast, then moderate peace until her and her brother were shipped home. No burnings.

Rossa took Bevan's hands and looked closely at the tattoos. Where was all this confidence coming from? How could he just reach out and touch her like that? Didn't he just call her a lanky bitch, and now he was touching her? Reels of old dreams about Bevan's large hands played behind Mae's eyes, and there was her brother, just touching them like they were any old hands at all. Outrageous.

"They're amazing," Rossa marveled. "I've always wanted a tattoo."

"Have you?" Mae couldn't help but snap.

"Yeah, actually, Mae," Rossa responded, not letting go of Bevan's outstretched hands, looking his sister dead in the eye.

"Well, it's the first I've heard of it," Mae sneered. She knew she was being unfair, but she didn't stop herself.

"I draw tattoos all the time, in my sketch pads. You've seen them!" Rossa was scrambling now, caught out in his flirtation. Stung, thought Mae. A minor victory.

"Oh! I totally forgot that you like drawing. Will you show me some of your pictures?" Bevan's earnestness was utterly alien to Mae. She sounded like she was actually interested.

"Sure—my sketchbooks are in my case." Rossa smiled at her, casting a split-second look to Mae that read *I'm not stung. You're stung.*

"Right! Let's go get them, yeah? I'm sure Mae won't mind taking care of the dishes—will you, Mae? I'll owe you one!"

"I suppose . . . sure . . . yeah." Utterly blindsided, Mae watched Bevan and her brother stand up from the table.

"You're such a dote! Come on then, give me a look at these notebooks, Leonardo."

Rossa didn't need to be asked twice—he and Bevan scarpered out of the kitchen so quickly that steam was still rising from the dregs at the bottom of their teacups. The kitchen door closed behind them, their footfall and chatter drifting away in the hallway. Two empty soup bowls and Rita and Mae remained, Bobby watching them from his panel of light.

A moment passed, too awkward for Mae. She looked at her great-aunt. "Rita, what in the fresh hell was that?"

The old woman was already lighting a cigarette. "Since her old bedroom closed that summer, she's become more lively. I prefer her this way. I take it you don't?"

There was something in Rita's frankness that refreshed the air around them. Mae snorted a laugh, genuine. Trust Rita to treat magical catastrophe and violent spellcasting as a finishing-school technique making Bevan more palatable to be around. Trust Rita to clock that Mae was uncomfortable.

"I—oh, Rita, I don't know." Mae sighed, putting her face in her hands. "God, that was so weird."

Rita chuckled, dragged on the smoke. "It's been stranger than that around here."

"I know." Mae didn't look up.

"Don't be jealous," Rita teased. Mae's knuckles in her eye sockets pocked the black behind her eyelids with white.

"I'll try." Her voice came out very small.

"Have you had any time to practice with the cards, with all the goings-on at home? I would have asked you on the phone at Christmas, but I didn't want to draw too much attention to it."

Mae lifted her head, the beginnings of a smile prickling the sides of her mouth. She'd been holding this secret close; she'd been waiting for this chat. "I have, actually. A lot."

Rita slapped the table, the cutlery taking a small jangling leap up in the air from the shock. "That's my girl! Show me what you can do?"

Stubby cigarette pursed between her lips, Rita pulled

that same old silken bag from her cardigan pocket and removed her tarot deck, corners softened and rounded from use, monochrome backs thumbed, faded, loved. Mae wished she could tell her all the hours she'd spent with her own deck, which still looked good as new compared to these old soldiers. Back home, Mae would sit with headphones in on the bathroom floor, the only door with a lock, and pull reading after reading while thunderous arguments raged elsewhere. She became fluent in the symbols of the cards, a private and soothing language as her home fell down around her, as her brother stormed out to stay at one of many friends' houses night after night after night. It was just her and the floral bleach of the little gray bathroom and the security of the locked door.

Mae took Rita's cards and performed a few shuffles, wrist tricks gleaned from internet videos digested on loop. For a second she was a card dealer in a casino, all paper flare, not a seventeen-year-old kid crumpled by the mere presence of her first crush.

Mae asked softly, "Should I read for you or for me?"

"For yourself, dear."

Mae had been waiting forever to show Rita this one magic trick.* Sometimes it gave her a migraine, other times it made her eyes water but it wasn't water it was blood and she couldn't think too hard about those times without

---

* Just like a magic trick, Audrey told the bartender, that's what it felt like when Bevan had shown up holding Rita's mug. Audrey had been waiting forever for a sign that Rita was still out there, but she'd heard nothing since. The bartender told her she wasn't listening hard enough.

feeling like she was going to faint. Regardless of what it took to get it right, this one good trick would blow her aunt away, of that she was certain. She drew three cards from the deck and placed them facedown on the tabletop. She gathered all of her focus, refused to allow the lurching dread of her brother and Bevan poring over sketchbooks in a room above them to intrude. She shooed it away, past the periphery of her mind's eye, same as her mother's roars, her father's Olympian name-calling. Like a single beam of light, she pulled her strength toward the three cards. Three cards, facedown. She wouldn't even need to touch them, she could feel them giving way to her already.

The Tower. The Two of Cups. The Fool.

"You three again," she whispered. Mae had drawn these cards every day for a fortnight.

The images flicked in and out of her sight, not fixed necessarily, but in flashes they were crystal clear. She was certain. She said their names aloud.

Rita took a sharp intake of breath, and Mae smiled up at her, her ears ringing (another side effect, much milder than it used to be).

"Mae," Rita spluttered, reaching across the table, her ringed fingers turning each card over.

"Not bad, right?" Mae gave Rita a wink. Rita's eyes were wet, her freshest cigarette a long, untipped pillar of ash, drooping tablewards.

"I am sorry things have been so bad back home, but I am so proud of you for taking what this house gave you and nurturing it. It would have been so easy to forget."

"I couldn't forget." Mae shuffled the usual three cards back into the deck. "Though . . . there's less magic back home. I'm not sure there's any at all."

Rita rose from her place at the head of the table and embraced Mae tightly. "This house got into you. You have it, too." She gave a deep, broken sigh and held her a second longer, before releasing her.

"You'll have to describe your reading process to me." Rita straightened herself out then, wiped her eyes, and shifted her demeanor up a few notches.

Mae began to clear the table. "Sure. And you'll have to explain to me what exactly the story is with Bevan's transformation into the Rose of Tralee!"

The two witches tidied up the kitchen, and Bobby rolled onto his back, showing his snowy belly to the sun. His ear twitched a little. Upstairs, there was laughter.

TWO

Y OU unscrew the top of the bright blue pot of face cream. Rita swears by this brand, and of all the advice she's given you over the years, "Moisturize. You'll thank me later. Don't forget your neck," has sat with you. On the radio, Alan Maguire's sharp, dismissive voice slices down another caller who became too aggressive on air. You love this show. The night shift, all yelling about whatever happens to be grating Alan on any given day, whatever's splattered over headlines—long into the black hours. Your world is small, just how you like it—manageable—but the radio makes you feel a little less removed.

Your phone is off. You've been keeping it off more lately, especially since you and Gus parted ways. You prefer your days without it, the internet a hall of mirrors, the constantly open channel of conversation too overwhelming. After the breakup, Gus had posted a forlorn missive on Facebook— as if you'd been the one to jump ship. Not that that was the problem, more that every girl you half knew had rushed to your private messages with some prying variation of "You okay, hun?"

You hadn't been okay, not for a while. Then, month by month, you were. You'd learned to keep away from the phone during your not-okay times: then, during the okay times too.

Alan Maguire is talking about ways parents could stop teenagers from sending naked photographs of themselves to one another. A taxi driver with a booming voice named Carl is insisting that all cameras should be taken off all mobile phones and that anyone caught sending nudes should be arrested.

"We had plenty good sex before cameras were even invented!"

Alan quips back, "Sorry, how old are you exactly, Carl? A hundred and fifty?"

You chuckle. Alan talks about this at least once a week, it really gets people riled up. You'd never call him yourself, though you were tempted just after the end of things with Gus to plea out anonymously—how do you mend a broken heart?

(You know how to mend a broken heart. You keep all your fairy tales to yourself in the future so nobody thinks you're crazy, or breaks up with you, then unbreaks up with you so you end up breaking up with them. You stay busy. You don't try to touch the wall.)

You separate your hair down the middle of your scalp, comb out the tangles from your bunches. Three thick strands and you start to braid the left side—keeps it out of your face while you sleep. These quiet routines help you switch off in the evening long enough to get a full eight hours so you can be up in time to cook breakfast for the twins and Rita.

You can't remember exactly why you were so irritated by the twins the first time they stayed here. Likely it was just because they were fourteen. You couldn't have anticipated Rossa becoming the cute one and Mae becoming so grumpy—a little pang of guilt ripples through you as you remember what an awful bitch you were that first summer. You were thralled to the thing in the wall—you know that now—but still. The piercing. The tooth—*God*, the tooth—you'll have to apologize. Make it up to them somehow. They know it wasn't you, don't they? They must know. Bobby talks to them. He must have told them it wasn't all your fault.

You feel a little sick then at the recollection of how hungry the thing in the wall was for them. How desperate. How you caved so easily to whatever he wanted, fed him their pain, fed him your own pain. How for weeks after your old room closed down you lay in bed, bereft, hollowed, your mind not your own, just full of the brutal memory of him. It must have been so strange for those kids, all of it.

You fasten a bobbin at the end of one long, thick plait. You'll make them some extra-nice breakfast to make up for it. Food is a good, quiet gift.

Alan is saying something, something like "You can't protect teenagers, Carl, they'll do what they want, they're not really children anymore," when his voice runs a shade deeper, repeating, **they're not children anymore.** The radio crackles and hisses, **you can't protect, you can't protect, you can't protect** glitches like a record skip over the airwaves. The light flickers above you. An electric scent is in the air and Alan says, **i've missed you,** but it's not Alan anymore.

You know who it is. Your palms are scorching from the inside out, you can't keep braiding. You can't scream. You know this feeling, this hit of something you've long stopped craving, this delicious, this awful.

You look at your hands. The blue pupils of your tattoos, perfect little rings, turn triangle. The triangles blink up at you. Through the mirror, you see the wall over your shoulder. The ivy leaves of the wallpaper flutter as though in a breeze, even though the air is so still you aren't even sure if you're breathing anymore. This is impossible. He's gone. He's with her. He doesn't want you anymore. This is a different room.

Behind the ivy, something is crawling. Moths. Dozens and dozens of moths in the paper, gray wings patterned like more eyes, too many eyes. It's not Alan on the radio, oh, no, no—it's *him*, laughing sweet and low. You spin to face the wall as the moths begin to cluster, two vast eyes, one long beak. Like bone and mirror, hunger and sharp. Like you're trapped.

"You didn't want me anymore," you whisper. "I have nothing left to feed you, I don't want what you have to offer—I don't want to go there again. Audrey took you away and you're supposed to be gone." You choke, you can't sound brave, your voice is high and airless against the brutal melody of his laughter.

audrey stopped showing up for work, bevan. she did or i did or maybe we both did, but either way that isn't how things are going to work anymore. if you don't feed me, they'll feed me. the girl will feed me.

"No, she won't!" you shout to the moths that are almost his face. "She's—she's a smart kid. She's too smart for your games!"

what about the boy, bevan? you like him, don't you?

"You don't know what I like!" You clench your burning fists, how *dare* he—

i know what you like, bevan. i always have. you should show him the other rooms. don't you remember how that felt?

A moth leaves the wallpaper, flutters across the room. It hovers a moment, graceful, before your nose, then lands on the very tip. You are frozen. The moth's wings are very slow, eyes that swing opened and closed, obsidian pupils dilating. Voltage under your skin.

rossa would like to sleep with you. so, as it happens, would mae. that, or break your nose. isn't that so funny, bevan? she can't decide. you would like to walk out of this world and never come back. you still want that. i know it. i would like to eat. we can all have what we want, bevan.

That was it. Too much. A girl possessed, you pick up the

radio and throw it against the wall,* your hands aflame. It makes an ugly sound and splits into pieces—and the moths glitch out of sight. Blink, they are gone, the ivy leaves just as they ever were, flat, an empty green. You scream. You paid for this, this was supposed to be over. His influence cleansed from you, cauterized from your palms, then wept out like a broken heart. Audrey. Audrey who just came in and took him, who walked in and took a story that was yours. Audrey had assumed herself into something that had belonged to you. She had taken Sweet James and made you ordinary. How dare he pry about the twins that way, how dare he try to get you back—

Hair half done, you storm out of your bedroom, broken radio littering the carpet. The corridor twists before you like a cruel joke, the floor spiraling up the walls, bad living architecture—but you march along heedless of the nausea it gives you. It rolls and unrolls itself, precisely how your insides felt for weeks after your room closed—your room, there, the empty spot in the corridor where your door used to be. For a second, it blinks.

A flash, a glitch, a tease. It flashes again, holds, like the door's really there, like he and your old room are waiting for you just past the threshold and maybe things can be just like they used to be, maybe he's done with her and it's your turn again—you extend your hand and

---

* "Listen harder," the bartender told Audrey. And Audrey listened, and listened, her hand wrapped hard around her glass. Somewhere past the soft, regular chirping of the bird in the cage by the piano, she swore she heard a crash. A distant sound of something breaking.

it is gone. You are left, a fool ready to step off a cliff. You close your eyes and take a deep breath, you try to dampen the sick need for him, for neon lights and moths and baths and endless possibility.

His voice thrums and the door flickers one last time.

bring me the boy.

Something wakes in you. Some old, bad need.

In the bathroom, you run your hands under the cold of the taps—steam rises from your palms, the eyes of your tattoos back to their old shape, like they'd never moved. You look out the window over the garden—it will still be warm out, July holding strong.

Why did nobody come when you smashed the radio? Did nobody hear you scream? You dry your hands and close your eyes. What is it about this house that eats cries for help?

THREE

THE garden was alive with motes, soft buds of strange on the air. The last fluorescent strip of sunset was muted to the mauve that comes before night in July. Rossa rolled himself a joint with the remnants of his weed.

He sat on the bench, which was a little farther from the house than he remembered it being three years ago. He had thought that growing up meant things felt smaller to you, not still so vast—but maybe not at the house on Iona. Things weren't quite fixed here.

The wisteria hung heavy almost over him, drunken peonies bloomed in beds about the bench, petals like silk, too heavy for their stems. He sparked the joint, irritated that he hadn't brought his pencils and sketchbook. He'd have to pick some of the flowers to draw when he was finished. Rossa inhaled deeply and held the smoke in his chest.

Mae was in funny form, he thought. She'd been coping okay so far, given the circumstances. Maybe it was Bevan making her uncomfortable. Bevan certainly had that disquieting air, too gorgeous for her surroundings. A runway model collaged into an Ikea catalogue. Rossa had no idea how he hadn't fancied her when he was fourteen. Maybe it had been just before he'd figured out how to fancy anyone. Upstairs in his room, her curls brushing the pages of his sketchpad, he'd thought how easy it would be to sweep one away from her face and kiss her. One hand on her lower back.

He took another drag from his joint. This was the end of a scarce supply now: he should have made it last a little longer. Should have shared it with Mae. She was always real funny after a smoke, her laughter like it had been before their mam and dad had gone septic. Didn't bear thinking about. Besides, Rossa was beginning to feel the exact dose of *I don't care anymore* that he needed, leaning into the high.

The patio door slid open, his twin's boyish silhouette in the frame.

"Perfect timing, Maemae," he called, waving the spliff, a little cherry-red beacon in the growing dark.

"You sly dog," she called back, soft, closing the door behind her. "But Rita's not gone up yet. She'll be raging at you for getting stoned!"

"I somehow imagine that Rita's had her fair share of potions and concoctions in her time, I hardly think a cheeky joint would offend her."

Mae fell back onto the bench, reclining, exhaling. Like, Grand, just us now.

"Should we get Bevan and offer her some?" Rossa wasn't thinking when he said it. His sister's face fell.

"Give me a break, would you? You were all over each other at the table earlier."

Rossa passed his sister the joint. She took it, and as they touched fingers briefly, he noticed she'd painted her fingernails. Apricot pink, a little messy. That was weird.

"I wasn't all over her. I was just trying to, like, establish something! We're here for three weeks. Just because she was possessed or whatever last time doesn't mean we should hold it against her."

Rossa was surprised by how easy it was to talk about the strangeness of the first summer, now that they were here, at the site of it. Some parts had caved off in his memory, some parts of it felt like they hadn't really happened. They didn't talk about those days too much, he and Mae. Their shared experiences in the house were hard, sometimes, to put language on at all. Mae inhaled, held the smoke in her throat, and puffed out two, three delicate rings. They drifted in the air, and she closed her eyes. "That's not bad at all."

"All right, Gandalf the Gray, hold your horses." Rossa reclined, rolling his eyes at his sister's performance, and she gave him a soft elbow in the ribs. "It's really something here, isn't it? So quiet."

"Ah, yeah," murmured Mae. "Nothing's getting thrown at the walls tonight."

The pair laughed darkly—hushed remarks like this they could only share with each other. Neither of them saw any use in telling their friends what was going on, drawing the wrong kind of attention, drawing pity. Their parents separating was one thing, that much the whole housing estate knew, but the rest—well, the rest wasn't anyone's business.

Rossa took Mae's hand on the bench and squeezed, but the peace and silence didn't last. A crash lifted them right out of their skins. In the bedroom farthest to the left of the house, the lights flickered, brightened, then switched off.

Mae swore, all color draining from her face, her breath quickening.

"It's grand, shhh." Rossa rubbed her arm, her grip on his hand now a vise, her apricot nails almost breaking his skin. "Shhh," he soothed. "Look, it came from the side of the house that Bevan and her ma used to live in. You don't think—"

Mae wrenched away from her brother and wiped her eyes. "And I suppose you're going to go gallivanting into the house and save her from the creatures in the walls, are you? I'm pretty sure she's on good terms with them—she took a tooth out of your mouth, for Christ's sake."

"But shouldn't we be going up to see what's going on?"

"Absolutely not." Mae shook her head firmly.

Her brother narrowed his eyes at her. "Is this because you're feeling weird about seeing her again? That shouldn't stop you helping her, Mae."

"Look. For a second, can you imagine you're me? It can't be that hard. Imagine if you saw her again and she was totally different. Got that? Right. Now, imagine that you saw her again and she was totally different and your twin was flirting his hole off with her." Mae was always frank.

"Ah, come on—" Rossa began, but she cut him off.

"So now that you have that delightful image, imagine you saw her again, and she was totally different, and your flesh and blood was putting the moves on her, and oh. The most important thing. You were in a magical fucking house with your witch aunt and a talking cat. And! The house was full of weird bad spirits and that girl was the center of all that malevolent energy and—look at me—imagine all that. Imagine that was the case. Now. Imagine hearing something smash and seeing the lights flicker. Are you with me now?"

Mae was vibrating with anger. Rossa saw flashes of their mother in her when she got like this, wondered if he should tell her that. If that would make her stop and calm down, or wind her up even more.

"Mae, we should go and help even if it was something strange. We're older now, we're probably better able for it too."

"Oh, I'm sure you're well able for it, all right." His sister took one last pull off the joint. "I'm going in to check on our aunt and the cat. If there's something up, Rita probably knows the ins and outs of it. Bobby probably knows its birthday and favorite color."

Mae stood up in front of Rossa for a moment, hugging herself tightly as though it was cold, though it wasn't. She sniffled. "Do you want a cup of tea? Toast?" An olive branch.

"Yeah, actually. I'll follow you in a second."

As Mae wandered back up to the house, Bevan greeted her in the garden doorframe. Rossa saw his sister flinch. Felt it for a second, even, some weird twin reflex that had been dormant since they were single digits in age. Or maybe it was just the weed. The stiller he stayed, the better he felt it. Bevan was advancing down the garden toward him, and his pulse hopped. He could see the gooseflesh on her bare legs before he saw her face, blotchy and red. Her eyes puffy, her hair a mess. She sat down beside him and wiped her nose on her wrist.

"You're not here to take another one of my wisdom teeth, are you? I've only three left."

It was out of Rossa's mouth before he had even a second to filter himself. Surprisingly, Bevan laughed. The sound of her was unreal; Rossa felt a wave roll over him.

"Kiddo, you have no idea. I'd say I was sorry—I mean, I am, I really am—but at the time . . . at the time it was worth it." The girl shrugged. "I know that probably sounds awful. I feel awful."

Rossa asked, "Did you smash something off the wall upstairs earlier?"

Bevan nodded, her eyes prickling with tears again, her lip trembling. Rossa looked at her throat, her clavicles.

"I can't tell you about it just now. Will you . . . will you come to the glade—look, there's this place in the woods I'd like you to see. Come in the morning? Please?"

Before Rossa could answer, his heard his sister's voice. Mae was on the patio holding Bobby. "Are you two saps coming in or what?" Rossa sensed something behind her jovial tone, something forced. Bevan however, didn't. She called, "Coming, Mae!"

Then she turned back to Rossa. "Meet me here at six. We'll get going before Rita's up, go down to the cut, then come back through the village. We'll be back by nine, and it'll look like we just went off down to get some fresh bread."

She rattled it off so quickly, so quietly. Then she got up, waving to his sister with one hand, wiping her running eyes with the other.

"Let's see if we can get Rita to stay up late." Her tone switched as they approached the house, from one kind of conspiratorial to another in a single breath. "I'd suggest Cluedo, but someone always ends up peeking through the paper and ruining it for everybody, don't they, Bobby?"

Bobby chirruped, "Not you though, Bevan. Butter wouldn't melt."

"Butter wouldn't dare. Sure, I've never done a single thing wrong in my entire life."

Rossa let himself believe her. Just for a second.

FOUR

L ATE the following morning, Mae was listless. She lay
on the bed scrolling through her phone. No internet.
Just a few saved songs. Rita was with Bobby, holding court
in the living room with a clutch of young women, reading
their tea leaves and tarot. Mae wished Rita would tell her
her future. She read her own with her cards, sure, but it
wasn't the same as the hope of handing over big, heavy
questions to someone far older, far wiser. For once, Mae
would just have liked answers. What would become of
Mam and Dad, their house? Would she ever feel the same
way about anyone as she had about Bevan? Would she and
Rossa stay close . . . actually—where *was* Rossa? What was
going on in this house? She swore she could feel it, an
uneasiness in the air. No amount of incense could mask
that oily electric tone: an infestation taking place.

She sat up, a determination to investigate blooming in
her. Where was Rossa? Had he gone off someplace with
Bevan? She focused intently but couldn't quite see him.

Of course. She'd been cultivating what little power she had, her senses keen from years of exercise with the tarot. She didn't have sight, she couldn't throw books off walls with her eyes (no matter how many times she'd tried), but she did have something. Something small and unnamable and most likely deniable to anyone she'd try to explain it to. She'd always had it, more so when she was little, she felt like she could hear her brother's thoughts, what he needed. That channel had been long closed, but the half sense stayed there. Maybe it would be more someday if she worked hard enough.

She got up and ventured out into the hallway. She was sure her brother was just behind one of these doors. Mae closed her eyes and ran her hand along the walls, where was he, what was he doing? The walls were covered in paper, and paper wasn't all that different from cards, and the cards held up structure and stories the same as houses, didn't they? Maybe the hum she was feeling in the walls was just her imagination, but even if it was, she wandered after it, down the too-long hallway to the other side of the house. The carpet even changed halfway along from bold, hotelish geometrical patterns of Rita's taste to Imelda's neutral beige.

Mae peeked around a doorway—another bathroom, nothing useful. She didn't know there were two bathrooms up here. Two doors left. She listened hard, but the house was mute in return. That meant nothing: the house ate noise, something in the architecture dampening cries for help. It probably also muted any sort of cries of pleasure.

She realized that she was not only looking for Rossa; she was looking for Bevan, too. To see if they were together. To see if it hurt.

The next peek into an unexplored room showed her a bare double bed, an empty open wardrobe: Bevan's mother's room. Imelda the escape artist. Mae had never seen her; there weren't even photos around. Mae assumed she was beautiful, if Bevan was anything to go by. She looked around at the unused space, the hollow of it. She tapped her fingers lightly on the door, heard it echo. She imagined her parents' bedroom this bare. This abandoned. A pang of sorrow flashed through her, and she quickly closed the door on the empty room and on those unbidden feelings. Not for today.

Next was the too-large space on the hallway wall, the room that Bevan used to stay in, the room they'd watch disappear that night. She tried hard to remember more from that late, strange scene, but she couldn't wrap her memory about it. It felt just beyond her, but she knew this was the place she'd seen the door close up. The farthest room from the kitchen. The house's heart. Mae was drawn to it like a magnet, pulled by curiosity or something else. Something worse.

She stood in front of the blank space, and in a blink, the door was there. In her memory of the first summer, this door was a place she had desperately wanted to go but never could. Bevan's room. Had she called it? Had it come just for her? Her mouth was dry and her heart too fast. She didn't even think before opening it up and walking in.

The room was spare, but not as barren as Imelda's had been. The bed, under a window facing the garden, was made. Pastel and neat. The wallpaper a muted rose garden. The dresser scattered with cosmetics. The air stale. One wall of the room stood without a stick of furniture up against it, the wallpaper an ivory garden. The air hummed ugly around Mae. She had seen this door close, this room get eaten up, with her own eyes. Some things you misremember, sometimes big old houses that aren't yours feel strange when you think of them years after—but the house on Iona, Mae knew, was all wrong.

Mae felt a little woozy: at any moment she could be caught trespassing here. She was an interloper. She had no excuse for being in this room other than the undeniably creepy truth that she had been wandering the house expecting to find her twin with the first girl who broke her heart—technically she was just following a feeling to its source. Maybe that wrong feeling was only heartache. The metallic dark of the air in the room was almost indistinguishable from the pain she had begun to feel when she first noticed her brother's eyes on Bevan. It was almost enough to make Mae feel a little drunk—a very heady gradient of pain.

Where was her brother? Where was Bevan? She ran her fingertips down the rosebuds on the wallpaper.

She closed her eyes. "Come on . . . where are you?"

A silence fell, thick, the afternoon dense all around her. Maybe she could plant the pain in amongst the flowers, nurture them to grow into what she wanted to see: her brother, Bevan, wherever they were. As she thought it, every hair on her skin lifted. Something was arriving.

"Mae Frost." Bobby stood in the doorway, aghast. "What are you doing?"

Bobby was as big as a Labrador, wavering in the light, his form uncertain, rippling. "Leave this room immediately and never come back. You can't reckon with him!"

"Him? Who's—"

Mae's fingertips sank into the wall and she jerked back, shocked. The roses turned black, then white again. The air smelled of copper.

"Please, Mae, he'll drink your fear and get stronger— come to me, please—" Bobby was almost shouting.

but bobby will drink up all your love. The voice came down thunder-deep. **it makes him strong, it is delicious.**

The room rippled, colors warping, furniture trembling. The bedsheets were mercury liquid, the ceiling was mirror, the floor below her was sand. Everything was wrong. Mae had no scream in her. She looked at Bobby, at the flowers now assembling into a beast, a face—an owl, a great owl in the wall. The roses around the white feathers trembled as though in a rising gale. The carpet went from sand to silk, then gravel beneath her feet. The ceiling stippled white then mirror then dark, old-blood red. The air reeked.

Mae took hold of her terror and twisted it, forced it to become courage. The heightening and deadening of every nerve became bravery just long enough to get her to the door, stumbling over Bobby, then slamming it behind her.

From inside she could hear her name called by Doris Day in a sick chorus.

Bobby nuzzled his long face against her and she did not stop him. Let him take whatever it was that was coursing through her. Let all this be over, instead of happening again.

FIVE

T HE garden felt almost too long as Rossa and Bevan walked. Longer than it had any right to be. Past the bench and the tearful falls of wisteria, purple and gushing. Along a hodgepodge cobbled path, stones loose, a little dangerous. There was long grass, a shed that looked like it hadn't been touched by a human's hand in years: windows wintered by cobwebs. It was a forgotten structure from a time when more people lived in the house on Iona Crescent, oddly quiet against the circus of flora all around it, the roar of wildflowers in high summer. All these parts of the garden Rossa had never seen. His allergies began to flare up, his eyes watery, but he didn't say anything. He didn't want to dampen this clandestine morning adventure.

Rossa's garden at home was a sixth, an eighth of the size of this rolling suburban oasis. How unjust it was that they got a tiny square of paving with a washing line in it, and Rita had this—this wild, this countryside end of suburbia. Maybe having a garden would have made a difference:

surrounded all the time by so much green, how could people hate each other like his parents did?

Bevan pulled open the gate at the back wall; it wasn't even locked. She beckoned him to follow her and disappeared behind the stone. Rossa peered through first, as though this simple exit was a portal to someplace else. At home, out past his back door was just the next street over, identical to his own—but here there was a riverbank, a busy ravine, then, beyond the farther bank, a forest. Tall, skinny firs stood in an endless row. Rossa could smell them, feel them in the back of his nose and under his eyelids. Still, when Bevan sprang elegantly over the ravine, Rossa followed her.

He should be nervous about following a girl who might have been a vessel for a malevolent being into the mountains with no map, no signal on his phone. But he wasn't shuddery or nauseous or uncertain at all—nothing felt that way to him anymore. The air still had a newness about it, almost a chill, and Bevan was a doe, loping through the lean trees.

He followed, though he couldn't move as lightly as she. He was a lad of footpath and streetlamp and tarmac, not fallen branch and wet soil and loose stone. He'd have to pay attention so he didn't fall on his face and make a sap of himself in front of her.

"The cut is a little ways farther out today, I think," she said, wrinkling her nose a little, staring into the middle distance. "It'll take a while to get to the glade. You don't mind, do you?"

Rossa wanted to say, "Of course I don't mind, I'd follow your every step until the end of the world," wanted to say yes, yes, yes; wanted to say, "Is it too early in the morning to kiss you?" Wanted to say, "When did this start feeling so huge, it's only been a day?" But he said, "Yeah, cool, that's grand."

Bevan looked at him a second, silent. Her eyes flashed, a tiny smile curling at the edges of her mouth, as if she knew something he didn't. He pushed down the beginnings of discomfort and they walked on.

When had he wound up in so deep with Bevan? Had she always looked this way, made of so many splintering details that his eyes couldn't take her all in? As they walked, the warp of infatuation made her taller, bigger, more. He didn't know how to look at her, exactly. She was fascinating. She was too much happening at once.

"Do you come out here often?" Rossa asked her, the undergrowth crunching softly beneath his sneakers.

Bevan hummed. "Not really, no. Only on special occasions. I just thought you should see it. It's where Bobby came from. It's why the house is, well—you know."

Special occasions. Rossa reeled. He was a special occasion! Bevan laughed sharply then, in a way that disoriented him a bit, but he didn't address it. Instead he asked, "Do—do you know what I mean if I ask if it's going to feel like the house?"

The girl nodded. "It is, yeah. The whole glade. Like it doesn't agree with physics or something."

It took them forty minutes, almost tripping and

215

squeezing through narrow rows of slender trees before they started to clear. A glade opened up ahead. Rossa's tongue moved to the spot in the back of his mouth where his tooth had been. The air was dark and magnetic all around him as they stepped forward.

There it was, then. A split in the world, the scarred fabric of the universe. It was gorgeous. It was wrong. Like when a television is broken, or a photograph held up to heat, the surface of the world had ruptured. Not the ground, the earth—but the air, hanging in the middle of the glade. Scarred white light, casting fat prisms on the grass. A cut, suspended.

On the ground beneath it was a small stone structure, open and facing them. A grotto, wherein stood a statue of the Virgin Mary, her face pallid, her gown blue, her halo a yellow that wanted to be gold. Plastic roses all at her feet. It looked like a poorly made child's toy below this incredible anomaly. A plaque was fixed to a stone,* but he couldn't make it out. The air all around Rossa was too warped. The morning light took on an almost ultraviolet quality, the rubber in Rossa's sneakers glowing, his clothing rippling in a wind his skin couldn't feel.

Bevan was, undoubtedly now, a foot taller than she had been when they left the house, her hair a chaos of gold rings. All of her bigger. She leant down and picked a stray long-stemmed daisy from the forest's edge, and it was tiny in her hand. She laughed at it and plucked a few petals

---

* In Loving Memory of Deborah Hurley and Baby, By the Grace of God Eternal.

216

before throwing it over her shoulder and stepping into the meadow. Her hair lifted around her.

Bevan sat down a few feet away from the scarred and shattered slice of sky, and Rossa followed suit. The grass was soft beneath them, the day just starting to warm—any trepidation Rossa had felt was replaced by sheer awe. This giant girl, this tremendous place.

"You should stay at the end of the summer," Bevan said, quite suddenly.

"What?" Rossa couldn't keep it in his mouth. "Are you serious?" If he'd thought a little longer he would have said something slightly more dashing.

"Yes, you should stay. I know there're awful things happening at home for you and Mae. So, stay. We could do with a man around the house."

Man. What a massive word. Rossa felt like anything but a man here in the shadow of a closed-up portal, beside Bevan. Boy, he felt like, for sure. Boy. The least magical thing for miles.

"I . . . I've only been here a day. I'm not sure you or Rita would want to put up with me for much longer than a few weeks."

Bevan shook her head. "No, I think we would. You could draw pictures, we'd feed you—you could keep me company, fix things around the house for Rita. Think how nice it would be."

Something like an alarm went off somewhere in Rossa's head. A faint warning—something a little greedy in Bevan's tone. But it flattered him more than scared him.

217

"That's a sweet picture. But . . . what about Mae?"

Bevan trilled a laugh. "Oh, Mae doesn't want to be here at all, can't you tell? Besides, you're hardly going to hang around your twin for your whole life, are you?"

"No . . . but I can't send her back to Mam and Dad on her own. That wouldn't be fair."

Bevan tutted a little. "Perhaps she can stay, too. She likes studying with Rita, I suppose. I wouldn't mind her being about as long as you were here."

Rossa's chest was tight; this was more than just flattery, this was out-and-out flirtation. He felt, for a second, embarrassed that the statue of the Mary had eyes at all, like some deadened audience, watching what was beginning to feel quite intimate.

"Has being out here made you bolder?" he asked, giving her a little nudge. As he touched her, he realized that he just about came up to her shoulder. Mere contact felt seismic. She took the knock for effect, then nudged him back.

"Something out here just makes everyone . . . well . . ." She gestured. "*More*, I suppose. So yes."

She grinned but didn't look right at him. "It's the same thing that makes Bobby grow. Sometimes he gets as big as a lion, can you imagine that?"

"Are you a lion, too?" Rossa's voice almost came out a whisper.

Bevan laughed. "Maybe."

She bared her teeth a little at him, and he could have sworn her pupils switched from circles to slits to triangles—then back. But then she kissed him. And her mouth was shocking, and her hands tender on the sides of his face, growing and shrinking at once. If she was a lion, then he was a ball of string in her giant, dangerous hands, happily undone.

She only stopped kissing him for a second to ask him again, her voice low, to stay in the house after the summer ended. Rossa said yes—at that moment, her fingertips skirting the edge of his T-shirt, he would have said yes to any damn thing she asked of him. Anything at all.

SIX

MAE sat at the kitchen table, head between her hands, rattled. She was mortified: getting caught by Bevan would have been better than this, Bobby's judgment and disappointment—and now Rita's. What did she think she was doing creeping around that closed room? God, how Rita's face fell as Bobby led her into the kitchen and said, "Found her in Bevan's room. Sweet James must have opened it. I got her out just in time."

How steely the old woman's eyes. Mae saw her own failure reflected back in a face she loved—the first time disappointing someone was undoubtedly a heavy thing. She could barely muster an "I'm sorry," still breathless with shock, vibrating with adrenaline. She reckoned she'd better just cry it out while she could: take a moment to feel sorry for herself before whatever punishment her great-aunt and the magical cat would dole out.

Rita handed her a clump of floral tissues. "Dry your eyes, girl. You can tell me what happened when you catch your breath."

Mae nodded, and balled the tissues to her nose and eyes. The stinging heat of humiliation was one thing, but crawling under that was something else: what had the strange man's voice meant—Sweet James? Was that what Bobby had called him?

Bobby padded along the table and sat at the corner, watching Rita lean down into the stove with the poker, rousing the red coals.

"The wall started to transform under her palms. We should clean her hands."

"Did he talk to her? Did she answer him?" Rita didn't turn away from the fire, and her tone was clipped.

"I don't know if she went looking or if he called her. Maybe a little of both things." Bobby shot her a look, and Mae had the distinct sensation of being on trial, like getting called to the principal's office in school. She hadn't been looking for anyone but Rossa, but she had trespassed. Maybe she deserved this.

She shrank in her chair, waiting for the eruption. The scolding. Maybe a glass would be thrown to the floor, a wall punched, a table shoved, plants knocked from their stands. The logical part of her brain knew that there was no way her great-aunt would ever shout or break things near her, but she couldn't quite shake the specter of her parents' war zone.

Rita picked up a small pair of bellows from beside the stove and began to pump air into the hearth, coaxing smoke up out of the scarlet gut of flame. As it thickened, she kicked the door closed to stop it from spilling into the whole kitchen. She went to a cupboard, fumbled around, before removing an empty jam jar, the words "Raspberry Sweet Preserves" blown into the side of it, the lid red and white. She opened it and cracked the stove door, then dipped her jar inside, as though the fire was a bucket of dishwater. When she removed it, the jar was full of swirling white smoke. The old woman locked the stove door,* screwed the lid on the sweet preserves jar, and turned to the table. Mae had just about stopped crying but was still sniffling, steadying her breathing. Rita looked at her, then at Bobby, then at the jar of smoke.

"This should be enough for now. Bevan didn't tell you to go in and do any of that, did she? You need to tell me the truth." Rita's coldness was melting into concern, but that didn't make Mae feel much better. If there was one thing she hated more than pissing people off, it was worrying people. How had she managed to do both?

"No, she's barely spoken to me at all."

"How did you know to touch the wall?" Rita pulled out her chair and a cigarette, and Bobby stepped into her lap. Her lighter clicked and hissed. "I didn't know to. I just did it. I was following—I felt something and I was following it."

She wasn't technically lying, and she was sure that Rita could read what she was thinking anyway. The old woman raised her eyebrows.

"And you're sure the owl hadn't come before Bobby showed up?"

---

* It hadn't always had a key.

Mae nodded.

Rita picked up one of the shining little geodes from the table and began to worry it, with her thumb. "What if he wasn't coming for her, Bobby—what if he was coming for you?"

Bobby laid himself down flat, his body liquid cat. "That's a fair point. He hasn't seen me in a few years."

"Who is he?" Mae asked, voice small. She had known there was something bad, but she didn't know it was a person—or if not a person exactly, a life. A monster.

Rita held her cigarette by her mouth, not smoking from it. She and Bobby exchanged a glance. "You should probably just tell her, Rita. She heard him. He talked to me in front of her." Bobby's tail flicked.

"Oh, should I now? Why don't you? He's an old, dear friend of yours, isn't he?"

A coldness swelled between the witch and the cat for a second. You tell her. No, you tell her.

"Will one of you please tell me?"

Bobby looked at Mae, his eyes so human, then gave a long stretch, leaping onto the table, settling in for a story.

"When I came here, I came here with an old friend. We're—well, we're very much alike, he and I, but the way we get along with human beings is quite different. His name is Sweet James."

"Why didn't you tell me before?" Mae felt sick. That weird night at the end of last summer hadn't been a one-off. There had been something—someone else creeping around the house this whole time, and nobody had thought to let her in on it. It had a name. It wasn't just some amorphous strange or bad thing, it had a name that nobody had told her. There she was thinking she had been let in, the littlest witch in the house: but no, they had her blindfolded the whole time. Her face burned.

"We needed to make the badness smaller for you. You never would have set foot in here if you knew what was happening behind the walls. But we both know you're better off here than you are at home, no matter Sweet James, no matter the strange. Aren't you?" Rita's voice was a blade.

The scale of Mae's disgrace towered. She felt like a child. Rita had been so good to take them in, and she was right. Mae hated this feeling but would take the weird of this house over what went on back home any day. Magic—even something like Sweet James—is a more honorable secret to keep than, well, the other thing. Whatever her parents were.

Rita held out the jar of smoke. "This is a tiny protection charm to keep you a little safer from him. Put out your hands."

Mae obeyed, laying them on the table, sticky with tears against the oilcloth. Rita mumbled rhythmically to herself, eyes half closed, before unscrewing the lid of the jar and placing it at Mae's hands. The beat of Rita's whispering increased as, following the command of her fingertips, the smoke danced up and out of the jar, over the table, and onto Mae's hands.

It was hot, and she flinched, but she let the gray magic

lace around her fingers. It pulled and it wove, braiding itself this way and that. The heat fluctuated in time with Rita's whispers, obedient to the incantation. For almost a minute, an intricate matrix was built around Mae's fingers. Her flesh turned pink under the heat. She wasn't at all afraid of it; rather, transported by it. A world less intense seemed to fold around Mae.

Rita's incantations reached a fever pitch, the heat seared a second; then the smoke dissipated, leaving the three at the table in silence. Mae turned her hands over and over, inspecting a tiny even grid of white scars left behind, so faint that they were barely visible at all.

"You won't be able to summon him now, Mae, intentionally or not. It's for your own good. The spell is temporary, but will last you until the end of the summer, maybe longer, and is designed to stop you from seeking a depository for your fear. Though you're not a girl full of fear at all, are you?"

Mae didn't feel afraid exactly. Or particularly protected. She looked at her hands again.

"Now. I've a session to host in an hour and need to meditate, I can't be going in to this group of women anything less than serene. Don't want to alarm them."

The old woman got up and tapped her fingers on the table three times.

"Join me, Bobby?"

Bobby shook his head.

"I'll stay here with Mae for the moment."

"The other two will be back in three minutes. Do

your best, won't you, not to tell them? Though I can't imagine you'd want either of them knowing you were looking for them."

Rita walked out of the room, clutching her shawl tightly around herself, the door closing sharply behind her with a deliberate click.

"Do you think she'll be pissed off at me for long?" Mae couldn't even bring herself to look at Bobby; she still stared at her hands.

"She's not. Neither of us is." Bobby padded over to Mae and settled down into her lap, purring deeply. "The last thing we need is Sweet James getting out of there again, trying to feed. There isn't enough of you to go round. Shh now, though. They're about to arrive at the door."

And he was right—Rossa and Bevan rolled into the house laughing, rustling bags of groceries.

"We got pastries. Pastries are basically cake for lunch!" Bevan announced as she strolled into the kitchen, brandishing a croissant, flakes coming off it and catching in her hair, on her sweatshirt.

Rossa carried two big bags. "And we got two absolute skulls of cauliflower, you should see the size of them, Bevan's going to roast them for dinner."

The two continued to announce each item they pulled out of the shopping bags, capering around, distraction distraction distraction. Mae knew immediately something had happened between them. Sometime recently enough for them still to be slightly embarrassed, fresh in new knowledge. Their nervous energy, their laughter at nothing

in particular, a secret neither could quite manage to hide—
Mae could read them. This was no psychic signal. This was
plain as day—boring, obvious fact. Her brother had laid
down with the girl she couldn't get over, and he was so
happy he couldn't contain it.

Why did this feel worse than Rita's disdain? Than
being caught out? Mae stroked Bobby's fur and said
nothing. Their energy was sickening to her. Fear flipped
jealousy flipped rage flipped defeat, a flatter and heavier
color than any other feeling. She was suddenly too tired
for this. She looked at her hands, their new tiny white
pattern. A delicate protection that would do nothing to
ward off the toxic flare of Bevan and her brother. Why
couldn't Rita have cast a spell to prevent this feeling?

They flitted about the kitchen, using each other's first
names twice a sentence: "Rossa, would you like a cup of
coffee, Rossa?" "Bevan, look, Bevan, can you reach this? I
can't get this jar down!"

Mae scooped Bobby up, unwieldy and soft. She quickly
stepped out the big glass doors to the garden.

They didn't even hear her go.

"Are you all right?" Bobby whispered. Mae just nuzzled
the top of her head with her nose.

She didn't say anything until they got very, very far
away from the house. The garden was exceptionally long
that day, twisting in strange directions. It felt convenient to
Mae, a grace: like nobody would ever find her, if they came
to look. It took her ten minutes to reach the bench.

When she eventually started to talk, Bobby grew a

little bigger by her side, his eyes marigold and beaming. Maybe he was feeding off her, but if he was, she didn't care. She told him exactly about the jealousy and rage and the flattening of defeat. And Bobby drank up every word. The old crush was shaped enough like love to give him exactly what he wanted.

SEVEN

A FAT book of crystal analysis sits open in front of you at the kitchen table. The radio buzzes classical. Rita sits across from you, working her way through a birth chart for a new client. Rossa's at the end of the table, drawing something you can't quite make out into his sketchbook. Hushed evening time. Mae nowhere to be seen, Bobby missing with her.

Not that you aren't well used to lying, but you'd be lying if you said you weren't actually quite happy. You enjoyed your day with Rossa. He made you relax in a way you aren't used to at all. Even Gus had never paid you attention like Rossa, listened wholeheartedly to everything you said. Believed you. You could maybe tell him everything, couldn't you? It is so pleasant having him sit there at the table with you and Rita. He's a lovely addition, his energy gentle.

You hadn't intended to kiss him, let alone do anything else to him. With him. You'd just thought it would make your case for him to stay a little stronger. And it wasn't like all parties weren't willing and enthusiastic. You hadn't expected to like him more afterward. To spend most of the day laughing. You aren't sure if you'd do it again, but the memory and the potential of a reprise will keep him here, won't it? It will keep all those gorgeous feelings alive in him, and you are sure now that how he feels is making you stronger and stronger. That owlish thing is awake under your bones again and you can't stop yourself. Sweet James will be very proud—or at least you hope so.

You know that's bad, but sometimes bad things make the most sense.

Of course he'll stay. Even as he sits there, just a couple of feet from you, you can feel a little glow of contentment radiating off him. It is delicious. How can he walk away from something as gorgeous as this, this quiet life? He has no propensity for magic whatsoever, which is so... healthy, or something. How sane that must keep him, you think, watching his pencil ghost down the page in a deliberate, gentle arc.

You flip your book shut dramatically, as if you'd actually been reading it at all the last forty-five minutes. "My eyes are falling out of my head. I'm going up to sleep."

Rita nods. "Rest well, girl. I won't be long after you. You can come in with me tomorrow with the next party of women, if you'd like—take notes. See what you can pull."

You smile broadly. "Ah, nice one, Rita! Thank you!"

She normally keeps you at a room's distance from the women who come in—this is a step hard-earned. That'll give you something to leap out of bed for in the morning, given that it's a bit too late to make a date for another dawn excursion with Rossa. Besides, that might be too much too soon. Draw it out, even though you don't want to draw it out, you want all Sweet and all James right now, but you'll tiptoe, you'll go soft. By the time the leaves are crisping red on the trees outside, Rossa'll be moving his things in: he'll be part of the house. You'll be able to eat, Sweet James will be able to eat, everything will be delightful.

He looks up at you, those gunshot pupils again, round and black, pushing back a dead-giveaway smile.

"Good night, Bev." There was something hopeful in his tone. Something trapped.

"Sleep tight, Rossa."

You wink at him, the bunny in the snare, and whisk out of the room, proud of yourself. Away up the stairs, and to your room, which is still a wreck, you think, still a disaster area with the broken radio. You scuttle along the corridor, light on your feet past the room Mae's staying in, the noise of her and Bobby having some hushed conspiracy beyond the door—good luck to them.

You notice immediately the radio is back in its place. Did Sweet James fix it for you, a mea culpa for his unbidden return? You run your fingers over it, not even a crack or a loose wire. You hate this room. You wish for neon. For moths. For endless possibilities.

Then you look at the wallpaper and down at your hands. Is it so awful that you wish he would just show up? You'd been doing so well, God, you were almost normal there for a while, but tiny empty cavities in his shape are breaking through you and you need to fill them. You don't resist it. You let the want roll through you, ugly and sour. It just about undoes all the good energy Rossa had given you, drains his adoration from your body.

For the next hour you sit on the floor with a heap of magazines, contemplate turning your phone back on—but don't. You do, however, turn the radio on, late-night chatter a distraction. You will interference onto the radio, another voice, a familiar voice, his voice, just his voice even for a second—but nothing comes. You prepare for bed. You listen to the rest of the house moving towards their own, the footsteps on the stairwell, doors opening and closing. Then the house is silent. You're not even tired. You wonder, just for a second, what you might be doing on a Thursday night if you were in college. If you had stayed in touch with the girls you went to school with. If it was, perhaps, worth having a life outside this house.

Something clicks hard against the window, and you jump out of your skin. You spring up and run to the window, fling your curtains wide, searching the garden—did something land, did something hit the window in flight—

There. Down in the garden you see him. Gus. His beanie hat, his hoodie, his skinny jeans, flailing his arms for your attention, one hand full of gravel. Alarm flickers through you, on and off, a broken light, your heart races— what does he want?

You push open the window, and lean out.

"What the fuck do you think you're doing here?" you whisper-shout. You can't wake the house. Romeo and Juliet this is not.

Gus puts his hands on his hips, head tilted up to you.

"Would you ever learn to turn your phone on, Bevan?"

"Would you ever go the fuck home, please?" you hiss.

"Not until you tell me who that dope with a ponytail was. You walked by my shop today! The audacity! First thing in the morning, walk of shame!"

He's getting a little loud. You blink.

"Are you being serious? We broke up in April. Go. Home."

"Christ's sake, Bevan! Ignoring my texts, walking around with someone else right in front of my shop? In front of the whole village? That poor young fella's going to find out you're a crazy slut in no time, you mark my words—"

Slut. Crazy.

Crazy slut.

The words are out of his mouth at a pitch slightly higher than the rest of his tirade. Those words raise something in you and in the room behind you. You don't take your eyes off him. He's still talking but you're not listening. His imperfections are amplified to hideous now. How could you have ever wanted him? Maybe you never did want him. Maybe you just let him distract you from the only thing you've ever really wanted.

The air turns to molasses around you. The radio flickers, the lights dim and rise—oh, here we go. Here he comes.

"Well? Aren't you going to say anything?" the boy in the garden yelps, pathetic.

You pause, let the demand hang limp in the air.

"What do you want me to say? Why are you here?"

Something electrical warps your voice as you speak,

but Gus doesn't notice. He's here to prove something to himself, not to prove anything to you.

He starts talking again, so absorbed in his own perceived injustice that he doesn't notice that the lamplight glowing from your room turns neon. That a breeze takes up. He talks and talks and you can't hear him anymore at all because out of the corner of your eye the swarm of moths is gathering on the surface of the wall. The warmth of Sweet James's presence flicks through you. His voice isn't in the room, but in the conch of your ear. Just for you, an unearthly whisper.

do you want me to help you?

Yes is an impulse firing through you. You were never over this, you were never clean of him. How could you ever be when he made you feel this alive?

Gus is crying now, his anger turned vulnerable.

"You can be so cold," he insists.

But, no, you are a lantern in the window. Your skin is golden and your eyes heavy with light. Your palms feel hot and strange, but any semblance of pain is in the distance.

Gus finally ends his monologue on a question.

You do not have an answer. You were not listening.

He finally sees you, an unholy idol glowing from what Sweet James is doing through you, and he gasps and swears. You laugh and your laugh erupts eighteen colors into the atmosphere and all of these colors are a shade of gold. The sound of your scorn ripples.

You raise your hands over your eyes and the marks you once asked Gus to make on you shine like your veins are running rich with liquid star. He falls to his knees. You can feel the molten crystal ink beneath your skin change from circle to triangle. Like Sweet James's eyes. Like your eyes. The owl is laughing. The boy is afraid. You love this. A conjuring of sickness.

Words like "crazy" and "slut" mean nothing. Language means nothing. His terror is so satisfying. Somewhere in the distance, you hear him whimper, "Please, no—" Then, "Bevan, you're scaring me," and you repeat these phrases back down to him from the window, no longer afraid of being caught by Rita or Rossa or Bobby or Mae.

Call the cops. Call your mother. You dare them. You'd shatter each one of them—you could split the air open, and Gus, poor stupid Gus who really believed that he had any power over you, is there on his knees, bawling in the grass like he's seen God and God is the girl he walked away from and she is beautiful, she is vengeful, she is laughing.

"Go home, stupid boy," you roar. "Do not come here again."

He scrambles to his feet, his knees stained and his hands dirty from clawing the lawn. He runs and you wail a gorgeous and sickening cry into the night. For years to come, the residents of Iona may say it was the banshee herself warning them that there was worse, much worse to come. But the house eats your roars. Even if the neighbors rouse, nobody within these walls can hear a single thing.

The luminescence and power begin to leak out of you when Gus is clear of the garden, vaulting over the wall at breakneck pace. He doesn't break his neck, though. You hear him land with a thud and begin to run again until his

237

footfall becomes nothing in the sable of night. Your flesh comes back to being just flesh. Your eyes, just membrane and blue. The comedown is so steep it knocks the breath out of you. You slump away from the window, doubled over, your ears beginning to ring, your hands—you look at your hands.

They are blank.

They are the soft girl hands they were before. Before you were burned. Before the inky, rebellious reclamation. Just your same old hands, all recent history eaten out of them. Healed.

Sweet James flickers on the wall now. He is ivy leaves, not roses, but all the same he is like the old days. An old friend: you suppose you've earned that by now. You are buckled and exhausted on the carpet. "How did you know I needed you?" you say to the owl. He says nothing.

"Thank you, for—for that." You gesture weakly to the window.

i am sated. we have dined and shared. tell me how it felt.

You don't need to say it felt good. You can feel Sweet James in your head so you just think it. Good, good, so good. The owl laughs, a song you have missed.

this does not have to be the last time.

You still don't have to say anything at all. He knows.

i expect you to bring me the boy twin's heart. all of the rewards i offer you—you are such a lucky girl, bevan.

His thunderous voice fades as the wall restores. You lie

on the floor, spent and charmed. On your hands black ink crawls back across your palms. Nobody will notice anything is amiss. A new hunger already gnaws at your belly. You are ready for trouble.

EIGHT

MAE lay in the grass, sun beating down on her. She imagined this was what it must be like to be Bobby, a solar panel, soaking up light. She'd laid out some of her tarot, the Major Arcana, on the grass in front of her, spinning out the centuries-old lore, as it always had. An ancient storyboard. Sometimes she enjoyed just looking at them, memorizing the details of their legend, something slightly new arising for her each time. The Fool walks off a cliff and look at all the things that happen to him as he goes down, down into the world.

She was still trying not to think about what had happened in Bevan's room the other day. But pushing it out of her mind was exhausting, and nothing could quite distract her from replaying it over and over again. She let her cardigan sleeves fall over her hands, just in case Rossa, sitting cross-legged beside her, noticed her new matrixes of scars. But Rossa wouldn't notice. He was absorbed in his drawing. He'd barely spoken to her all week, he and Bevan locked in some new camaraderie that she was excluded from.

But for now, he sat with his unwieldy, thick sketchbook in his lap. He'd sketched a disembodied hand, suspended on the page, clutching a bouquet of wildflowers. He was just beginning to touch them with color.

The garden was large today, an expanse of green, turning the lawn more meadow. Rita had her clients in the living room with Bobby and Bevan. There hadn't been much point in hanging around the kitchen, getting in the way, and it had seemed like such a shame to miss the sunshine. Yet even in all this fresh air, Mae felt stifled.

"What do you think we'd be doing if we weren't here?" she asked. "Would we be at home just doing normal stuff?"

"What even is normal stuff?" Rossa answered, eyes still keenly on the page. "It'd be dull at home. I'd be having cans with the lads. I don't know what you'd be at. Probably . . . having cans with the girls? We'd be dealing with Mam and Dad all the time and our heads would be wrecked. It's nothing to be homesick* for."

Mae shifted onto her side. Was this the moment to ask him exactly what the hell he was doing sneaking around with Bevan when he was supposed to be in all of this with Mae? Her stomach lurched. She swallowed the argument. No use in making it awkward. Tread soft, she thought, breathing calm back into herself.

"Since when are you so fond of it here?" she asked

---

* Not the word, exactly, Audrey would use for it. Rita sick, maybe? Was that how to put it? The bartender told her, "Lovesick, that might be the word you're looking for."

242

instead. "You didn't like it so much the last time. The house freaked you out."

Rossa still didn't look up; rather, changed his pencil to an earthier green. "Don't you like how calm it is? How nobody's yelling or crying? How we don't have to pretend everything is normal to our mates? It feels like a blank slate. A clean page. Sure, it's weird. But weird I can manage."

"I mean, yeah, but we're getting a blank slate when we go to college," Mae said.

There had been no talk of college until now. Not a word. It left an ugly silence.

Mae plucked blades of grass and rubbed them between her fingers. Their parents' crumbling marriage had brought both twins up against a hard wall of not caring when the time came to study. Mae had only written her name on her math paper, not a single number, just sat there for hours until the bell rang, staring into space. College was no certainty.

"I'm just finding it hard to distract myself out here, Rossa, that's all."

"Keep at those card tricks then." Her brother shot her a wink, and she threw a clutch of grass at him. His pencil dragged on the page, and he said, "We could probably stay here, you know, if we wanted. If we asked Rita."

Mae was torn. A life ahead here, in the house full of monsters with the walking heartbreak machine of Bevan Mulholland? "I'm not so sure," she said. "That's a big ... big choice to make so quickly."

"Why? We're away from *them*, away from the divorce.

243

Rita'd benefit from having more people around. You could keep studying under her and be, like, a medium or whatever. I could work on my portfolio for an art course a few years down the line. It'd be an easy life, like."

He still wasn't looking at her. Still looking too hard at the drawing on the page. He wasn't telling her something.

What Mae tried to say was, "I can't stay here watching you and Bevan fall in love. It hurts." What came out was, "We can't just run away from our parents, Rossa."

"Why not? Seems to me like they're running away from us."

"You know as well as I do that's not the case at all." Doubt flickered through Mae, though. Get the twins out of the way. Out of sight, out of mind.

Rossa shrugged, changing pencils again. "I just feel like it'd be a nicer place to be. You're welcome to go home to those two, if you want, but I'm going to try and stay. I'll ask Rita sooner rather than later."

"You aren't seriously considering sending me back* to them on my own, are you?" Mae felt a little outside her body as she spoke. Her brother, her twin, sending her back to all that noise and rage alone. The rain of smashed crockery, the thunderclap of slammed doors. The tragedy of only ever being collateral. It'd just be her. He'd get out. She'd be trapped.

---

* "I don't like it. Sweet James didn't show up this week and I'm worried about her, about the house—I think I should go back there." The bartender poured Audrey another drink, and she downed it in one, for courage.

"You can't," she managed. "You can't just leave me."

"Well, Mae, what's the alternative? One of us is going to leave the other at some stage. You could stay here with me and Rita, and I'd still leave eventually. We don't get to stay together forever. We're not one person. We come apart."

Of course the pair of them wouldn't stay together forever. She wasn't an idiot. She just hadn't expected it to be so soon, this way, over a girl whose name was a glaring omission: Bevan, Bevan, Bevan.

"I suppose I'm . . . well, the house is making me feel a little weird, this time. Does that make sense?" Was it so hard to say, "I saw a door, I went through the door, I touched something from another world"? She was only keeping this secret for Rita and Bobby. Still, she couldn't seem to summon the words: they wouldn't translate from her brain to her mouth, like something was blocking her, a thin film that wouldn't let the truth burst through.

"I mean, yeah, there's something a little off all right, but I reckon Rita has it under control. I've seen weird things up in the mountains, but they didn't make me feel bad. Weird, sure. Weird I could get used to." Green pencil to pink, eyes never leaving the page.

"So, you'd be happy to live in a house full of spirits with a talking cat and your great-aunt for the end of your teens? Something else must be keeping you here." Admit it was Bevan, she willed him, but he did not.

"There's more here for me than back there." His steady hand slowly filled the delicate flower pink. Mae wanted to knock his elbow, leave a fat fuchsia stripe down the belly of his drawing. Snap him out of it. But she didn't. She gathered her cards up from the grass and mixed them back into the deck with her wands and cups and pentacles and swords, the whisper scratch of her brother's pencil in her ear.

"You're welcome to stay, too, Mae. I'm just not going to force you." The pink grew darker on the page, the flower becoming hot and unnatural.

Mae shuffled the heavy cards, her body roaring *no* but her mouth closed tightly. She pulled a single card from her deck, a knife slice of potential perspective.

The Hanged Man. Stalemate, paralysis, a problem nobody is willing to solve. Great. Mae rolled her eyes and stuffed him back into the deck. These paper things had a great sense of humor when they wanted to.

In what seemed like the distance, the kitchen patio door slid open. Rita and Bobby stood in the frame.

"Tea?" Rita's voice echoed down the garden, and Mae accepted that as her signal to quit.

"Leave it with me," she said to her brother, standing up and stretching. "I'll think about it."

He didn't look up. "I'm all right for tea. Going to head up to my room soon."

Mae watched him curl the letters B and E under the bouquet, in dippy hopeless affection. She turned away from him as he began the slope of the V, filling in the name missing from their conversation, silently, all for himself.

NINE

THE woman with the red hair had been the most frightened but had shown it the least. You think about her, now that you're lying starfish sprawled on your bedroom floor, after all of them have left. It had felt good, all right. A different color to how Rossa had tasted. Maybe that was because the redhead was a stranger and Rossa was, well, in love with you or something. How funny.

Redhead had sat with three of her friends around Rita's coffee table, held rapt by Rita's work with the cards and bottom-of-the-teacup leaves. They'd been there for hours, receiving all manner of predictions. One of them was pregnant. He would be a Sagittarius, a heartbreaker all his life. Another, being cheated on (that, she already knew—it had been gorgeous, the budding of tears in her eyes, the cloying blotchy pink on her neck, her breathing irregular as she said, "I'm fine, girls, I'm grand"). One didn't believe in the whole damn thing and said nothing and felt nothing other than a constant urge to take out her phone and start scrolling. Cynics are so boring.

But the redhead, she was sick and hadn't told her friends. You read the depression off her, numb gray tones. You drank them up. Redhead didn't want her friends to know what she was feeling, or not feeling, so when Rita took her palm and looked at it, then up into her eyes and said, "Talk to someone," Redhead jolted, the first acute emotion she'd experienced in months. She wasn't going to tell any of the girls in the room anything. How fortunate you'd been to watch all these ugly little betrayals unfold.

You'd sat in the corner with Bobby. Rita had expressly told the women you were her student and they'd cooed over you, shocked that a suburban medium could have an apprentice. They'd giggled. "How many points in your leaving cert did you have to get for that one?" You'd replied, "Well, I took eight subjects, failed economics, and answered a few of the exams in Irish, so the points tallied up to, I think it was, 666?" The girls had screamed with laughter. They were charmed enough not to mind that you sat, a notebook in your lap, watching this strange and intimate session, visibly taking notes, invisibly harvesting their fears. Bobby curled up at your feet. He didn't notice a thing. Not so magical and all-knowing now, cat. Not so clever.

You'd gotten away with it and you are glowing now on the deep shag of your bedroom floor, wiggling your toes, gleeful, full of absorbed emotion. Sweet James bubbles behind the wall, letting you bask in the things you had stolen. He doesn't quite come out, but he is there, nearby enough for you to feel his electricity.

You'd missed this. His ambience.

It isn't even dinnertime yet. You have a whole day to enjoy it. Maybe he will even let you back into those old other rooms. What will you talk about with him? What will he tell you? Had he missed you these past three years? It is almost romantic, you think. A reunion, a rekindling. You, the girl, and he the great and terrible interdimensional beast. Tale as old as time.

The tea in the bottom of your mug has gone cold, you've been daydreaming so long.

"Do you mind if I head away for a hot one?" you absentmindedly ask the ivy on the wall, and the shadowy creature behind them rustles their leaves. "Thank you, darling." You stand up, arms stretched over your head, cracking your joints. Gruesome and satisfying.

Out in the dark of the hallway, as you swan toward Rita's side of the house, the corridor extra long today, you spot Rossa, twenty paces ahead of you. There are no windows in the hallway, and all the doors to the bedrooms and bathrooms are closed. It could be night up here. He turns, startled by your sudden appearance. As you walk toward each other, it feels for a second like the house is deliberately keeping you apart. The cheek of it. You scowl, as each step you take seems to hold you in place, the corridor a treadmill. He doesn't seem to notice.

"Bevan, do you want to buzz downstairs? Mae's cooking, I think?" Rossa's voice is far away.

You speed up a little, but that only seems to paralyze the corridor further.

"Why are you just standing there?" he says, and you speed up again, the house pushing against your momentum.

You stop abruptly, furious, and stomp your foot, fists clenched. "Stupid house! Do as I say!"

Then, with a jolt, Rossa is nose to nose with you, the corridor folding at your will. Good.

Rossa's eyes are wide and rain-cloud gray. He smells like soap and cotton. He thinks you are going to kiss him and his heart beats in your ears, anxious, pleading, "Kiss me again like in the woods." You smile a little. Sweet of him, that. He waits for a signal from you, but you don't give him one, just cock your head to the side and say, "Hey. I have something really cool in my room that I think you might like."

Rossa raises an eyebrow in a way that makes him look quite handsome. He thinks you're talking about sex, and you are not going to correct him, even though what you are talking about is absolutely not sex.

"Oh, have you now?" His voice is confident.

Your heart stutters and you stop it, bat that away.

"Yes. Come on." You grab his hand and lead him the few steps back to your room. He squeezes your hand tightly. Through his palm you feel a surge of emotion, a braid of excitement and infatuation and ah, yes, there it is under all that new love, fear. Fear, the color of his eyes. Fear like a cold winter day. Perfect.

He's so wrapped around your little finger he doesn't notice that the door you lead him to is an old door, a door that should have been swallowed and closed for good—a door that out of the corner of your eye you saw flicker back into existence. Silly, silly boy.

You kick the door open lightly and draw him into the spare landscape of your old bedroom. "This is where the magic happens." You spin away from him playfully and throw your arms wide.

Rossa mimes snapping pictures with an invisible camera, not registering that the room hasn't been slept in in years, not realizing it is on the wrong side of the house. He's too in the game, too in the seduction. "Bevan, I just love what you've done with the place."

"Here's where I perform all my unlicensed dental surgeries." You laugh, pointing towards the untouched bed, and Rossa chuckles. He can't help himself, he has to laugh at the terrible things you've done to him, because in these walls he belongs to you. "And here, Rossa, is my best friend. My dear old friend. James, come and say hello to Rossa!"

The room lurches, and Sweet James rises out from the paper, those good old paper roses, beak sharp and eyes white as bone, clicking and groaning against the flutter of thousands of gray moths. You've never seen him so big before. It's almost as though he's adjusting the size of reality to accommodate his greatness.

Rossa blanches and staggers back. "Bevan, what are you doing?"

You place your hand on his shoulder. The fear ripples off him. You could almost gasp from the sheer delight of it. "Doesn't he make you feel huge?" you whisper.

All the desire rains out of those stormy eyes of his as he stares at you, then at Sweet James.

hello, rossa.

The boy clasps his hands over his mouth, you squeeze his shoulder.

would you like to see something?

Sweet James grows bigger and bigger. He is eating. You are dining together.

say yes, rossa.

Rossa is vibrating with terror, and it brings you such bliss, you can do nothing but stand there and absorb it, feel it build under your skin and roll through your nerves. It is not like anything you have ever experienced. It is not like pleasure, it is not like satisfaction, it is new and you do not have language for it but right now, here, you do not need words.

Rossa only needs one, and he says it, breathless, "Yes."

Sweet James roars and splits into a cyclone of roses and paper and moth and bone, rearranging himself into that old familiar door. You squeal and leap forward. "Oh, Rossa, let's go, come on, you'll love it in here!"

Rossa's mouth opens and closes but he does not say a word, so you grab his wrist and lead him across the room, through the charged air. You pull open the door and the neon glow rolls out. You lean your head in and inhale the smell of fresh water. Yes, yes, this was the feeling you'd missed. The endlessness of the other worlds, right there. And this time you have a companion to take with you! You're not alone!

But he stops, frozen to the spot. You lean in to him, summon some of the light you stole from him, and whisper, "Come on. You can be a lion, too."

Warmth rises in his face, and he looks at you again. "Can I trust you?"

His earnestness is alarming. Of course he can't trust you. Look at what you've done.

For a second, there in the space you've torn in reality, on the threshold of the endless other rooms, the doors upon doors of newness and exploration and sensations that defy anything you've ever known, something very old and very new comes over you.

Guilt, like rot, cold and damp. Guilt like, what are you doing, what have you done? You are feeding on this boy, feeding him to the monster in your house, using him as a toll to pass into the next world. Trying to get him hooked on the same damned infinity you're hooked on. Dragging him to hell with you.

You can't shake it off. You feel sick.

And before you say it, before you lie to Rossa again, before you tell him of course he can trust you, he can trust you with anything, he should stay with you so you can prove to him how much he can trust you, before you start to talk and ruin everything, the next door opens.

A girl stands there. The last girl in the world you wanted to see. Cropped hair and a black-and-white suit. Audrey O'Driscoll.

TEN

MAE held a sharp, heavy grater in one hand and dragged a pale potato along it. Dinner was on her. They had a heap of leftover mashed potatoes in the fridge that wanted a second shot at the table, so boxty it was. Mae had watched her mother do this time and time again, mix last night's potatoes with thinly shredded new ones, crack in an egg or two for hold, then palm the mix onto a hot buttery pan, frying them into dense potato cakes. The cooking was calming and repetitive. The food was hearty. The routine was just what Mae needed.

Smoked salmon was chilling in the fridge, and she'd picked fresh dill from the garden and chopped a red onion to teary-eyed confetti. Mae loved cooking, the alchemy all of it, but the kitchen at home had long been a fraught site of conflict, a no-man's-land where the closest thing to witchcraft lately had been a frozen pizza turning crisp and golden under the grill, then scooped onto a plate and eaten in the privacy of her room.

The grid of scars on her hands seemed to ripple ever so slightly as she worked, a subtle iridescence like the scales of a fish. She held a hand up to Bobby, who was curled on the kitchen table amidst the crystals.

"Are my hands shimmering, or am I cracking up?" she asked.

Bobby opened one daffodil eye. "Yes. They'll do that. Don't be alarmed."

He closed his eye again, gold slipping away into the snow white of his fur.

Mae tutted.

The extraordinary things that went on in the house were treated as mundane, humdrum. She'd barely been outside the garden and house for days. Maybe she shouldn't keep herself so confined. She could most likely find a bus that would take her back into the city. It'd take an hour or more, but at least she'd be able to meet her friends for the day. Touch reality for a second. But something in the thought of that was sour to her. What if she left and something went wrong? What if she turned her back on it for a moment and it all crashed down, a rickety illusion? What if when she returned, her brother wasn't her brother anymore, what if he became something different too?

She gathered the shredded potato into a paper towel and wrung out the wet, then emptied it into a bowl with last night's mash. Cracked an egg. Dashed in the onion, her eyes stinging. Garlic flakes and salt. Black pepper in a tall wooden grinder. Stir. Shape into disks. A little flour for structure, not too much. She'd keep her hands busy, keep her head busy, not think too much of her brother and Bevan and the thing in the walls.

"How was the session this morning?" she asked over her shoulder. Maybe if she did stay and study with Rita, one day she'd be allowed to host sessions of her own. Maybe she'd learn how to keep James away, and other things like him, too. She laid a huge, unwieldy pan on the hob over the furnace, the holy fire glowering in its locked gut, as always. Gas on, match struck, the pan beginning to warm, a shallow pool of olive oil glugged from a green bottle.

"Strange. Bevan did something to the energy in the room and the women were very unsettled. She was showing off—and worse, she thought she got away with it. I'm very tired, and a storm is coming." Bobby flopped over onto his side and stretched, a small feline noise escaping him.

"What do you mean, a storm?" The oil began to hiss, and when Mae lowered a potato cake into the pan, it fizzed. Explosive, delicious sounds.

"You can feel it too, if you try. Look for it. Open your eyes."

"What, like now?"

"Yes, now."

The cakes sizzled in the pan. Mae held a spatula poised, ready for the flip: no magic wand here. She opened her eyes a little wider, unsure of what she was supposed to be looking for. Her hands gave a shimmer amidst the rising steam. Three thick halos edged the boxty now. She flipped them, one, two, three.

The past, the present, the future.

As Mae looked down into the pan, for a second, she saw something on the crisp moons. The disks winked up at her, glistening with hot oil.

"What was that?" she spluttered, holding up the spatula like a katana, poised for a fight.

Bobby rolled over and sat up, a monochrome sphinx.

"The harder you look, the more you see. You might not like all of it."

"Bobby, would you come on? You don't usually talk like this!"

"These aren't usual times, Mae."

Mae sighed and peered back into the frying pan. No glyphs, no symbols, just potato flecked with onions, crisping in the heat. Had she been fooling herself? How much of magic was just fooling yourself, anyway? Giving wiggle room for belief. Still the boxty stayed as it was. So she fished the cooked cakes out of the pan and placed them on a plate lined with tinfoil to keep them warm, then started all over again.

The sizzle, the scent. She tapped her fingers on the kitchen counter, waiting. Then she flipped them: one, two, three, and yes—there it was again—but it was gone as quickly as it had arrived. It was just beyond Mae's vision, but she was thrilled by the proximity of a new ability.

Rita interrupted her then, decked out in black leggings and a vest, hair scraped into a bun, padding in from the garden. Strangely small in the absence of her usual cardigans and shawls. She looked spritely and modern: a yoga teacher, not a witch.

258

"Bobby, I'm going to have to have a word with her," Rita said, as if midconversation. "I feel something. He has his talons into her again, and poor stupid Rossa's going to follow her wherever she tells him to go. She'll eat him alive."

Mae's stomach dropped. Rita sat down at the table in a heap, procuring a cigarette from somewhere and lighting it, heedless of the food cooking on the stove.

"You said Audrey had this taken care of, Bobby," Rita continued.

"I thought she did," Bobby retorted, licking his paw and roughly cleaning his ear.

"What's happening?" Mae asked, refusing to be left out any longer, standing like a dumb piece of furniture behind the drama.

Rita leaned back in her chair and posed her cigarette elegantly by her jaw, her wrist slight, her fingers long.

"Bevan was eating the sorrow of our guests, Mae. Inhaling it like smoke. I've never seen anything like it, not in a long time. She didn't learn that from me."

The steam from the pan soured. Mae inhaled sharply; she'd left the cakes there too long. She hurried to flip them from the pan, and three bright silver symbols stared up at her from the metal.

The icon for cups. The tarot in her frying pan. Three cups. Three cups suggested—or forewarned—of a union of three women. Three witches. Macbeth's beginning, Hecate's faces. The card always seemed celebratory to Mae: three girls dancing, toasting full chalices, victory and unity and friendship. The crone, the siren, the—Mae supposed she was, as always, the child. Mae didn't draw Rita's and Bobby's attention to the vision: it was hers. She should work with Rita, it said to her, and even with Bevan. This house had called her and she would answer. She wasn't even scared. No, she was brave.

Something lurched in the atmosphere around them, then. Rita leapt up out of her chair and Bobby's back arched.

"Something is happening," the cat cried.

Rita flew across the kitchen, grabbing a black wrought-iron lantern. She knelt by the furnace and, to Mae's horror, opened it wide and thrust her hands inside. She removed hot coals and some odd, glassy shapes that Mae couldn't quite make out, and placed them in the lantern.

The air around them lurched again.

Rita, hands black, kicked shut the furnace door, not bothering to lock it. She stood up, the red glow somehow changing her face, her skin. "Well then," she said. "Up we go."

Mae didn't even think to put the spatula down. Or turn off the stove.

ELEVEN

A THICK, dark streak of blood led from Rossa's nose to his upper lip, but he couldn't even move his hands to wipe it away. Before him, the mouth of an owl split open to reveal a room beyond the wall. He couldn't think or feel. It was like the cut in the woods but worse, far worse. The girl inside was slight and sharp featured, dressed in a black-and-white suit. Saddle shoes. She stopped at the lip where one world became another, hands on her hips, scowling.

Bevan stepped forward, eyes flashing. "It's you again. You took him away before."

"Yeah, well." Audrey folded her arms. "You can make deals with devils, but you can't make deals with whatever Sweet James is. Sweet thing, are you there?" She peered around, theatrical.

James. What an ordinary name for a terrible thing, Rossa thought. As though naming it something usual made it manageable, instead of sickening.

The wall trembled and spewed moths. An almost-voice said, **i grew tired of you, audrey.**

"Surprising absolutely nobody," Audrey spat. "There's a hunger in you that won't ever be sated. Not even by this girl. Not even by this boy. You'll just keep eating and eating."

you have always known this.

"Well, Bevan knows it now too. Girleen, I think you and me should have a little talk. Why don't you come back here with me?"

Bevan glowered. "Why would I go anywhere with you? You took him from me."

Audrey closed her eyes and shook her head. "I did. But he's never going to fill *you* up, either. He'll just eat away. You still have a chance, you know."

"I don't want a chance. I will follow this—I will follow him as far as I can go." Bevan scowled and Audrey smiled, wry and knowing. "Ah, you sound just like me."

"How am I like you?" Bevan leaned away from Rossa now, her body inclining toward Audrey and the wall.

Audrey's and Sweet James's voices were a chorus:

because there is no place for you here.

"Because there is no place for you here."

Audrey jumped a little. "James, don't do that to me! Ugly old parlor trick!"

The owl laughed, and Audrey rolled her eyes. "Now, if I can speak—thank you, James—because there are things back here that are bold and strange and enough for you. Because you'll never again be able to live in this world without them."

"Audrey O'Driscoll?"

Rossa turned and there, in the wood-and-brick doorway of Bevan's room, stood Rita and Mae and Bobby. Rita was between the huge cat and the girl, holding a lantern full of fire. The room swayed and color flipped negative to positive to negative again, the air reeking of medicinal sage.

Rita stared past Rossa, eyes only for Audrey. "You came back."

The old woman stepped across the sandy carpet scattered with gray moths, and the closer she came to the portal, the younger she turned. Audrey took a slight step back, her mouth open, pupils black and huge. Rossa could move again, finally, so he edged out of the way. He shot a look at his sister, standing in the doorframe behind the cat that flickered lion. But Mae was not looking at her brother. She was gazing at the three women at the edge of the world, and she was chalk in the face, fists clenched.

Rossa was struck then. None of this was ever about him or his sister. He and she weren't even pawns on the chessboard. They were teacups that happened to be on the same table where the game was being played. The floor wavered beneath his feet and he almost lost his balance.

Rita barked, "Stay still!"

The house obeyed.

The closer she came to Sweet James's door, the more it flickered, reality unable to sustain itself. She faced Audrey, two girls on two different planes of existence.

"Have I given you enough time yet?" Audrey whispered.

"I . . . I think so. I don't . . . mean to ask—but . . . you won't stay here, will you?"

"No." Audrey was barely able to keep her balance as the floor on her side gave another nauseating swell. "Rita, you know I can never come back. But you can come with me. These—these aren't your children, are they?"

"No," Rita said, almost sounding scornful, and Rossa felt a sting from how sharply this reply cut. "I'm so old now, they're Brendan's *grand*children. Can you believe it?"

Audrey laughed suddenly, high and bright.

Rita laughed with her for a second, like it was just the two of them there. When the laughter stopped, a thick silence sat in the air a moment before Rita said, "This can't be goodbye again. It can't be."

The wall winked ordinary a second, wallpaper blank just as it had been. When it opened up again, Bevan gasped and leapt forward, past Audrey and Rita. She was away then, becoming smaller in the strange perspective of the other room's neon glow, opening and slamming a faraway door that shouldn't be there at all, that led who knows where.

Audrey groaned. "Rita, I've to go and get her. I'll have a talk with her about Sweet James. Meet me in the woods. At the glade. I'll try and open the cut there. I'll deliver her back to you. This door needs to close, or it'll take the whole house down. Bring me some smokes, won't you? Oh—and actually, Bobby?" The girl waved. "Looks like you're winning. Congratulations." With that, she turned on her heel, and the wall slammed back to normal—or more normal, at least. Merely shifting and twisting vines, rather than a mind-bending hole in the world.

On one vine sat an owl. It blinked and turned its head almost all the way upside down.

bobby, he said. **rita. you have become very, very strong. well done.**

Rita held up her lantern, some kind of defiance. "Don't you try anything, Sweet James. I'm not afraid of you."

Sweet James laughed low. **i believe you. you are not afraid of me. but you need me. you need the rent i pay, you need the power i bring. look how strong i've made you.**

Bobby took padding steps into the room, quaking with energy, growing and growing.

tell the humans to leave.

Bobby looked around at Rossa, Mae, and Rita.

Please.

Rita turned on her heel and took Rossa by the arm to lead him away. Mae was already gone. The door slammed on the owl and the cat, and the corridor stretched limitless before the Frosts. Mae was a hundred paces ahead already. Rita did not let go of Rossa's arm, the lantern lighting their way. The air was hot. Rossa was sure he could smell smoke.

TWELVE

THE second the door of the neon room slams behind you, you scream in delight. You laugh. You roar yes, yes, yes! What if you never went back? The air of the other world crawls all over you—there in the long white corridor, great trees of gray moths are a forest, undisturbed by your jubilee. They seem less sinister, you think, dancing forward, arms outstretched. You grab fistfuls of them and eat them like paper candy. Mine, mine, mine!

You pelt on, through the next doorway. The room with the twelve white baths where you'd met Audrey for the first time. If she wanted to talk to you, she'd have to come in and find you. You stroll around, hot steam rising from each of them but the last on the left. You trail your fingertips over the hot surfaces, leaving ripples and wakes. You promise yourself a long bath in each one, someday. You stand at the end of the room, a door to your left, a door to your right. You close your eyes and remind yourself you will be able to go through all the doors eventually. You can't hear Sweet James's voice anywhere, outside or inside your head. You almost—a little—wish he'd give you instructions. As you listen hard, trying to will his voice into existence, you realize that nobody will give you instruction again. There is no strong gust to pull you from this world. You are a tiny pioneer, a girl adventurer tumbling through the unknown.

You feel very strikingly alone. Is Audrey actually going to come after you? Does she really want to talk? Will she be able to find you? Your eyes bead with panicky tears. Is this stupid? Is this really what you wanted?

You cautiously open the door on the left, lean and black. You step into the next place, eyes wide, hoping that some new wonder will distract you from the panic hatching under your diaphragm, crawling up the inside of your rib cage. It doesn't. It's an office.

A small, poky office full of paper. Stacks and stacks and stacks of white paper filled with black ink are piled from the floor to the low ceiling. A huge wooden desk, gargantuan. A hat on a hat stand and a door behind the hat stand. A blanket heaped on a swivel chair. On the desk, more paper. Pens snapped in half. The place smells of pine and chemicals, and the sharp and sudden feeling hits you that you shouldn't be there, that you chose the wrong door. The blinds are drawn on the narrow window, so you step over the carpet to peek through, to see if there's a world out there. But a small, high sound scares you so acutely that the jump almost hurts your bones. You swing around— what was that, what was that? It happens again.

A canary perches in a cage, hanging by the desk. It

peeps again. You laugh in relief, double over to catch your breath. *Peep peep.*

You go over to it for a closer look. *Peep peep.*

"Hello, little buddy. You aren't going to start talking to me, are you?"

Peep peep.

"Good."

Peep peep.

"I'm going to look out that window, then I'm going to leave."

Peep peep.

You turn to the window and open the blind, expecting a street, a meadow, an outdoors.

You are wrong.

This is a mistake.

Your breath leaves your body and you slide down to the floor, holding your face. The blind swings closed. Your eyes, your brain—what have you just *seen*? There was too much out there. Too much. The inside of a body, the outside of the galaxy—you don't know which it was, but it was not a street, it was not a meadow. Your stomach lurches: you can't throw up in someone else's office, you have to get back to the room with the baths—you crawl across the floor and the canary peeps and peeps and the sound of it pierces through you. You crawl out the door. *Peep peep.*

The tiles are blessedly cool on your skin. You close the door behind you, on your hands and knees, then lean against the door and press the heels of your hands into your eyes. Your ears are ringing.

"Well, you weren't ready for that, were you?"

Audrey's voice is a surprise and a relief. You are glad not to be alone.

"Was that your office? Your bird?" you ask, not taking your hands off your eyes.

"Ha. Oh no, no, no. *He* wasn't there? That's probably better for you. Bet you didn't even knock before you went in."

You groan, "I feel so sick."

"You looked out the window?"

"Of course I did!"

"Was the canary singing?"

"Yes!"

"Well, that's something. Here, let me look at your eyes."

She leans in, her cold hands removing your own from your face. The world is a blur, and light is only abstract as you try to focus. You can see, at least you can see, though you wouldn't be surprised if what lay behind that window had rendered you blind. Your brain feels like it is full of static. Your ears still sing a terrible, high note. Audrey's sharp, small face comes into focus.

"Oh, it made a right mess of you. You're very bloodshot. Can you see me?"

You nod.

"Well, lucky you."

"What was that?"

"The rest of things. Do yourself a favor and don't look out any closed windows while you're back here, please. If a window is draped shut, there's a reason. Not everything

270

is as even as these rooms." She tucks your hair behind your ear. "You've a lot to learn."

"Whose office was that? Why was there a bird?"

"It doesn't matter. You might meet him, you might not. There's lots of folks back here. He keeps birds so that if I drop by, I know quickly enough whether the room is safe to be in. Some spots have less breathable air than others, some spots have—well, things in them that would do away with a canary pretty quickly, for food or for pleasure. So no singing? No go. It's very thoughtful of him, actually."

"There are some rooms that aren't safe?"

"None of this is safe, Bevan. You haven't been safe since the first time Sweet James set eyes on you. Come on. This room isn't the place to be recovering."

She takes your hand and leads you to the other door. You squeeze her hand hard, and she squeezes back. Your eyes hurt and the light in the next room makes them sting, a high summer midday light. You're outdoors, walking a long grassy path lined with shrubbery, but there's a ceiling above you. A black ceiling, hanging as though it were installed above the ground—a roof that shouldn't be there. Light shouldn't be this strong without a sun or a source. You can't see any doors, or what is beyond the shrubbery, only pale blue sky that ends sharply where the hard dark of the ceiling closes off the world.

Audrey leads you along the grass to a bench, painted white. It feels familiar. She sits you down and rests at the other end, folding her legs up. She produces a nail file from a pocket and begins to run it along the edges of her fingertips. The ringing in your ears is fading. Your eyes still sting. But you're not so sick, not so afraid.

"We can't stay long. I've got to go and meet Rita at the cut. You can ask me anything you want, for now, though."

"Do you know where the cut is from back here?" You rub your eyes again. A little blood comes away.

"Don't touch them, you'll only make it worse. Of course I know where the cut is. I've been back here for more than twice the length of your life. I know where lots of cuts are."

"Is it near here?"

"Not really. But I know a couple shortcuts."

You summon the big question in the silence that follows, and ask it.

"Audrey, why did you take him away from me?" You aren't looking at her. The sound of the file against her nails stops.

"Because I thought if he'd left you be, you'd find a place in the world for yourself. I was wrong. You can either go on living out there with all the questions of these rooms alive in you, eating you as you grow—or you can come here. Stay here. Adventure on alone."

You both stare straight ahead, not at each other. She's right. Even in the years he was gone, you were haunted, batting away the flutter of moths at the back of your eyes, distracting yourself from the pull of neon.

"And you? Why did you leave—you couldn't have known all this back then."

"I left because I had to make a choice. Run away or get put away."

"Who was going to put you away?"

"The nuns. My ma."

"Why? Did they think you were crazy?"

Audrey gave a cold laugh, "No. They thought I was queer. They were right, too."

You gasp a little. "They couldn't put you in jail for that!" She scowls at you.

"Yes, they could. But it wouldn't have been prison for me, that wouldn't have looked good on my ma. One of the laundries for girls. That way it looks holy. Just like they did to Deborah."

Laundries. Places where women who didn't fit in went. Homes for girls, run by nuns, holy prisons they were signed into for the rest of their lives. There was an old one by the church in the village. The year your ma got pregnant with you was the year it shut down. She would have been done for otherwise.

"I'm . . . I'm sorry." You can't think of anything else to say, but a gentle query. "Who was Deborah?"

Audrey's brow furrowed even further, and for a second she looked terribly old. "Rita never mentioned her?"

You shake your head. You've been by Rita's side for your whole life, and it seems you knew so little about the old woman. But then again, you have secrets from Rita too. So much could go unsaid in a house like theirs. You feel the sorrow rise in Audrey, potent in the air—but you do not drink from it. You let it sit in the space between you.

"Deborah was taken away to the nuns. She was our best mate. Mad curly ginger hair, laugh like a magpie. The three of us were great as kids, a little gang. The nuns always had their eyes on us, though, even from when we were small things. They were waiting for one of us to put a foot wrong, for something to happen. Deb got herself in a way, you know. Pregnant. I told my ma, my ma . . . well . . . asked the sisters for help and they took Deborah away and we didn't see her after that." Audrey closed her eyes. "They found her, and the baby, dead out by the grotto in the woods. We were so young. Just like that, me and Rita and no Deborah. Then, quicker than I can tell you, it was me and Rita and James and Bobby, but they only came because after Deb died the world got split open. The wrong of it tore a cut in things. That's how it happens. Pain opens the world, and things come through."

You reach across the bench and squeeze Audrey's arm, for only a second, then let go. Of course Rita had never mentioned Deborah. How does anyone find the words for that story, or the moment to tell it?

You summon your breath and say again, "I'm sorry."

"Stop apologizing. There's no need. Cats and owls aside, those nuns were monsters. They ran that town. I'm glad I left. There was nothing there for me."

"There was Rita, though."

She snaps her head around at you.

"Of fucking course there was Rita. Rita wasn't going to get sent away. Rita was a better liar than I ever was. She could have a normal life out there. I couldn't. She never set foot in the rooms. She wouldn't know freedom if it kissed her on the mouth."

"But you loved her."

"Not enough to stay. And she didn't love me enough to leave."

"Why meet her at the cut now then? Why not leave her?"

"Because . . . because I love her enough to ask her one more time. Because I think she's ready, and that—back there, that can't be the last time I see her. And you can't just disappear without saying goodbye. Trust me, I've done it, and you don't want that over your shoulders."

"I don't think I want to go back and say anything at all. I want to keep going."

"Well, make up your mind quick, because I'm not your ma. I'm just saying you owe some people the word goodbye. You don't want any regrets out here. They weigh hard and heavy, and you don't need to carry anything more than yourself."

The pair of you sit in the quiet for a while. Your eyes hurt, your head feels strange. The cat. The owl. You want to ask her everything she knows about Sweet James. You want to tell her everything you know about Sweet James. Did he ever mention you to her over those years in between? Had he missed you? What was he like when Audrey first met him? What was Rita like when she was young? What was Deborah like?

But you don't ask anything at all. You can't. Audrey owes you nothing. Least of all her stories, her pain. A small yellow bird bops along the grassy path towards you.

"Is that the canary from the office?" You squint.

"This place is riddled with them." Audrey stands up and stretches. "Lucky for us."

She leans down and takes it in her hand, stroking its head. It peeps softly at her touch, in the way a wild bird shouldn't. She releases it and it keeps itself steady in the air, beating its wings.

"Right. That'll follow us. Just in case."

Your ears ring and each *peep* brings you right back to that window ledge and the things you shouldn't have seen. You cringe, taking steps after Audrey as she goes. You do not know if you want to stay with her, nor do you know if you have a choice. She leads you down the grass, on and on until in the distance: a door.

The next room is again not a room at all, but a dark, cobbled street. That black ceiling pervades, claustrophobic. Shop windows are lit dimly. You see bodies moving behind their dusty surfaces, hear the murmur of voices. Streetlamps suggest, rather than shine, amber. It might be nighttime here, you think, slowing to look around.

"Come quickly," Audrey says, grabbing your wrist. "Now's not the time to be making new friends."

The street runs uphill ever so slightly. She ducks around a sharp corner into almost liquid black. There is a door marked with a green light. Opened and closed.

The next space is a room, narrow and short, almost a closet. There is no visible ceiling, only a long pull upward into dark. Falling from the dark are too many strings to count. Tied to the strings are small, slim white bones. They graze against your forehead. Audrey swears under her breath as the two of you crowd in, the canary peeping, fumbling with the walls, looking for something. *Click, thud,* she finds the door. Onward.

A library, void of people or books, the ceiling a high painted dome. You don't get to stop long enough to look at it. You think it is painted with flowers, but you could be wrong, it makes your eyes hurt. The bird peeps and peeps.

A kitchen, the tap overflowing and the water up to your ankles and freezing cold. Audrey strides through; you almost slip, but don't. *Peep peep.*

The next space is green. A tunnel, budding with fauna, clusters of canaries like rows of daffodils. There is no end in sight. You have to stoop, almost crawl, to get through. The door this time is below you, and you hold your breath and follow Audrey into the black.

A room with red curtains and two empty chairs.

A hotel lobby. (Audrey rings the bell, playful for a second as she passes the reception desk.)

A string of hotel corridors—unopened door after unopened door.

The carpet moves and changes beneath your feet.

Somewhere along the way, you decide you are not afraid anymore. You think, Is this what infinity feels like? You never want to get off this strange carousel, it dazzles you so.

"Can you feel that? We're getting closer." Audrey slows down a second and extends her arms, reveling in something you can't feel.

"What am I supposed to be feeling?"

"Listen harder."

You stop. The canary peeps. You listen. There's your own heartbeat, the inhale and exhale of your own breath… then glowing past the edges is something good and warm. Almost a melody, but not quite. It's familiar. A rising tone that falls just when you need it to, if you could call it a tone. The aftereffect of a tone, maybe. A feeling. A moth's wing rising and falling. Gray becoming gold. Circle flicking to triangle. A light coming on slow, like a breath. You are not afraid at all. You have never felt braver in your life. The glow is coming from somewhere you can't see but yes, you can feel it.

"I feel it, but I don't know what it is."

"The house is burning down. The wall between worlds is thinning. Let's get to the cut. I don't want to miss my girl."

Audrey takes off at full speed and you fly after her, the source of the glow pulling you. For a second you think your arms could be wings. For a second you think you could be a moth, an owl. You are anything but human and you are, as you race, caught by delight. Maybe you are happy. Maybe, just maybe, you've been lucky.

THIRTEEN

MAE knew the corridor was misbehaving, that space wasn't working right, but there was nothing she could do about it. All she could think of as she tried to get to the stairs was that she wasn't the third witch. Her role had been usurped by the mysterious interloper in a tuxedo. Audrey. Audrey was the third cup. Mae bit back tears as she sped up.

Where had the stairs gone? The windowless shade manipulated what was and was not possible as on either side of the hallway new doors slid into existence, the world effortlessly extending itself all wrong. Mae looked over her shoulder: Rita and Rossa were still far, far behind her. The carpet underneath her feet was warm in a way that made her skin crawl. Like maybe the house had turned flesh, like maybe she was in some new organ of the place, or traveling down an artery through a fresh limb, or as though the house was eating her, digesting her, like she'd become a part of it and never get free.

Bobby had gone inside to banish Sweet James. He would, wouldn't he? That's what had to happen. Bobby was kind and loving and Sweet James was greedy and hungry and controlling. Love always wins in the end, doesn't it? Where were the stairs?

Mae stopped and opened the door to her left, as a test. It should be a bathroom—that's what the first door by Bevan's room was.

But when the door swung open, a closet lay before Mae, dark and shallow, packed with flickering candles, stacked with hundreds of tiny idols: the Virgin Mary, over and over in different blue cloaks, her heart bleeding, snakes at her feet. Mae gasped, peering in, unable to take her eyes off them. She had never seen this before. The nest of holy statues looked back at her, their tiny judgmental eyes flickering in what was barely more than a closet, but shouldn't be there at all.

Mae looked back up the corridor, expecting Rita and Rossa to have advanced, but they were static in the distance, almost eaten by shadow. None of this was right.

She broke into a sprint toward them, called her brother's name, but somehow he and Rita descended. They had found the stairs. She cried out, her chest tightening, she couldn't just keep running, the corridor wasn't getting any shorter. The air felt hotter, the ceiling lower. There was a smell of smoke, she thought, though that could just have been the candles from the grotto.

She flung open another door, and what lay beyond the threshold took her breath away—a bar. An empty dance floor, pumping music low and dissonant. Red light soaked down over empty tables and thick striped drapes on the wall. A mirrored globe hung over the proceedings, dousing the place in flecks of white. A shallow stage, an unmanned piano. A stand with a birdcage, home to a tiny yellow bird. Behind the bar, there was a man whose face she couldn't quite see. He stopped polishing his glasses to take a look at her. Mae shivered.

"Come in and watch the show!" he called.

Something pulled Mae's body, but she resisted. "I have to get outside!" she cried, clinging to the doorframe. "Let me go!"

"You can't just yet. There is something you need to know. Let me pour you a drink."

"No!"

The bartender sighed and lifted his hand. Mae's feet left the ground. She shrieked as the door slammed behind her and she landed on the hard, cold tiles with a crack.

He pulled a tall, dark bottle from the shelves behind him and twirled a long glass in his hand. Mae still couldn't quite make out his face, but his voice was deep and familiar.

"You're going to need this." He poured the drink with flair. From behind the bar he procured three ice cubes and a tiny umbrella. He slammed the drink down. "This one's on me. Only rule is, you gotta get up and get it yourself. No drinking on the floor. At least sit at a table if you're not going to sit at the bar."

Mae looked over her shoulder. The door was gone. Just wood paneling in the red light. She pulled herself up off the tiles and dusted herself off, her elbows and knees sore. She sat up on one of the high stools and leant over the bar. Beer taps and unmarked liquor bottles. Lemons in a jar. The bird over by the stage chirped softly. She tried to look up at the bartender, but his face wasn't a face. His eyes weren't eyes. His form was absent. He was obscured in the red light. His suit was most definitely a suit, but that was all the light gave her. She wrapped her hand around the cold glass and thought, Well, why not die this way—and drank. It was thick and sour and good.

"Stay for the show, then I'll let you be on your way," he said, leaning over the bar.

"Do you promise me?" Mae asked. "I have to find my great-aunt and brother."

"There are no promises here. You'll just have to believe me."

The bartender handed her a cigarette from an unmarked white box. She hesitantly took one, murmured a thanks, and he lit it for her with a long match. She held it in her hand, too nervous to bring it to her lips. It looked right, but it didn't feel right. There was too much smoke already. She didn't want anymore.

A cloth in one hand, a glass in another, the bartender resumed cleaning. Mae drank again, wondering if she should ask him what the hell was going on, or just let all this happen around her, not resist it. She had no power to fight. Her party tricks were no use here.

Mae took another drink, and the light reddened, then blackened.

The bartender said, "It's starting. You'll want to listen."

Mae turned to the stage, expecting some slinky lounge singer to emerge, but that was not what happened. Smoke rolled from the slim gaps between the wooden paneling on the walls and coated the stage, like fabric caught in air. The small bird in the cage gave a *tweet, tweet*.

The smoke became a screen, and licorice-black tendrils began to illustrate something on the surface. The swooping wings, heart-shaped face, and savage talons of an owl. The serpentine tail and piercing eyes of a house cat. Sweet James and Bobby Dear. The owl perched high above the cat. They spoke.

long time no see. you don't visit enough.

I'm trying to win, not trying to waste time.

do you feel as though you are winning?

I no longer care. We've made a terrible mess of this one.

what a waste.

What a waste. This was a dangerous game.

you picked the right hand. love makes them pliant and comfortable.

Fear keeps a good handle on them until it doesn't. Fear gives until it snaps. A volatile meal. Love, however, quietens and fades.

next time let's choose different things to taste. we must leave here soon.

I know, friend. I know.

we have broken this house.

Pity. It's only bricks, but I had gotten quite used to it.

you grew to love her, too.

Yes. And you never feared her for a second.

will you miss her?

Don't ask me that.

there will be other feeds in other places. other buildings stronger than this.

So who wins this round?

let's call it a stalemate. hangman. the next point counts double. the next place will be different.

Mae is listening.

then she should get out before she burns alive.

The smoke dissipated.

Mae was left with the strange, faceless bartender in the red light with knowledge she didn't want. Couldn't the cards have spelled this out for her? Bobby hadn't just been eating her love, he'd been competing with it. It wasn't just sustenance, it was entertainment. A game. Her love like currency, Rita's love like checkers on a board. Poor Rita. Rita had been betrayed far worse.

"You have to leave now, girl. The house is on fire."

"This isn't the house. This isn't anywhere." Mae stubbed the cigarette out in a flat steel ashtray, never having brought it to her mouth.

"You can stay back here if you like. But I don't think that's what you want."

This was where Bevan had gone to, wasn't it? A temptation came over her: she could just go looking for Bevan. The other world offered her something the real world never would: the company of that tall, terrible girl. She'd have to leave Rossa behind.

Rossa would have left her behind. He'd said as much in the garden. And he'd have done it for the same reason: for the possibility of more time with Bevan. The very thought made Mae's stomach roll. But no, Mae was not going to slink out of this earth quietly and turn her back on her family, despite the mess they'd found themselves in. Mae would leave the house with her head up.

She pushed the empty glass back across the counter to the bartender and said, "I've to go find my family now."

He picked the glass up and examined it. "You're welcome here anytime."

Mae paused. "How did you know about all of this? That I'd need to see them, that I needed help?"

The glass melted into liquid in his hand. It dripped, thick water, onto the bar.

"Walls are very thin. Thinner some places than others. Nobody in that house was listening for what's been going on, but you can hear it all from here."

Mae blinked and dipped her fingertip in what used to be the glass. It was warm, gelatin.

"Thank you for the drink. And for the information. I've nothing to tip you with."

"Make it up to me, someday."

For a second Mae thought she could see a face there, a smile, perhaps, in shadows where the bartender's face should have been. She smiled back.

"Maybe I will."

She leapt off the stool and walked across the tiles, smoke rolling down by her ankles, like she was wading through a shallow, dangerous pool. The bird in the cage had not chirped since the shadow show had ended. The door unfolded in the paneling and swung open before Mae even touched it. She walked back into her own world— thick, foul-smelling haze in the air, yellow flame licking the corner of her vision. Mae was not just a score in a game, she was whole and alive and human—greater than any monster. She was going to run through the fire.

FOURTEEN

THE hallway was mineshaft dark and mostly on fire, but Mae could tell she was at the top of the stairs. At least fire made sense. Fire would let you go if you moved fast enough. Behind her, the door to the bar ceased to be. Just wallpaper, now curling at the edges. The heat and smoke in her nose and eyes and throat were quicksilver hot as she bounded down the stairs. She stumbled down the last few steps, careless. She had to get out of this house.

She landed in the hallway, her breath short, the air filth in her mouth. Mae clamored towards the front door, her arms outstretched. She grieved the kitchen as toxic belches of smoke poured through a crack in the door, half of it already eaten by the flames, like they were taking some strange pleasure from the consumption of this haunted place.

Mae would never see that kitchen again. The holy stove, the crystals scattered on the table, Rita's carved-glass ashtrays littered here and there, Bevan taking up too much air, lighting incense, boiling the kettle. Towering, like a suburban colossus. Bobby lying on the floor, belly to the sunlight. Grief twisted in her gut. Bobby, he'd betrayed them all. He'd only been playing a game, and she'd let him feed, again and again.

She bumped face-first into the hall door, which hung, thankfully, ever so slightly ajar. Rita and Rossa had left it open for her. She put her hand on the doorknob and the heat scorched her, but the momentum was enough to nudge the door wide and escape into the summer evening. She left the door ajar (for Bevan, just in case) praying nothing bad would escape.

Though, she supposed, as she rounded the house to the gate that led to the back garden, the bad things had their own doors. What use had they for any other?

From the outside, the house was painfully ordinary; the only tell of the carnage within was a plume of black, spiraling smoke from the chimney. When would the fire department come? Nobody outside that house could see how bad the danger was on the inside. She climbed awkwardly over the back gate, a graceless leg up on a bin and over the top, the clumsy landing sending a shock wave of pain through her knees. It wasn't until she landed on the other side that she saw how badly burned the palm of her left hand was from her exit of the house. The scorching brass handle had ripped the skin right off her palm. How had she not noticed she was bleeding? In the small alley beside the house, Mae tore a strip from her shirt and wrapped her hand. She couldn't feel anything, but red pooled into the denim blue and turned it a wet, violent purple.

She turned the corner and came upon the back garden—but now it was large enough to be a meadow. Standing in the center were Rita and Rossa. She sprinted, her legs bright agony and the long grass tearing at her then, at last, pounced on them, sobbing their names. They stood there clutching one another, watching the windows of the house turn black.

"What'll you do, Rita?" Mae cried. "Your house, your house!"

Rossa said nothing, only held his sister as shock overtook her.

Rita ran a long hand over Mae's hair and said, "That was never my house. First it belonged to my parents. Then it belonged to James and Bobby. I just lived there."

Her serenity in the face of this horror did nothing to quell the blaring alarm running through Mae. "But they were using you, Rita! They were feeding off us, like a game between them!"

"I know. And I made sure they never went hungry." Rita should not have been smiling, but she was, thin and long.

"What do you mean?" Mae asked, a terrible logic unfolding.

"I mean, if those who came to my house were full enough of love, or full enough of fear, or young enough that they were experiencing both for the first time—it helped Sweet James, it helped Bobby Dearest. It made them strong and warm, and in turn, they kept me strong and warm. Think of all the things I can do because of that power. They gave me so much."

Mae had no idea who this woman was, for a second.

Her jaw was hard and her eyes were cold and Mae almost had to take a step back from her, recoiling from the embrace she had only moments ago leapt into. Rita had been poaching monsters and using Mae and her brother as bait. The witch had known. Worse than known. She'd run the show. Honey in the trap.

"Is that why you took us in?"

Rita nodded, slightly weary. "And Imelda, but she was a tough one. Had no idea how to love anyone and wasn't afraid of a damn thing. Thankfully, Bevan made up for that in spades. It was never going to work out neatly, but I came as far as I could manage."

"Why? Why did you—"

"For her." Rita pointed into the wood. "For Audrey. I needed time. I took time, I took strength. When we are together again I will protect her, I will see all of the possibilities of the things out there that could hurt her. I was not brave or strong or wise enough when I was young. And now I am. Don't tell me you wouldn't do the same."

Mae's heart faltered. All this horror, all this brutality, just so Rita could find a way to Audrey again.

Rossa said, "All along. You've known all along."

Rita tossed her hair over her shoulder, grazed her fingertips across the bark of the trees she passed, said, "You'd have known that from the beginning if you'd been listening harder."

"We need to call the fire brigade, the whole house will come down!"

Rita sighed deep, and Mae's eyes threatened tears but

she rubbed them away with her hand of denim and blood. She opened her mouth to explain now, to tell her brother everything, ready to denounce Bobby for what he had done to them all, when Rita cut in, sharp, casual. "I have seen all of this, time and again in my dreams, but the clocks are always covered. Someone will eventually call the fire service, but until then, flame will continue to clean the house. Until that ground is razed, until the weak point Sweet James left has no wall left to hang on to. This is a boiling flood, and this place will be pure in its wake. You can come to the cut with me, or you can say goodbye to me now."

Rita was magnificent and undeniable in her power. Ageless. Mae still, despite it all, would have followed her anywhere. Rossa wasn't so sure, Mae could tell by his face. The boy always had had trouble with magic.

"I'll come with you," Mae said. "I want to see—" She stopped. "Do you think Bevan will be there?"

Rita's thin smile again. "You might get to see her one last time."

Mae didn't bother trying to conceal the need she had to see Bevan again. To, perhaps, convince Bevan to come out of the other side. To stay here, with her.

Rita thumbed Mae's face with an off-tenderness, and the love in her voice was at odds with the ordeal she had orchestrated. "You're covered in soot. That'll look proper, I suppose, when the police pick you up."

Mae and Rossa followed after Rita down the meadow sloping toward the garden wall, which, when Rita raised her arm, crumbled away like chalk.

Down through the grass and over the deconstructed stone that was once the garden wall, past ridges of bush pocked with white roses that Mae had never seen before. Over her shoulder, the gushing wisteria fluttered a goodbye in the breeze over the disused shed. Farther over her shoulder, flames had begun to lick out of the windows of the house, scorch marks bleeding down onto the outside brick. Smudged mascara at the end of a long, long night.

Rita stepped over the skinny river and into the trees. Rossa, too, seemed to know where he was going in the labyrinthine corridors of nature. Mae followed him closely, listening to air in the woods. On the breeze she could hear a high, glowering sound.

"I want you to know that despite everything, I love you both more than words can say," Rita began, not looking at either of them, still making her way surefootedly through the forest. "You have given me far more than you know. I come from a time when big houses held old secrets, and that's just the way our people were. I became an old house full of big secrets, and I wish there had been a way for me to share them all with you. But secrets are kept, sometimes, for good reason. And you have to believe me when I say that, and you have to promise me you won't tell anyone about what happened this summer."

She didn't look over her shoulder as she spoke. Her tone didn't have a soft inflection of question: Rita wasn't asking them to keep it secret. She was telling them to keep it secret. Commanding them. And they were going to do it.

"What you can do here is preserve legacy. You can

protect my good name. Bevan's good name. She has a mother out there in the world who, God love her, knew nothing of how corrupted her daughter became, knew nothing of what I was when I invited her into my house. If there is one thing I have learned through all my years with my hands in other people's futures and pasts, it's that nobody ever really believes in magic. We are but one room in a grand cosmic hotel, and if you try to tell them, they will call you crazy, call you liars."

Mae mourned as they walked. How could she ever tell anybody this story, how could she build enough rooms inside of her for it to live in?

"Silence isn't that high a cost, really," Rita says. "For survival. For who you will become as a result of all of this, after I have gone."

A terrible hex. Mae's tongue cut out. A last bodily theft.

"Does that mean you're just going to leave us? Let us go back to our parents alone?" Rossa's grip on Mae's hand was a vise. "You can't just leave us. We wanted to stay."

"This was only ever temporary. There is no respite that lasts forever. This is not how either of you will leave your home. Though it will give you the courage to try." Her regal tone faltered a second. "I will give you this truth. Just once, just this last time, in exchange for your promise of silence. I have allowed the cat and the owl to take from you, and I have given you nothing in return, so I will give you something priceless. Proof that you will survive this. A prophecy, each." Rita turned. Her eyes bright, mad jewels in her hard, gorgeous face.

"But first I want you to promise me."

Silence landed in the forest for a beat too long, but Rossa broke it in his most serious of voices.

"I promise," he said—but Mae could tell his uncertainty, and so could Rita. Mae held her silence.

Their great-aunt shook her head. "A verbal promise is not enough. Mae, take that bandage off your hand."

From the forest floor, Rita picked a sharp rock, and without pause or reflection, dragged it down the center of her palm. A red shock of fresh blood there; she did not even flinch. She handed it to Rossa. "If you like, I can do it for you."

The boy offered his palm and the crone marked it open. Mae unspooled her denim bandage, wincing at the pain. Each twin held forth a wounded hand, side by side, a mismatched pair. Rita, whispering low, placed her long, bleeding palm down, and neither twin felt anything at all but the sting: an ordinary pain contrasted starkly with the sheer paganism of Rita's murmuring. She was spellcasting there in the narrow corridor of trees, as in the distance, sirens began to wail.

She looked up at Mae and Rossa and for a second. Mae could have sworn she saw a glittering flash of triangles in her pupils: unmistakable wrong in her face. But it was too late by then. The reek of copper rolled over them, and the twins withdrew their hands. Rossa wiped his on his shirt. Mae wrapped hers in her soiled bandage.

Rita said, "You may speak to each other about this summer, and the last—but nobody else. And in return for your silence and for what I allowed Bobby and James to take from you, I will tell each of you one thing that will give you hope."

How could one thing make up for all that Rita had stolen? Mae thought. But nothing more would be offered. She knew that. So when the old woman leaned in to whisper in her ear, she listened hard. She needed hope like air.

FIFTEEN

THE remaining walk to the cut was spent in a holy
silence. Rossa clutched his hand, stinging in the sleeve
of his hoodie, the scarlet of his blood turning copper in
the air. Rita's prediction sank into him. The brief glimpse
into the future was reassuring, certainly, but what would
tomorrow look like? What has this time done to him, and
his sister? Would they ever be the same again?

These women had a capacity for pain that he wasn't sure
he could even imagine. Whatever it was that Bevan had
tried to do to him in that bedroom with the owl—Christ,
even the thought of it threatened to lock his joints with
terror. The undergrowth of the forest crunched beneath
his sneakers, but there was grass in sight. The glade was just
ahead of them. Rita seemed to hover above the ground,
such was the force and determination that led her. She was
hard to look at, full of some new fury.

Rossa could smell smoke in the air. That was the reek
of a home destroyed. All of his things—his gut flipped

suddenly. His notebooks. His drawings. The preparation he'd done for college, all gone. Eaten up by fire. He would be seeing his parents tonight. How would they react to this? Mae's face was streaked with black, around her nose charred from breathing in destruction. Her wounded hand was a sick thing to look at.

His twin. The other half of him. This could have been the end of them, and he felt his eyes prickle with tears. He blinked them away.

The forest split open into the strange, evening-light majesty of the glade. Thin, dark-bodied trees with splintering arms and thick crowns of green were a somber crowd of bystanders, rustling low in what felt like anticipation. The cut hung there in the air, glassy and static, not beautiful enough to be crystalline but shining all the same. Below it, the grotto holding the stone Virgin. The plaque at her feet shone in the strange light. Rossa, without thinking, reached his uninjured hand out to take Mae's, a silent plea to not be in this alone. Mae flinched, but then squeezed back.

Rita walked toward the cut, arms raised, antigravity buoying her hair like a cloud as she approached. Rossa expected her to sweep it open like a curtain in reality, revealing another place just hanging there in the forest, like how there had been a pink-lit room on the other side of Bevan's bedroom wall, like no big deal, like this is here and always has been. But she didn't. She just stood, looking up at it, in silence, as voltage rippled through the air. It hit Rossa almost in a rhythm; the old woman—or was she young, he couldn't tell—was spellcasting, and the weight of it through the air was vertigo. He had seen some bad things in the house, and lately, from Bevan—but what was happening before him now was different. Bigger.

Something moved behind him and he clenched Mae's hand so tightly she yelped and pulled away. An owl as big as a five-year-old child. A cat the size of a golden retriever. Both all wrong. Both more oil than hair, more bone than feather. Four yellow orbs that could have been eyes if Rossa had known less, or if their pupils were circles rather than three-pointed triangles. Two vile beasts. Two hungry things.

"Bobby, how could you?" Mae was on her knees in the grass before Rossa could stop her, her bloodied hand a fist against the earth. "How could you have done this to me? To us?"

The butter-yellow eyes on the cat thing flickered, and it padded towards Mae. Rossa braced himself. If the creature attacked her, he would throw himself between them. He would defend her at all costs. An ache in the bridge of his nose resurfaced—the unmistakable sour of blood in his nostrils.

Mae extended her arms to Bobby, fresh tears leaving tracks of almost clean down her filthy face. The thing walked right up to her and let her hold it, for a moment flickering to something more domestic, something like soft white fur, and then back to the shadow-slick impression of its truer form.

You are an uncommon creature, Mae, he said to her. *There is so much love in you, I could have drunk it for the rest of time.*

"I love you, Bobby," she whispered. "Even though

you're bad. Even though you did all this."

We are leaving the same way we came in. We have a course to follow. I cannot apologize, but I will not forget you, he said, and Mae leaned her face into the otherworld soft of his body.

The owl thing made a noise, a clicking and breaking that rounded out into a deep, human laugh. Rossa's stomach lurched.

you're welcome, he said. **you're welcome, mae, you're welcome, rossa, you're welcome, rita. we took, yes, but we gave and gave, too. what would your lives have been otherwise, without us?**

"You should have burned!" hissed Mae. "You and that house are one and the same."

no bricks can contain me. that site is corrupted now, unstable. a cut all its own. two so near each other spells trouble for whoever comes here next. clever rita finally knows when to run.

The crone turned toward the twins and the beasts. She was a house on fire, ablaze with what she had cultivated, year after year under the same roof as these calamities. All she had sacrificed at the altar of Sweet James and Bobby Dear rushed back here, in a burning flood.

"Would you like me to open this door for you, then?" Rita asked the calamities before her, almost mocking them.

The owl clicked and let out an ugly laugh, and Bobby shook his head, chuckling.

do you really think you can do that all by yourself?
Come on, Rita. Don't be silly.
Rita moved toward the blue-gray grotto, the smallness

of it striking in this cosmic spin. She knelt there, spine curled over, praying, summoning all the love and agony she had felt, that she had harvested. She was still a moment too long,* and Rossa felt like maybe nothing would happen after all. He was afraid, for her, for him, for his sister. For a moment Rita was just an old woman, praying at the feet of a false idol.

Then the air split like silk and the world separated. All about them sang some high, bad note, all color and texture unsure of itself. There, hanging from just above the ground to the crowns of the trees, was the cut. A door to someplace else. Mae clutched her brother in the shattered opal light of the opening world.

Beyond the cut the sky was nighttime ink, a slice of deep blue against the evening dusk of the glade. The stars hung in thick clusters, no elegant and spare constellations in that world. The ground had long grass, too, but it stood in strands of black and white. A glade beyond this glade, moving in a strange breeze.

well, well. we may have been worth it all along.

If a beast could sound surprised, Sweet James sounded just that. Bobby didn't say a word. He gave Mae one last nudge: an affectionate gesture, a goodbye—then walked past her toward the cut, toward Rita. He grew and he grew, reality flexing around him, accommodating him. Sweet James took flight, slow, like a stingray gliding through thick water, his wingspan longer than a human reach, longer than

---

* "Deborah," she whispered, she prayed, she called. "Deborah."

301

a kitchen table, than a kitchen, than a house. Rossa had never felt so small and made of flesh in his life, nor would he again. Bobby stood on Rita's left and Sweet James, enormous, flew above her right, each beat of his wings a clap of eldritch thunder. Mae retched into the grass at the sound of it, and Rossa dashed to her side, stroking her back as she sobbed.

The two of them knelt there at the feet of a witch and titans. The owl and the cat exchanged looks, either side of the gleaming weak point in the world. The ground trembled, and Rita screamed. Not in terror, but in command: be gone, be gone, be gone.

Two figures approached the cut from the other side, two girls, one giant, one small. Rita cried, "Audrey!"

The small girl broke into a sprint. A singing yellow bird beat its wings behind her, its song a quiet rhythm of trills. The other girl followed slowly behind. Audrey stood at the edge of the cut and extended her arm through the void, trembling as the air of this world hit her skin.

"Are you coming, now, Rita?" she asked, and the smile on her face was a thing of hope.

"I am." Rita Frost reached up and took the shaking grip of Audrey O'Driscoll and stepped into the other world. They embraced tightly in the glow, on the edge of two worlds. Audrey pulled away from Rita after a long moment and said, "You're different, somehow."

Rita knitted her brow, and brushed a stray curl from Audrey's forehead. "We're all different."

Bevan approached cautiously, aglow, her hair a mane of

302

golden curls, too tall. "Sorry, sorry, don't mean to interrupt, but—Rita, I'm not going back. I'm staying back here. I'm going to walk the corridors."

Her voice jolted Rossa. He would never see her again after this night. Whatever he had thought was beginning between them was nothing more than a move in a game he didn't even know she was playing. He was unraveled. Mae gripped him tightly as Bevan spoke, and Rossa could swear he felt a grief much like his own rolling through his twin's body.

Rita touched Bevan's face. "I know."

From either side of the three witches, the cat leapt and the owl flew, with oily silence, and disappeared into the night inside the cut. Audrey, Bevan, and Rita looked up at the dense sky, and even from where Rossa knelt, he swore he could see their shadows swim across the stars.

"I'm going to find them," Bevan said, head tilted to the stars, her hands clenched into fists. "I'm going to find Sweet James, and Bobby too. They will not feed on anyone like they did on us. No new games will begin. I will be slow and I will be sure and I will meet them again."

Rita placed a hand on the girl's shoulder. "I have faith that you will come upon them again, but I will not help you. I have been playing their game my whole life, and have no wish to begin it again, now that it is finally over."

Bevan shook her head. "I didn't ask for your help. I'm going alone."

"That's dangerous," Audrey warned. "You've barely seen a handful of rooms, that's nothing of what it's like out here."

"Fine, then I won't go alone." That bright, capricious spark in Bevan lit up. She looked out of the cut and down into the glade, where the twins were cowering. Rossa gazed up at her. For a second he waited for her to call his name, to summon him to be her knight on this quest for cosmic justice, on her journey through landscapes unknown—but his sister's breath caught. Bevan was looking at her.

"Mae. Come on then. You've a good run of power through you. You'll be well able for it out here. I'll make a witch of you yet."

Mae made a small noise and got to her feet. She was ragged and skin filthy, one hand all but destroyed, but in the maddening light of the cut, she still almost managed to look heroic. This was how Rossa would lose her, he realized. She would be called upon a grand adventure. He never thought it would be like this. That she would be the one to walk away.

He steeled himself for goodbye, for walking alone past the burning house and into the street. For the fire brigade. For their parents. He would tell their parents that he could not save her from the flames—which was not entirely a lie. He could not save her from the bright thing that called her away into another world.

"No. I'm staying here."

Mae's voice was small, but it was brave. Human.

"I can't leave my brother to deal with all of this alone. Not now. There is a time to leave and a time to stay, and I know the difference. Good luck out there, Bevan. Goodbye, Rita."

Rossa leapt to his feet and went to his sister, taking her hand again in his.

Bevan sighed. "Suit yourself. See you again sometime, Mae. Be safe out there, Rossa." And as though she was just walking away from the kitchen table to go to her bedroom, she turned on her heel and left. Over her shoulder she called, "Audrey, meet me in the bar later. Rita, I'm glad you're here."

The edges of the cut began to contract, like the weight was too much for whatever force was keeping it open.

Audrey said something inaudible into Rita's ear, and Rita laughed, and she was nobody the twins knew, then. Someone else. Someone gone.

And then, before Rossa or Mae could say a word, the cut snapped closed. The lavender night of the meadow was just that, and the cut was just a scar wavering iridescently in the air. The fog around them could have been smoke as they walked out of the forest and back into the gray world, saying nothing to each other.

The police found the twins sitting on the path at the front of the lawn as the house smoldered against the firemen's efforts. Rossa couldn't manage to say a single word to them, and Mae just wept silently, writing down their parents' phone numbers on a piece of paper.

They were led in great silver shock blankets to an ambulance, where two paramedics put oxygen masks over their mouths and sat them up on a stretcher. There was so much noise, and the adults all around them were frantic, but the twins were strangely peaceful.

Rossa reached his hand across the stretcher to find his sister's. Her fingers crept across his and they were linked there, in their silence. They sat outside the burning house full of secrets. The time would come for talking later, but for now they just breathed, unburdened by smoke.

What Rita Said to Mae

Yᴏᴜ will fall in love, again. On an island full of tall buildings. It will be with a woman who will not need to know all of your secrets to choose you. You may never know true peace, Mae, but you will find something close to it with her. You will craft yourself a new family. You will not want often for company. Your gift will get stronger, but it will be up to you to nurture it. You will have to keep listening, keep peering hard through paper for what is on the other side. One day, your mother will apologize. I cannot see if you will accept the olive branch or turn away, but the branch remains, regardless. Listen close to me, Mae. You will receive another call through the walls someday. They will rumble with false promise, but you will know when it truly comes. You may not stay in this world for good. You, page of cups who beat* the hierophant.

---

* Almost.

What Rita Said to Rossa

I NEVER told you this, but you are a boy of swords. You'll put your weaponry down in time. You will flee as far as you can from this island, farther than anyone expects. You will find who you are amid orange groves. You will forgive* your parents. I suspect, in fact, that you already have, but you will not tell them this for many years. They will be grateful, and far away enough that you will be safe from them. Love will come to you in those citrus fields. There is a chance you may look past her, so I tell you this now, that she is your family and she will bear you daughters. Your home is a way off yet, but you will find yourself a backbone and become a man who is generous of spirit and tender to the core. Draw this hope into existence. The swords of you will grow into wands, and someday, Temperance. I am sorry we did not get to know each other better.

---

* Almost.

EPILOGUE
Fifteen Summers Later

THE air seared with an unmistakable energy: just for a blink. Short enough to make Mae doubt it, though even in that half heartbeat she knew what it was. She was filled with the dread that comes when something you believed to be gone is—*whoosh*—resurrected.

Her first thought was to call Rossa—but she didn't. She'd call Rachel, but her wife couldn't know. Would never know. Everyone has secrets.

She couldn't take her eyes off the wall. The wall with the monochrome zigzag tile that she and Rachel had constructed together when they first moved in. Something in the tiles had moved. She was sure of it. An inconsistency, a ripple, a glitch.

Then it was just a wall again. The air clear. Chevron tiles, a bold accent wall in the otherwise Scandinavian quiet of the loft. The canary singing in the kitchen. Her loft. Her home.

So Mae waited. She waited for the wall to open. She had been told this would happen again.

She picked up her old, well-worn tarot deck, the gift

from Rita, and drew three cards, placing them facedown on the table. She doesn't need to turn them today.

You three, again.

The Fool. A young man holding a white rose and a bindle, carefree, naive, dancing towards the edge of a cliff. Teetering on the abyss. Always, just about to fall. At his ankles, a tiny dog nips at his heel. The Fool is frozen there, about to embark on the deep dive into the blue. Rossa leapt that jagged end of the world, in the end. Settled far away on the other side. Mae always saw herself reflected back too. Sure the pair of them weren't that different after all.

The Two of Cups. A pair of lovers, one with hair cropped short, the other long and flowing; each raises a golden chalice. Above the chalices, Hermes's staff. Two snakes entwined, culminating in a lion's head with great thunderous wings behind it. A caduceus: the symbol of medicine, of healing. The lovers toast their successes, their future, their union. Mae runs her fingers over the card, a warmth rising in her, despite it all, for her great-aunt and the woman she loved. Somewhere far- flung, safe in each other's trust. Somewhere, dancing.

Mae glances at the last card.* She shuffles it back into the

---

* The Tower. Ablaze, but not with fire, with energy, gold and red and bad. Atop it, a beast, roosting. A titanic owl with a beak made of diamond. This feathered thing, far hungrier than any dragon, glowering down at the vast plain of his realm. On the path, a mighty lion, monochrome, wearing thick reins of gold, a heavy chain on his neck. On his back, his master. A girl with his chains clenched in her fists. A girl with bright blond hair and triangles for pupils, a girl with eyes on her hands. A girl who eats love and fear. She is alone and ready. The door to the tower is open.

deck, not letting it sour her day any further, just when she was starting to feel better. Mae does not live in a burning house anymore, nor is she on fire herself. Some days the hearth in her burns a little too bright, but she knows that heat could give her energy and protection, if she let it. Today she feels more like a building full of beasts and flame than a woman, but the elements would settle. They would not make ash of her.

ACKNOWLEDGEMENTS

ONE gal can't find her way through a labyrinth alone, and I had more than a little help in excavating the winding tangle of this book out of myself and into something that made sense. It took three years, but we made it out alive.

Thank you to my editor, Martha—for your vision and patience and for making sense of this haunted old house. Thank you to everyone at Greenwillow. Thank you to Ella and Lydia at Titan for having faith in me and in this project—thank you to Brian Martin, too.

Thank you to Simon Trewin and the team at WME for being at the other end of the phone with answers and support. Thank you, Vanessa, too, for always having an eye out for me.

A vital thanks to Sarah Davis Goff and Lisa Coen, for incredible mentorship. I don't know where I'd be without you. Thanks also to Sinead Gleeson and Doireann Ni Ghriofa; I am deeply fortunate to be in the way of such kind and wise women, dare I say witches.

Thank you to my dearest, maddest art friends, to Roe McDermott (a great witch) and Helena Egri (to whom this book is dedicated); thank you to Dave Tynan and Erin Fornoff and to my Doomsburies, Dave Rudden and Dee Sullivan. This book made me more than a little difficult, and every pint and walk and text message mattered. Making things in the world can be lonely and ye make me feel like part of something bigger.

Thank you to Ray O'Neill, for everything.

Thank you to the folks at the Booksmith in San Francisco, and in the old JAM offices on Synge Lane. This book was begun at a bookshop counter and finished at a desk in a renovated garage, and everyone in orbit of those spaces mattered. Thank you especially to Mike for the big hug the time my tooth shattered—the tooth made it into the book, in the end.

Thank you to Paula, Paul, and Chrissie Duff, and to the Coen family. I am extremely lucky to have found peace and space in your faraway homes when I needed it, and this book wouldn't be what it is if it wasn't for ye having put me up during deadlines.

Thank you to the Arts Council and Maynooth University for your support; it is meaningful to have two such institutions at your back and it made all the difference to me, and to this work—and to more work coming down the line, too.

Thank you to everyone who fought to repeal the Eighth Amendment in Ireland, and who continues to fight for women's rights and intersectional equality in this country.

Thank you to my parents, Sean and Patricia, and to my gorgeous sister, Katie. Thank you to Paula & Dave & Teresa & James & Steo & Daithi & Deirdre & little Niamh and Conor—and of course, Nana Sheila, for always showing up and having my back. I am from a good tribe and you were the making of me.

And most of all, thank you, Ceri Bevan. You are my home. I love you.

ABOUT THE AUTHOR

SARAH Maria Griffin is a writer from Dublin, Ireland. Her nonfiction has appeared on *The Irish Times*, Buzzfeed, *The Rumpus*, Midnight Breakfast, *Guts* and *Winter Pages*. Her collection of essays about emigration, *Not Lost*, was published by New Island Press in 2013. She was the recipient of the European Science Fiction Awards Chrysalis Award in 2017. She tweets @griffski.

SPARE AND FOUND PARTS
Sarah Maria Griffin

In a city devastated by an epidemic, where survivors are all missing parts—an arm, a leg, an eye—Nell has always been an outsider. Her father is the scientist who created the biomechanical limbs that everyone now uses. But she's the only one with her machinery on the inside: her heart. Then she finds a lost mannequin's hand while salvaging on the beach, and inspiration strikes. Can Nell build her own companion in a world that fears advanced technology?

"Reads like a piece of mechanical poetry, an intricate machine with a fierce and fearless heartbeat"
V. E. Schwab, author of *A Darker Shade of Magic*

"A sweet and darkly hopeful tale of what it takes to build love"
Kiran Millwood Hargrave, author of
The Girl of Ink and Stars

"A dark and fierce thing"
Joseph Fink, co-author of *Welcome to Night Vale*

TITANBOOKS.COM

For more fantastic fiction, author events, exclusive
excerpts, competitions, limited editions and more

VISIT OUR WEBSITE
titanbooks.com

LIKE US ON FACEBOOK
facebook.com/titanbooks

FOLLOW US ON TWITTER
@TitanBooks

EMAIL US
readerfeedback@titanemail.com